Tomorrow's Paper

Tomorrow's Paper

Richard Allen Wunderlich

OakTara

WATERFORD, VIRGINIA

Tomorrow's Paper

Published in the U.S. by:
OakTara Publishers
P.O. Box 8
Waterford, VA 20197

Visit OakTara at
www.oaktara.com

Cover design by David LaPlaca/debest design co.
Cover images © iStockphoto/ Andrey Prokhorov/Kiyoshi Takahase/
Knape
Author photo © 2008 by Craig Pulsifer (www.craigpulsifer.com)

ISBN: 978-1-60290-068-4

Tomorrow's Paper is a work of fiction. References to real people, events, establishments, organizations, or locales are intended only to provide a sense of authenticity and are used fictitiously. All other characters, incidents, and dialogue are drawn from the author's imagination.

To
the world's best family,
most wonderful students,
and warmest community in the universe—
Salmon Arm, British Columbia

1

Lisa's eyes opened slowly. The dampness of the tear-soaked pillow cradling her head during the lonely night lay cool on her face. Lifting her head, she observed her nightmare, made real by the concrete walls that imprisoned her. She tried to move. Her body, stiff and sore, resisted initially, but by sheer determination she forced it to respond to her command to shift from the fetal position she'd been lying in most of the night. She felt as if her brain was somehow displaced from her body.

Drawing in a deep breath through her nose, she noticed immediately the air was saturated with the smell of disinfectant. It reminded her of a hospital ward. The thin mattress covering the steel bed frame was barely sufficient to protect her body from the cold probing of wire and frame. She ached not only from the inadequacy of the bed, but also from the extended time spent in the wooden shipping box she'd been forced into the night before. Terror overwhelmed her as she remembered the events preceding her being put in the cell.

Kidnapped? No, it could never happen to me, she had once thought. But it had. And now she was so afraid. Her body began to shake uncontrollably. She prayed, asking God to stop the nightmare and let her awaken.

She studied her surroundings. The concrete walls defining her cell looked clean and freshly painted. That was encouraging, at least. As she rolled over, her bloodshot eyes fell upon a small, wire-mesh-covered light, recessed in the ceiling. It looked strange somehow. She blinked her eyes, rubbed them, then forced them to focus on the steel door that held her inside the walls. Leaning over, she reached towards a steel bedside table for the small cup that rested on its surface. She drank the tepid water cautiously, allowing it to gently moisten her throat. Again she wondered where she was, and why she had been taken.

Lisa imagined she'd been arrested. Perhaps it was a case of mistaken identity? It was a fantasy that, strangely, allowed her some comfort, especially when compared to her imminent future.

Down the hall from the room that held Lisa, two women, dressed in starched white laboratory coats, spoke quietly so their subject, held only a dozen or so feet away, could not hear them.

"Make sure you follow the protocol," Xavier Lyon admonished the psychologist. "Don't stray from the questioning line that we rehearsed. Let her do the talking, let her unload her feelings and memories in as much detail as possible. We need that brain space cleared. We also need to stabilize her emotions. Try to get her to trust you, and to look to you for help. But you don't have too much time. The early results indicate that any more than five to seven minutes, and her brain will shift from short- to long-term memory. That will make the brain section too active, and it won't take the transplant as well. So timing is crucial. Doing the job in less than seven minutes will ensure that her brain is of the highest quality."

"I understand. I'll try to establish some reassurance as well. Enough time has passed since she was harvested that she'll want to believe anything that sounds like it might help her."

"Excellent. And don't forget to avoid looking at the camera that's hidden in the cell light."

"Done. When is the brain extraction scheduled?"

"Immediately after you are finished with her, so you don't have the luxury of a second chance. Don't make any mistakes, Doctor."

"I understand. I'm on my way."

The young psychologist walked down the hall towards the cell.

Lisa heard footsteps. When they grew louder, she knew they were coming closer. Sitting up on the edge of the bed, she waited, arms crossed, trying not to shake. She prayed for an angel to appear.

The door opened with an electronic whine, followed by a low-pitched clunk. Her "angel" entered, smiling. Lisa immediately smiled back. *Thank you, God,* she thought.

"Lisa, I'm Doctor Black. I know you are afraid and upset. I'm here to help you. Would you like some water?"

"No, no thanks. I already have some. What happened to me? Why am I here?"

"It's okay, Lisa. I know you're afraid, and I understand that. First, though, I need to know the details of what happened to you. Can you tell me? Start with what you were doing yesterday morning."

"Can't you tell me what's going on? When can I go? Is this a police station?"

"As soon as we have all the details, and the sooner I hear your story, the faster I can get you out of here. Tell me everything, and don't leave even the tiniest detail out."

Lisa settled into a comfortable position on the bed. "Sure, okay. Yesterday morning I got up, had some tea and toast in my apartment and rode my bike to school. I'm a graduate student in computer studies at the University in Brussels. I won a fellowship to go there while I was at MIT. Anyway, I went to my first two classes—they are both advanced computer programming. After that I left the computer science building and went to the student services facility, where I worked out in the Rec Center for about an hour. Then I met some friends for lunch, and we drank some cappuccinos. I went back to the com-sci building and worked a few hours on the semester's main assignment, the creation of a computer virus."

"A virus? Why would they have you working on making a virus?"

"The prof figures we'd learn more about the process of defeating a virus program if we built one for ourselves. I worked for a few hours, then got frustrated and left."

"Why were you frustrated?"

"Well, to be honest, my thoughts and ideas seem to move faster than the university's computer system is able to absorb. The technology slows me down in executing the program lines I write. If only I could think directly into the cyberspace that the computing system lives in, it would be way faster. Maybe I'll make that a doctoral thesis."

"Go on," said her guest, smiling.

"I went to get some coffee…stalling for time, I guess. Finally I made myself go back to work and logged on to the computer. Just as I was getting started, Lorne came by."

"Who's Lorne?"

"He's a new grad student who just arrived on campus a week or so ago. Already he's one of the main 'hotties' of campus life. He's Canadian and has that semi-British accent that's so cool. He's tall, in great shape, and what's more, he seems smart *and* sensitive. Most of the women graduate students like him."

"What happened next?"

"He came right up to me. We've been, I guess, seeing each other." She hesitated and swallowed hard. "A few days ago, Lorne and I had spent a whole afternoon together, just talking and laughing. I noticed right away that he didn't seem to mind hearing about my work, like so many of the other guys I've dated. He was such a good listener, kind and attentive. It all happened so fast."

Lisa took a sip from the cup. "After that time, he called the very next day. I couldn't believe it. I was thrilled. Since then, we've spent tons of time together. Sometimes I even skipped my favorite classes just to spend time with him, walking around the city. We shopped, tried on clothes, visited tourist traps, and enjoyed being together. There never seemed to be enough time for each other. When we left and were apart, it was like it took forever until the next time we could be together."

"He sounds unusual."

"Well, yes…he's the first guy who has seemed to like just being with me. It never felt like he was after my body, if you know what I mean. I felt warm, safe, and cared for when I was with him. He was perfect, I thought."

"You thought?"

"Until it happened."

Lisa's mind flooded with the memory of what had happened to her just yesterday. From the depths of her consciousness Lorne's image emerged. The past twenty-four hours unfolded. She closed her eyes and the visions appeared….

Lisa had been in the com-sci library for several hours when she saw Lorne Browne walking towards her.

"Let's go get some coffee," he said as he neared the library workstation she occupied.

She sighed. "I have to work."

"Please, Lisa?"

The subtle aroma of his aftershave drifted to her, weakening her will.

"Couldn't it wait for an hour or so? I need to test the virus program I'm doing for Professor Stannic's class," she replied.

"Oh, come on, Lisa. You can do the virus thing later. You deserve a few minutes off," he said, smiling. The dimple that appeared from nowhere on his powerful chin dissolved the remainder of her resolve. "Besides, I have to work later. This is the only time I'll get to see you until tomorrow. And there's something I'd like to ask you."

"And what might that be?" She reached up and toyed with her hair.

"Come and find out. I guarantee you won't be disappointed. But you will regret it if you don't come now. Please, Lisa, I don't want to wait a whole 24 hours to see you again!" he begged.

"Oh, all right. There, I'm shutting down the computer right now. See? I hope I don't forget where I was."

"Excellent," he said as he offered his arm to her.

How very gallant, she thought.

Lorne escorted her out of the building and down the concrete steps that led out of the com-sci building. They strode, holding hands, onto the cobblestone pathway around the building and entered the alley between the computer science building and the university library.

There, parked halfway down the passageway, was a plain brown van with its motor running. Two men dressed in workers' clothes exited the van slowly and walked towards Lisa and Lorne. The men spoke to each other quietly, then separated as if to allow the couple to pass between them.

"Where are you taking me?" Lisa said as she held tightly to Lorne's hand.

As the men from the van passed by on either side, Lorne let go of her hand and placed his arm around her waist. He tightened his grip, as if to protect her from something. She felt the tension of his muscles and noticed how secure she felt in his arms.

As they walked by the van, Lisa absently looked into its open door. Inside she saw a man. They locked eyes for a moment. And then he lunged at her.

She screamed as his hand grabbed her shirt and instinctively pulled back. But Lorne pushed her towards the man in the van....

"He was pushing you?" The voice from the present penetrated the past, dispelling it.

Lisa opened her eyes. The cell was back, and she was in it. She lowered her head as its reality washed over her mind.

"What happened next?" the doctor in the white coat interjected.

"Lorne pushed me into the van. The other two men ran up from behind and jumped in. They taped my mouth, my hands, and feet— and put a bag over my head."

Lisa began to sob again, rocking back and forth on the bed.

"What happened next? It's very important I know. Can you tell me?"

"I heard Lorne speak to the men. They asked for money."

"Money?"

"Yes, and Lorne said to them, 'It's all here. And Henry Rexan sends his regards.' Then Lorne said, 'Thank you boys, you do fine work. I'll call when I have another.' Those were the last words I heard him say. Next I heard them start the van, but I couldn't see anything because of the hood. It was so black. I could listen, though. I knew to listen. It was like I was super sensitive to the sounds around me."

"You were listening?"

"Yes. You see, once I'd watched on TV the story of a girl who had been kidnapped. She'd been able to free herself while her kidnappers slept, then used a cell phone she took from one of their pockets to call 911. Because she'd been able to describe the sounds she had heard on the trip to the police, they'd had been able to find and then rescue her."

"What were you thinking in the dark?"

"I thought I was going to be raped, or killed, or maybe sold. I had to block those thoughts out of my mind, so I concentrated on listening. We traveled for about an hour, I guess. Then they took me out, cut the tapes on my legs, and led me up some stairs. I heard the sounds of jet engines. I'm sure I was put on a plane. They shoved me into a small wooden box, like a crate. They cut the tape from my hands and told me there was a bucket to pee in. Then I heard nails being driven into the wood."

"What happened next?"

"A long time later, the plane must have landed...or at least it felt like a long time. They moved me out of the crate and into another van and drove me here. They put me in this room, sat me on the bed, and closed the door. The next thing I knew it was this morning."

"All right, Lisa, you've done very well. Rest now. They'll come for you soon."

"Don't leave! Please don't leave!" Lisa pleaded as the door opened and the doctor moved out into the hallway. The door shut with a loud clunk.

Doctor Black walked down the hallway and into the observation room where several people stood watching a TV monitor. Lisa's room was on the screen.

"You did very well, Doctor," Lyon Xavier said. "You've made her re-think and relive what happened so she's processed the information. Also, she has hope now, and that will make the operation go so much better."

"Thank you," Doctor Black said as she left the room.

The door to Lisa's cell whined and clunked again. This time two women appeared. They were dressed in green hospital scrubs and asked her in broken English to follow them into a room for a medical exam. There they stripped her, held her down, and shaved her head.

An obese man perspired heavily as he gleefully watched the shaving process via a two-way mirror. Henry Rexan loved secretly observing the macabre. "Why did you ask my assistant Lorne to take this particular girl, Doctor?" he asked.

"Lisa was chosen because of her very high I.Q. and impressive computer knowledge and ability. She is going to be the first human being to have living brain tissue removed while she's conscious."

"Surely other unfortunates have had brain parts removed—albeit, while they were unconscious."

"Yes, but in this case, the removed tissue will be kept alive, and then later fused with computer components. We are creating the first ever fused brain-computer technology. We call it COBRA, for **Co**mputer **Bra**in interface. We want to find out if the brain component can be kept viable long enough to grow into and become part of our latest wave of smart chips, those that create their own programs. We think that a brain already knowledgeable in computers might be able to make the brain chip fusion process occur more easily. This is our first go at using the procedure to mass produce COBRA implants."

The medical staff watched as Lisa was moved into the operating theater.

Strapped facedown onto a gurney, naked and terrified, Lisa turned her head and cried out. An orderly immediately taped her mouth shut.

"Why won't this part affect the brain tissue? She's certainly traumatized now!" Rexan said.

"We've found through experimentation that the last few minutes before the extraction don't make a difference, as long as the brain is pre-processed by the psychologist. It's just like when someone is involved in an accident. People most often don't remember what happened the few minutes right before. It's as if the brain eliminates the memory to protect itself from the trauma."

"This certainly looks outlandish. There is no way the public should ever hear about this."

"You are exactly correct, Henry...except that once people see the benefits of an implant, they won't care."

"It's kind of like watching an execution," said Rexan. "I'm so glad you invited me."

"If you don't mind, I'm going to go in and assist."

"Xavier, this must be costing a fortune. Is that why you asked me to come, and why you asked our people to arrange for the procurement of the girl?"

"You are a shrewd man, Henry. Truth is, I've been watching your work in Europe. I've admired what you are trying to accomplish, to bring back some pride to our country. My father was a supporter of yours, before he died."

"Really?"

"Yes. I believe in what you are doing, in trying to unite Europe into one strong nation. But I see the resistance, and I think my implant technology can help you and your cause. Perhaps together we can create the kind of manpower you need, with the kinds of skills and, shall we say, loyalty."

Rexan nodded thoughtfully. "I have read your material, as have my men. We agree this is an interesting possibility, if it works."

"It will work. I will not fail."

"What could I do for you, in exchange for your 'technology,' as you call it?"

"I need two things from you: money and volunteers to be implanted. I understand you have the kind of following who would be excellent recipients. In exchange for your help, I will make you an army. Not only will I make you an army, I'll make you a nation."

"Interesting proposal, Xavier, but I remain unconvinced."

"Just watch, Henry, just watch. It's time for me to go in now. I don't want to miss the end."

Lyon Xavier placed a surgical mask over her mouth and opened the door to the surgery.

Rexan watched her walk away, and enjoyed it.

The surgeon's voice now came from the operating room. "Let's begin the procedure by freezing the neck and head."

"Won't that affect the brain?" Rexan asked one of the Columbian staff who remained behind the two-way mirror.

"No, it's only a local anesthetic. It seems to lessen the struggle and make it less likely that the brain will be damaged as it's removed."

"When do you think you'll be able to mass produce the implants?"

"If this works as we anticipate, we could be mass-producing implants within the next few weeks."

"How many?"

"Well, we'll need to perfect the process to the point where it can be done at a factory level. Our engineers are working on that right now. But...the lack of funds has been slowing us up. I shouldn't really be telling you this, but I've heard from some of the department managers that this project is sucking the company dry. I've even heard that we won't last the month. Somebody said we shouldn't count on next month's paycheck."

"That would be a shame, wouldn't it? What if someone else took over?" Rexan grinned.

"Dr. Lyon is the brains of the operation. Only she really knows all the steps and procedures. She's brilliant, but holds on to the company for all she's worth."

Rexan smiled. "You've been very helpful."

Rexan took out a crisp American $1000 bill and a pen. He wrote something on the back and handed it over. The Columbian pocketed it immediately.

"Should you come across any more information that a potential investor such as myself might find valuable, you'll find my email address written on that bill."

The local looked into Rexan's eyes, folded the bill and placed it into his pocket, and walked away.

"Fool," Rexan muttered to himself.

2

Lisa had felt a coolness on her neck as the attendants shaved the back of her head and painted it with antiseptic in the operating room. She was too terrified to move, much less resist. Her body was shaking with fear. She felt so alone.

As she lay facedown, nurses taped various monitoring devices all over her body. She felt the prick of a needle as it was inserted into the now-bare skin that covered her skull.

God, help me, she prayed.

And suddenly, she knew she was not alone. Goodness and mercy was with her. God himself was with her. Phrases came to mind from all her years in Sunday school, with Mr. Motz. *Call on God in trouble. He is an ever-present help....* She wished Mr. Motz could be here, with her now. She wished she remembered everything he'd said.

Numbness crept over her skin as the anesthetic took effect. But evidently the chemicals only affected the very surface of the skin and didn't work on the deeper tissue. She felt slight tugs at her skin as the scalpel did its work and the surgeon uncovered the base of her skull. The sound of a drill came next. She heard her own muffled screams, echoing in the room, as the drill bit into the bone of her skull. The accompanying vibrations racked her very soul.

And then she knew. *I'm going to die...*

The drill soon broke through her tough outer skull. Mercifully, she passed out and missed the removal of the core of her brain. Her last visual image was that of the laptop computer sitting on a table just a few feet from her face. The screen saver absentmindedly produced an ever-changing three-dimensional image: *COBRA—Creating Your Tomorrow"* was the image her eyes recorded.

"That was great, just like the animal studies," said the surgeon who was performing the operation. "I told you we didn't need to knock her out. We now have an undrugged nerve matrix just waiting to be processed!"

It was over. The girl's last living brain cells now lay before them, existing as a core deep in a probe that had been inserted through the freshly drilled hole in her skull.

"Excellent work, Doctor. Now let's hurry and get it ready for processing," said Lyon. She was, at first viewing, not unlike the girl who was on the operating table. Her blond hair was arranged in a similar ponytail style. She'd arrived to work wearing jeans and a blue top that showed off her amazing physical features. She was built like an ice skater.

But now she was a scientist—an emotionally void, cold, and calculating scientist. She was perfect for the role. Earlier in life, she had learned not to care, not to trust, and not to get involved. Her father had taught her very well, by example.

So Dr. Xavier Lyon watched uncaringly as the body on the table convulsed, unable to survive without the base of its brain. Eventually the body came to rest, and lay still.

"Unfortunately, all of our donors seem to, well, expire at this stage. The trauma is too great for us to get another viable core," said the surgeon, pointing at the now lifeless body on the table.

Lyon walked over to where the doctor was removing the core from the extraction device. Bathed in highly oxygenated artificial blood, the cells of the girl continued to live, to fire, to feel.

"Any success with the new drug combinations I suggested?"

The surgeon carefully removed the white material from the coring device. He was treating it with far more care than he had shown the young lady while she was intact.

"No. We tried using various anesthetics, but they messed up our quality control. They seemed to help the donors, of course, but then we couldn't get the kind of unaltered drug-free tissue we need for the fusion process. Any drugs we used inhibited the process of growing into the silicon interface. Besides, she isn't feeling any pain now, is she?"

"Isn't she?"

"Actually, I don't really know, now that you mention it."

The surgeon carefully placed the brain tissue, which was the consistency of weak tofu, onto a small electric device. The device held the tissue submerged in the cooled liquid bath that kept the cells alive. As soon as the cooling process had made the tissue more solid and stronger, a moving arm held it against a scalpel edge and rotated it. The engineers had brainstormed the idea while watching an old-fashioned apple peeler at work. This infinitely more complex machine delicately sliced her brain into one long layer. The resulting strip was immediately passed into a bath that contained a supportive gel, which further supported the matrix of nerve cells that was all that was left of Lisa. After leaving the bath the strip was merged with a matching strip substrate of silicon/germanium crystal, then immediately sprayed with a fine mist that coated, set, and protected the structure. The strip was then cut into wafers. The final product of the implant machine was a workable material that was robust enough to be transformed into various implant configurations, all the while still being kept alive.

"Her particular shelf life, if kept refrigerated, is four weeks," the worker commented as he walked past.

"Her?" Lyon wrinkled her nose.

"I guess I think of her as being still alive in there," the surgeon said.

"How sentimental," Lyon said. "Update me on the fusion process."

"The process creates a living tissue fused to a computer chip. Within a few days, the nerve cells are able to grow into the chip and interact with it completely. We're using antirejection drugs to speed the process."

"Well done!" said Lyon. "What is the latest on the reimplantation process?"

"We wind the wafer into a spiral and then solidify it. It gets injected right into the base of the brain and grows and lives there."

"How long does it take to heal and become integrated with the recipient's brain?" asked Lyon.

"It used to take about two weeks working with animals, but now it'll probably be only a couple of hours. The move to eliminating anesthetic was a stroke of genius."

"What about the initial rejection problems you had?"

"The gel that coats the implant is hypoallergenic and also semipermeable. That means the nerves can transfer messages into the implant without creating major rejection issues."

"How many implants can you get from this core?"

"We estimate about one thousand implantable sections."

"Excellent work, Doctor. COBRA will be very appreciative of both your work and your silence."

"There's something else, something unexpected."

"What's that?"

"In the animal studies, we found that the DNA of the brain cells began to act as memory for the chip. It seemed to happen spontaneously. It's like a new form of memory. I think it's going three-dimensional."

"What does that mean to us?"

"Well, so far, all the memory architectures have been linear. By going three-dimensional, the capacity to hold programs, and even to create them, is hugely increased. It's a chip-maker's dream."

"What about the effects on the brain?"

"We're not sure. The evolution of the human brain is remarkable, but this is the ultimate in the evolutionary process."

"You've done fine work, Doctor, but tell me: are you personally ready to be implanted?"

"In a second, Dr. Lyon, in a second."

Dr. Lyon nodded in approval. "You've done remarkable work. Please send me the data as soon as possible."

"Thank you, Doctor," said the surgeon, who went back to his gruesome work.

Xavier Lyon moved away from the machine that was preparing the implants. She walked by the body of the student named Lisa, glancing briefly at the blue and horribly open eyes. Already they were drying out and glazing over. The girl was pretty, even in death, Lyon thought. She was probably a cheerleader when she was in high school.

"I wonder if your daddy came to *your* practices?" Dr. Lyon said to the lifeless body. She placed her hand on the still warm hand of the body. "Go team go," she said to no one in particular as she moved past the body of the girl and in the direction of her office.

As she approached the door, the smoke and body odors coming from the room nearly made her gasp. Henry was still there, as was his stench.

"So Henry, what did you think?"

"I'll need time to think..."

"Henry, if the tissue from Lisa performs as our studies indicate, and we have the funds we need to expand our operations, as fast as you send us recruits is as fast as you'll have your soldiers. The first thousand will be implanted, trained, and sent to you. That will clear my debt to you. After that, well, I'm sure you'll want many more at a reasonable price."

Rexan's instincts told him this was no time to hesitate—that he needed to say yes, and worry about the details later. "Dr. Lyon, your money will be here tomorrow, and your recruits, within a week. I'll send you a thousand of my best."

She didn't smile. That would have been uncharacteristic of her temperament. She simply nodded in agreement.

Rexan turned and noticed two security people waiting just outside her office door. They escorted him to the outside doors of the building and opened them.

Once outside, he was blasted by the heat, humidity, and fetid odors of the city. He strolled to the parking lot adjoining the two-story warehouse that housed the research facilities of COBRA. The building, built originally in 1956, was located in the southern part of Bogotá. Surrounded by nondescript, untended fields filled with low scrub brushes and grasses, it perched on the top of a hill. The tropical sun peeled old paint from the walls and window frames, revealing wood-bleached gray.

At each corner of the property, as well as at the road leading to the main entrance of the building, sat identical unmarked vans. There, lounging outside each van on lawn chairs, were several men. They appeared to be loitering and were smoking, drinking, or playing cards. At each of their feet lay a duffel bag. Inside each bag was a personal arsenal. AK-47 assault rifles with duel drum ammunition feeds, Uzis, and scoped M16s were all within easy reach of the owners. Brut strength seemed to be the forte of this particular class of security men. Clearly, no unexpected visitors could get near the building where the experimental surgery was occurring. The men appeared to enjoy the work…perhaps because of the pay.

On the roof of the warehouse, posted every 20 feet or so, Henry observed another class of security personnel standing watch. These were uniformed, and appeared to be the well-trained, well-paid men and women who clearly could ensure the building's internal integrity. The personnel here were armed with rifles, as well as shoulder-launched wire-guided missiles, capable of destroying aircraft as well as ground vehicles.

The research complex itself was a study of opposites, Rexan observed. The outside drew no undesired attention. Its facade was filthy and decaying, while inside it was completely renovated, freshly painted, and a technological flurry of activity. Closed-circuit TV cameras were everywhere. The operating and recovery rooms of the "hospital" were, in large part, as well equipped and modern as one might find in a university research lab. Except for the occasional screams that could penetrate the walls from the brain extraction rooms, the facility could have been located at a university anywhere in the world. Yet, because of the use of humans, the lab research facilities were highly secretive, as well as being highly illegal. Those outsiders who knew of the existence of the building assumed it was part of the drug trade in Colombia, a view not dispelled by the building's owners.

Henry Rexan smiled to himself as he thought of the opportunity unfolding before his very eyes. He had just been asked by Lyon to finance the final phase of the implementation process. It was a position he loved—to be the Savior of a promising company that was underfunded and about to sink. As he had done many times in the past, he could arrange for some high-cost interim financing in the hopes the troubled company could not make payments; then he would swoop in and take it over. Yet this particular company offered the opportunity for him to do so much more. It was everything he'd dreamed of. For the first time in several years, he felt the kind of excitement and anticipation that seemed unattainable without the shedding of blood. He felt truly alive once more.

The 120 percent humidity of the Colombian air was taking its toll on Rexan's nylon shirt, drenching it in sweat. As he pondered his next move, he subconsciously scratched at the rash developing between the folds of fat that made up his extensive stomach.

Sitting in her office, the elated Dr. Xavier Lyon waited until the door shut, and lifted her arms in triumph. She had taken her company from the brink of bankruptcy to a potential world technological leader in about 45 minutes. She deserved a break in order to celebrate. She decided she deserved to go on a good long run.

Lyon stepped from the office and into the adjoining private restroom. She removed her jeans and top, neatly folded them, and placed them on a chair. Reaching into her closet, she selected and pulled on a skintight jogging outfit. As she laced up her runners, she rubbed her knee. It was stiff, as usual, from a skating accident when she was fourteen. Next, she stood up and positioned a terry headband over her forehead and ponytail.

Reading the updates on the preparations for the production of prototype implants after watching the successful extraction of Lisa's brain had left her exhilarated. Already she could see that an earlier decision to begin the process of preparing for mass production was wise. In various places throughout the complex industrial base of COBRA, factories were being readied to begin a process that only now was being perfected. It certainly was the Japanese idea of "just in time" delivery of inventory, taken to the highest level. If Rexan agreed, the initial group of volunteers to be implanted with the "Lisa" version could arrive within two weeks. What a delight it would be to have Rexan's services, she thought, thrilled. She looked forward to a long run to burn off some of her excess energy. Despite the financial pressures, she was confident now that they could be overcome, even if it meant using Henry Rexan's money and power.

As she left her office, dressed and ready for her run, she passed by many of the workers who were making the research so productive. She uncharacteristically grinned and said hello to several. As she approached the exit that led out of the building, she nodded at the guards who were leaning against the wall near the armor-plated outside door. Several self-consciously looked away from the blond, tanned woman who was their boss. They did not want their eyes to give away what they were thinking. Their Uzi automatics rested comfortably on their hips.

Once outside, the humidity immediately assaulted Dr. Lyon's muscular body, and perspiration soon glistened in the sunlight as it emerged from her pores. The men in the vans strategically parked around the building, creating the defensive shell, stared but didn't offer the customary whistles and catcalls that would befall any other woman of her caliber. They feared her too much, and for good reason.

Lyon prepared for her run with several stretches that loosened and readied her legs for the assault that was about to take place on them. She expected perfection from herself and it showed in her obsessive warmup. She then began to run with the determination and passion that marked her existence.

As Lyon rounded the corner of the complex, she came across one of the guards, serenely asleep in the shade that protruded from a corner of the building. The young man was about nineteen years old and was dressed in a Nike shirt and khaki shorts. His right and left hand covered his weapon and walkie-talkie respectively. Lyon admired the lean body and olive skin of the guard for a moment, then she continued past without missing a step of her run.

Five miles later, drenched in sweat and breathing heavily, she retraced the path that had led her out earlier from the building. She found the guard, still asleep.

After reaching the air-conditioned coolness of her office, she grasped a towel and wiped the salty sweat from her face and upper body. Opening the door of the small refrigerator that was within easy reach, she removed and drank gratefully from one of the water bottles. She felt invigorated and full of life.

Reached for the desk phone, she tapped the security director's speed-dial button. "Jacko, one of your staff is sleeping around the Northeast corner," stated Lyon in a matter-of-fact tone. "I'd like him eliminated from the payroll immediately."

"I'm so sorry, Dr. Xavier. It'll be taken care of right away!"

exclaimed the head of security.

She continued, "Also, please deduct this month's salary from your wages. You don't seem to be earning it, do you?"

"No, Dr. Lyon. It will be done. I apologize. Is there anything else I can do?"

Lyon hung up without saying another word. She then removed her sweat-saturated clothes and threw them into the laundry basket in the corner of the spacious private bathroom that adjoined her office. She approached the marble lined shower. Reaching for the cold water tap, she turned it on full blast and stepped into the enclosure. The near ice temperature water shocked her body into greater rebellion, which she quickly quelled. Her willpower and determination kept her there.

Moments later she smiled as the sound of the running water that was refreshing and cleansing her body mixed with the muffled shots ending the sleeping guard's life. Turning down the force of the cold water, she reached for the hot water tap and began to add warmth to the mix, as if to slowly reward her muscles for surviving the punishment of exercise coupled with the icy shower. Soon the water was the temperature of a warm bath and her body was becoming limp as the muscle cells began to relax. Finally, she turned off the water completely and began to dry off, using the sweet-smelling towels her staff provided every day. She thought about the foolish guard and smiled again. It was a cheap lesson for the rest of the staff. They could even share his pay for the time he'd worked, up to his untimely death. Actually, his death was a good investment in several respects.

Outside, the guards watched as the fuming Jacko Rameze stood next to the still-quivering body of the young man. Jacko was angry at having lost a month's wages as a result of the stupid and fatally shot idiot that now lay crumpled on the ground.

Jacko held his trademark machete. He stroked the razor-sharp blade of the massive knife with his thumb as the others watched in eager anticipation. Swinging the blade high above his head, he paused, then accelerated the steel and wooden implement smoothly towards the back of the neck that emerged from the blood-soaked shirt. He felt satisfaction as the blade quickly and cleanly separated the body of the guard from his head. Jacko still had the touch…and he would use it to teach the other guards a valuable lesson about their employer.

He picked up the detached head and placed it in a white garbage bag. "Leave the rest of him for a few days, boys, to remind you of how to behave while you are here," spat out Jacko.

The bag containing the head was given to one of guards, who immediately delivered it to the laboratory.

There a technician nonchalantly said his thanks, put on some rubber gloves, and reached into the bag. He felt for and then grasped the head hair, pulled the grisly contents from the bag, and placed it in a bucket. Taking a plastic container to the ice machine across the room, he gathered some party ice cubes, to which he added prepared saline solution. He unceremoniously poured the contents into the bucket that held the head.

"Once it's cooled, you can use the brain to test the newest modifications of the neural slicing machine. It's more realistic than an animal, eh?" observed a colleague as he looked down into the bucket. He was just finishing off a large piece of chocolate cake, chewing it slowly as he peered into the bucket.

The lifeless head was bobbing slowly in liquid, its nose just barely breaching the surface of the saline and then slowly sinking below it. Finally, of its own accord, the head sunk into the pink slurry of ice, blood, and water, and came to rest on the bottom.

Brains, like cake, take about an hour to cool properly before they are ready for cutting.

3

D r. Lyon left the office and walked past the decapitated body of the lazy guard. Already flies had gathered and were using it as an egg repository. She looked up and saw a single vulture, soaring high above. It was a good sign, she thought.

She strode purposefully towards the parking lot and climbed into her jet-black BMW convertible. Her knee ached from the run. It was a constant reminder of her past, of her failure to please her father. When she reached her car, she sat for a moment, massaging her knee. She leaned her head back against the headrest. Closing her eyes, she remembered.

As a child in Switzerland she had tried to earn the notice of her parents by excelling at everything she attempted. An only child, she was raised in a family consumed with wealth and a passion for its accumulation. At age six she had entered the prestigious Dupree School for girls. Here her natural athletic ability and astoundingly good looks found its home in figure skating. She spent many years developing and honing her skills. Because she possessed such beauty, many thought she should model. Her five-foot-ten stature and stately manner accelerated her fourteen years of age.

By the end of the school year, she was competing internationally for the German National team, while at the same time achieving the top academic marks for her class. Rising by 4 a.m. each and every morning, she would practice with her team and then for several more hours with her private coach. Next, she would attend classes at school or work with a tutor throughout the day. Her evenings were spent either at the rink or in the library. Needing little sleep, she'd collapse on her bed at 11 o'clock and sleep hard until her alarm woke her.

Outwardly, everything was provided for her and what was there was the best. But neither her mother nor her father had seldom seen her skate in competition. As the head of a multinational chemical company, and a fund raiser for a secret Neo Nazi organization, the New Europeans, her father seldom took time to spend with his daughter. Occasionally, appropriately timed gifts would arrive from him. These were excessive and often signed by her father's administrative assistant. Her mother was usually off traveling somewhere or involved with her social clubs. Calls would arrive from her mom, but they were often during school hours or in the middle of the night. Her mother could not deal with time zone differences.

Near the end of the skating season, the final selection for the German Olympic team was in its last stages. Xavier was very much in the running and favored to win the current competition. The first two programs she'd skated had gone very well and essentially the win was hers for the taking.

She bent over in the preparation area located just off the ice and tightened her skates one last time.

The crowds were applauding the last skater. The girl had fallen twice, but had made a valiant effort and was holding on to second place. *She'll be the first loser,* Xavier thought.

Xavier's outfit was spectacular. Cleverly designed, it used her natural beauty in such a way as to draw the attention of both the male and female judges, although for different reasons. Her choreography was appropriately nationalistic and moving, yet clearly cosmopolitan. The music was dynamic while exquisitely simple. She was the best money could buy.

As the beautiful skater tightened the final knot of her skate, a voice sliced through the noise of the crowd. "We expect success, Xavier," was all it said.

By the time she looked up, all she could see was the tall image of her father. He was hurrying up the steps towards the top of the arena.

Moments later she stepped onto the ice surface. Slowly she drifted around the arena, awaiting her cue to begin. She looked up to the executive boxes and saw her father settle at a table, barely able to see the full ice surface.

Her heart was pounding. It was so unusual for him to attend…and very unnerving.

As her music began, Xavier mercifully had no idea her father had opened his briefcase and was reviewing his plans to acquire a new company in Central America. Clearly in command of herself again, Xavier was flying through her program. On fire and passionate, she landed jump after jump in preparation for the final and most difficult sequence. Her radiant eyes and perfect teeth flashed confidence as she passed, smiling, near the judges.

Her final jump was the quad toe. She would have to carry sufficient height and energy into the jump to rotate completely four times and then land cleanly and beautifully. It was extremely difficult.

Thrilled at her performance thus far, she glided across the ice and began to set up for her final leap. She completed her three-turn and set the pick of her skate deeply into the brittle ice. Shifting her weight to add to her already significant momentum, she left the surface of the ice and ascended into the air.

Time seemed to slow down for the young skater as her body completed the first three rotations. The crowd was silenced by the perfection they were witnessing. As she spun on the fourth and most difficult revolution, her skates neared the ice again. Orienting herself was difficult because of the speed of the spin. As she went to place her foot down, the voice of her father welled up from her subconscious. "We expect success...."

Whether it was a momentary loss of concentration or a flaw in the ice, she would never really know.

Whatever the reason, her momentum carried her body too far. Her skate caught the ice and began to bear her weight. As her momentum carried her upper body forward, the contradicting forces that had met at her joints twisted her knee like one might twist a wet washcloth in order to wring out the water. As the ligaments stretched and tore, pain sliced up her leg. Continuing to be twisted and now grotesquely misshapen, her joints and connective tissue virtually exploded internally. She hit the ice hard. Her head snapped back and crashed her skull down.

It was only then that her father happened to look down on the surface and see his daughter lying limp on the ice.

"Unacceptable," he said to himself.

He looked away and went back to read the last paragraph of the report that lay before him. When he had finished jotting down some notes, he rose from his seat, gathered his materials together, and walked down the stairs towards his waiting car. He stopped for a moment and watched as his daughter was lifted onto a stretcher.

She'd come to rest with her legs splayed across the ice and her foot pointed in the wrong direction altogether. As she was lowered onto the stretcher, pain seared through her grotesquely swollen knee. Her team doctor, kneeling at her side, whispered into her ear, "You'll heal, Xavier. Your performance was beautiful."

A tear fell from the cheek of the young skater as she was lifted into a waiting ambulance. As the rear doors of the vehicle opened to receive her, a tall man approached the girl. Sensing her father's presence, her face turned away in shame.

"You've wasted my time and money, little girl," he said, and then he turned and left.

At that moment, a new Voice was born. It was a voice that reminded her from time to time that she was not good enough, and that she would never be good enough as she was. She would have to find another way to seek perfection.

Rigid in the straps that bound her to the stretcher, she willed her eyes dry. She'd never hurt like this again, she vowed.

Although her body would heal, she would never again place her foot into a figure skate....

Dr. Lyon fired her car up and drove it at breakneck speed to the outskirts of Bogotá and onto the long road that led to the international airport. Her drive for dominance had translated itself from figure skating and now resided in a new, albeit more sinister, competition. This time the prize was the human soul itself. Surely her father would not be able to find fault in that, particularly if it forwarded his own political views on the New Europeans.

Once at the airport, she parked the car and walked past the guards who leaned against the building in the shade, fingering their submachine guns.

Waiting for her flight to be called, she sat in the airport first-class lobby. She passed the time by reading some recently published research papers on computer-neurobiology, the topic of the international conference she was heading to. One of the keynote speakers at the conference was Dr. Jerry Chen, an unusually gifted software writer and hardware engineer from Canada. His research was brilliant and his findings remarkable. He was currently working on a technology package whose purpose was to enable the user to think directly into the processor of a computer. The process appeared to be similar to speech-reading software currently available, with one major difference: Chen's work used brain waves rather than sound waves.

As she read over his research results she knew she must meet this Doctor Chen. Perhaps some of his work might be useful to her, particularly the software. She smiled as she realized that regardless of his capabilities and reputation, it was she who was going to create the first truly computer-controlled human. She leaned her head back on the hard airport chair and imagined her future. Moments later her flight to Zurich was called. She boarded and made her way to the first-class section of the aircraft. The flight was uneventful, but tediously long. She spent the evening working on her laptop, getting the latest results from her team in Bogotá.

The next day, at the conference, Dr. Lyon sat in a spacious and well-appointed conference room, waiting for Dr. Jerry Chen's speech to begin.

A short, overweight, and balding Asian haltingly approached the podium. He appeared to have yellow and white egg stains on his lime green tie. His hair did not look combed and his brown pants clashed with his blue sports jacket.

Yet, despite his appearance, when he began to speak, she realized his brilliance. His understanding of the complexities of the human mind and the potential of the computer chip held her spellbound. Software was not one of her specialties, and it became clear listening to him that he had much to offer.

When he was finished speaking, she watched as he left the stage and sat at a table near the speaker's podium. At that table was a strikingly handsome, tall man who helped Chen settle in his seat. She wondered who this appetizing being was and peered closely to read his nametag: Edward Calais, from Vancouver Venture Capital.

Lyon then rose and walked towards the podium as a stodgy professor of neuroscience introduced her. When the introduction was over, she took over the podium and began to speak.

"Ladies and gentlemen, it is with great pride that I announce that our company, COBRA, has successfully created the first computerized living brain implant."

The crowd of PhDs and high-tech business giants hushed. She hesitated, for effect, then began to speak again.

"Just recently, we successfully removed brain stem tissue from a rhesus monkey and fused it to a miniaturized computer processor. We then covered the implant in a permeable membrane derived from the skin of the recipient and installed the device into the brain stem of an unrelated subject monkey."

Lyon activated her laptop and a series of images depicting the procedures appeared on the overhead screen. The audience was captivated.

When she was finished her lecture, she watched with satisfaction as hands across the room shot up for questions.

A noted researcher from UCLA stood up. "Is the processor able to interact with the animal's brain?"

"Yes, we are able to wirelessly send commands to the subject and it has learned to respond, so clearly the processor is able to communicate with the subject."

Another offered the following: "Is the monkey able to access the processor itself?"

"Yes, our studies have tested the monkey's ability to complete a maze that it had never seen before, but the processor had the solution to. The monkey solved the maze with no mistakes. Yes, Dr. Greene."

26

She pointed to another raised hand.

"Dr. Lyon, this is remarkable. Tell me about its application to humans."

"We believe that a human implant will be created in the very near future. Its application? Consider the potential of a human who is able to think as fast as our best microprocessor, who can access the databases of the world in an instant. Think of a medical doctor who is operating with the help of an implant. The future is truly remarkable."

Dr. Jerry Chen rose in his seat. His eyes never left the floor as he spoke. His words were spoken as a child might, with little emotion and monotone, as if rehearsing for a play. His fingers unconsciously pulled at his tie or plucked an invisible thread from his pants. He looked almost mentally ill. "Dr. Lyon, the jump to human experiments...is an...ethical nightmare. How do you propose to...remove living human brain tissue?"

Lyon stopped. She then answered very slowly. "You are right, Doctor Chen. Unfortunately our learned committees and university ethics police are not quite ready to allow the advanced experimentation required to bring this technology forward. We must use animals for now. If I had my way, though, we'd be reading about such advances in tomorrow's paper."

Jerry Chen sat down and whispered to his business associate, Mr. Edward Calais, "There is something wrong with her, Edward. She isn't giving us the whole story."

"I agree, Jerry, she is a little spooky. One good-looking spook, though!"

The three of them never saw each other again at the conference. Dr. Lyon flew back to Columbia, and Jerry Chen and Edward Calais traveled back together to Vancouver.

The next day, as Jerry drove to the university, he pondered Dr. Lyon's secret.

4

"Oh no, look at Dr. Chen. He missed the turn again!"

The two grad students peered out of a window on the third floor of the computer research lab and toward the road that circumnavigated Simon Fraser University. It was raining and the concrete Stonehenge behemoth of the university was characteristically shrouded in a cold misty fog, some of which condensed on the grey concrete dampening not only it, but all those whose eyes fell upon it. The students watched as a dirty Toyota truck with a flat-bottomed fly-fishing dingy thrown in the back turned the corner yet again, then disappeared one more time into the mist.

"I wish he'd get here. I need to know what to do next, and these subjects are getting restless."

The subjects, two undergrad students, sat with electrodes attached to a variety of locations on their newly shaven pasty white scalps. The electrodes were wired to a complicated looking device that amplified the faint electronic signals produced by their brains.

"Maybe, while we wait, I'll enter our latest findings on the web board and see if anyone else has made any progress."

"Good idea. I'm sure he'll be up in a few minutes, once he realizes he has driven around the ring four times. It's a good sign actually; he is probably so obsessed with this project that he keeps missing the turn. Maybe he's making a breakthough!"

"I hope so. Besides, the subjects can wait. They are getting paid by the hour and they are only *undergrads* after all."

"Good point."

Dr. Jerry Chen finally negotiated the turn successfully, parked his truck, and eventually arrived at his laboratory door. He was soaked from head to foot. He had neglected to bring the obligatory umbrella or hooded raincoat necessary to cope with the chronically rainy weather of Burnaby Mountain, upon which the university sat. Thankfully, his grad student assistants were prepared for this highly predictable and regularly occurring event by having an old, patched, SFU emblazoned tracksuit of his stored on a dusty shelf. They got it for him when they realized he was shivering. Chen apologized and stepped into his private office to change. It would have been better if he had taken the time to close the door because the undergrad subjects were subjected to a rather unpleasant view of the professor's ample backside sliding into a pair of undersized fleece pants.

Emerging from the office, Chen noticed a noodle from a hastily consumed past lunch had perched on the belly of the tracksuit. What appeared to be a smudge of greasy broth or perhaps a dollop of plum sauce held it in place. Jerry reached down and plucked the dried noodle off his top, and since the wastepaper basket was more than a noodle-throw away, he popped it into his mouth and smacked his lips in appreciation. Apparently it was somewhat brittle in its desiccated state, judging from the crunching emanating from his open mouth as he chewed.

The undergrad students who had waited for the experiment to begin sat wired to the machine, watching the professor swallow. They paled perceptively as they observed his state of disorganized, disheveled, and almost dismembered approach to the proceedings. They wondered what such a man was going to do to their brains.

Dr. Chen plopped himself on his infamous three-wheeled stool and brought it up to maximum speed as he flew towards the bird's nest of wires that surrounded and clung to the undergrads. The grad students had already brought the computers and other technical equipment up to speed.

"All right you two, pay attention! I am going to hold up pictures of objects and I want you to think of their name. Focus on the object alone and try not to think of anything else," instructed Dr. Chen.

One of the grad students held up a picture of a basketball for the undergrads to view.

The computer hummed as Chen's software worked to interpret the brain signals being fed to it by the electrodes. The screen printed the word *ball* for subject A and *basketball* for subject B.

"Excellent!" exclaimed Chen.

The next picture was of a dog. Subject A and B's screens indicated the word *dog.*

"Wonderful! Well, I think we have done it! The software seems to be intelligent and fast enough to reduce the rest of the dribble that is probably racing around these young minds."

The grad students beamed. This was several months of trial and failure, of working and reworking the hardware and adjusting and rewriting the software. It seemed they had a combination that was able to read a person's mind. It was a huge breakthrough, they thought.

"Now let's try something more challenging. I am going to recite the first few words of a poem. You think the next few words."

The subjects nodded in agreement.

"'Twas the night before Christmas…"

At that moment an attractive young coed strode by the office door, looked inside, and stopped. Peering in, she smiled and waved at the students, whom she clearly recognized. The two male subjects responded as one might predict and Chen's software dutifully reported their thoughts and projected them on the computer screen as quickly as they thought them.

As Dr. Chen viewed the screen, the thoughts of the two young male subjects began to appear on the screen. He blushed initially at their lewdness. Moments later, he dropped his head in disappointment because his program had crashed under the weight of the unsolicited but entirely natural deluge of expressions that poured forth from the hormone-soaked brains of his subjects. The computer screen went blank.

"It failed again! We are using the most sophisticated software and hardware system available in North America, yet it can't keep up with the human mind. I can't seem to create enough of a buffer to block the unnecessary sequences."

"At least we know your hardware functions, Dr. Chen."

"I suppose you are right. All right, send these perverts back to their residences. Then go online and see if anyone out there is making any headway with telemetry and interpretive software. You don't need to mention how sensitive the hardware we've built is. Using artificial human skin as the sensor pickup was a brilliant stroke of genius, thanks to you. By the way, a researcher, Dr. Xavier Lyon, in Bogotá of all places, is using skin as well, only she is using the real stuff. Makes you wonder how a private lab acquired the amounts of real skin necessary to conduct the research. You might want to try there. It's a private lab, so perhaps you won't have any luck."

"Thank you, Professor Chen, but it was your idea to try the artificial skin, not mine."

"Really? Well, I guess it doesn't really matter who gets the credit, so it will go to you. You're a big help and very forgiving of a forgetful crackpot professor."

Chen took off on his stool and flew into his cluttered office, determined to improve on his work.

His grad student, pleased with the compliment, went to the computer in the lab and queried the web board yet again. He inadvertently added a small comment on the board about using a human tissue pickup for a receiver medium.

Someone in Bogotá Columbia noticed an intriguing comment on the web board and wondered if other body parts could be useful now that both brain and skin appeared to have their value. They emailed Dr. Lyon with the link to Dr. Chen's website.

The stewardess in Rexan's corporate jet brought him a cup of tea after his meal of calves' brains and tripe.

"I'll have some white cake for dessert, and warm it up a bit," ordered Rexan. He could not get the image of fresh brain out of his mind, and he was glad. Food always allowed Henry to think more clearly and recently he was particularly drawn to the look and texture of fresh cake, especially still warm, and preferably close to body temperature. When the cake arrived, he leaned over and inhaled the delicious mixture of ingredients. The glistening surface of the cake was so much like Lisa's cranial membrane.

With crumbs gathering on his lap and his stomach, he reflected on the day's events at the COBRA complex. It was far more than he could have conceived. It was as if everything he was working towards had been handed to him on a plate, all sweet and rich and moist. This was not just another acquisition project. This had turned into something new—something so filled with potential and excitement that he wondered in awe at the convergence of events unfolding before him. It was as if some unseen force was acting on his behalf, bringing these events, these people, and this history into one beautiful confection ready to be consumed. He wolfed down the cake, savoring its sweetness.

What Henry had not counted on, though, was the lovely brutality he had witnessed with the removal of sweet Lisa's brain core, all white and tender. He relished those images, running them through his mind over and over again. It reminded him so much of his younger days. The days when he and a few thugs could simply enter a restaurant in Russia or a computer store in Leningrad and beat the owner into submission, get him to sign the business over, and then slash his throat. He missed the times when another criminal, not equal to the task, had attempted to begin operations in Henry's territory. For situations like that, he liked to use a Canadian named Lorne Browne to do the work. Lorne's job was to kidnap the offender's wife, lover, or children and use them for extortion. Who would ever suspect a well-spoken and cultured man such as Browne was capable of removing a child's digits and sending them via courier to his competition's home? If that didn't work, a car bomb did.

When the intriguing message from Dr. Lyon had arrived, and it included a request for the kidnapping of a young computer student named Lisa, it was Lorne he'd asked to do the job.

Although Henry did miss the throat-slashing, he knew the risk was too great. He had amassed too much wealth and acquired too many legitimate businesses to put them at risk over a little warm blood being sprayed on a tile floor, regardless of how much that appealed to him.

Occasionally men who had built up a business or taken over a family operation were so crushed by the manipulations of Rexan and at the loss of their business that they committed suicide. For Henry, that was like icing on the cake. He did love his cake.

Those were the days. He missed those simple times when murder and money were enough to satisfy his passions. Now he needed more to meet his needs. He had become addicted to raw power, pure and simple. The more he acquired, the more he needed. More powerful than crack, more intoxicating than ecstasy, his lust for supremacy loomed greater by the day. He needed a fix, and apparently, soon he would have it, if he played his cards well.

Like his hero from the past, he imagined personally restoring his homeland to its proper place. While he had the makings of such a dream, including money, and a virtual battalion of henchmen, it was not enough to ensure a swift, lasting victory. Having an army sufficient to finish the job was essential as made evident from Lexan's study of history. Lyon's implants could provide him with that, and quickly.

The scattered limping Europe Economic Community, pathetically striving for the mediocrity of an American-like democracy, was ripe for such a man, such a leader as himself, but she needed discipline, the kind that only an army could provide and enforce. Also, his enemies needed to be eliminated. Once discipline was maintained and his enemies dead, Rexan's dreams for tomorrow could truly begin. He dreamed of leading a powerful military, completely dedicated and loyal to him personally. But progress was too slow for his liking.

He reviewed the technical report prepared for him by COBRA staff. The initial data on the implants implied that a motivated volunteer, implanted and properly trained and equipped, was worth the equivalent of at least ten regular men. He ran the numbers and the data Lyon had provided in his head. If he could get Lyon to mass-produce the implants, and if he provided her the recruits, he'd have a militia of one thousand in weeks, and his army virtually within months. He thought about such an army, goose-stepping in front of a giant grandstand with him at the centre, perhaps Xavier Lyon at his side. With an implant in her and him at the control of it, she would be so willing. Once his personal army was in place, he needn't use them to blitzkrieg across Europe with tanks and planes; he could use his army to ensure that the implanting of all the peoples within his domain was accomplished. Each person, once implanted, had no choice but to fall under his control, because the implant enabled it to be so. The technology didn't require him, or his armies, to break the people's will; his will became imbedded in them, downloaded as a live update.

"Thy will be done" was a line that came to Rexan out of nowhere and for no apparent reason. He wasn't even sure of its origin.

Rexan's mind began to drift to the images of Germany in the 1930s that he had seen as a child on TV...flickering black and white images of a leader he truly admired, giving speeches that even today caused scattered tributes among the faithful such as the New Europeans. He saw the admiring fans, the people who needed a savior to pull them out of the disaster that was post World War I Germany. This courageous leader had failed because he didn't have an army sufficient for the task. This time would be different. With the direct control of the people via the implants, Rexan would not fail.

The visionary in Rexan saw into the future, where a new grand leader would free his people from oppression. He saw himself as that grand leader sitting at a table, free to consume Europe's very best entrees. Xavier Lyon, beautiful slice of cake that she was, could decorate a plate at his table, a suitable dessert. He closed his eyes and rested as his plane reached American airspace. He needed Lyon, but he had to be careful how he went about acquiring her.

5

During the flight home, Rexan opened the newspaper and read about the U.S. Congress's involvement in the removal of a feeding tube from some woman who was in a long-term vegetative state. He wondered how a society as powerful as the United States of America even considered saving the woman's life. If he had his way, the weak, infirm, helpless, or lowly wouldn't be around to waste a nation's valuable resources. He'd kill them all. But countries such as Canada and United States were known for their weak-kneed inability to deal with the misfits of genetics. Survival of the fittest wasn't even applied to humans in those places. And that was going to be a problem.

Rexan's flight attendant approached him with a phone. "It's Lorne Browne, sir."

Rexan nodded. "I'll take it...Lorne, how are things?"

"I think we need to think about the political reality of what we are trying to accomplish, Henry."

"What do you mean?" laughed Henry. "We have always managed to purchase all the support we've needed in the past."

"That is true, but now we are dealing with North America."

"How is that different?"

"The Americans are the self-proclaimed police force of the world. When they find out how the implants are being created, and that their genesis was the necessary sacrifice of human life, they will act to destroy everything. It would be a huge political sidestep for the struggling Democrat President. He is currently plagued by his failure in the Middle East and could easily choose to divert the attention of the press off that and put it on us. He could cry that it was the work of the devil himself and that only evil would come of such accomplishments, no matter how great they are. "

Rexan closed his eyes and the pre World War II vintage flickering black and white images reappeared, except this time it was him making the speech. A grin crept over his face. "We'll just have to make sure the Canadians or Americans don't find out how we have done things until it is too late."

"I agree. We'll need to hurry things up. Are our computing systems safe from hackers?" interjected Browne.

"Absolutely. We have nothing to fear. Nothing sort of a miracle would allow anyone to get past our security."

"Excellent. We're poised to do something no one has ever done before. We are about to bring the whole world under one umbrella, and under our protection."

"I know, Lorne. It seems too good to be true. By the way, when are you getting implanted?"

"As soon as possible. How about you?"

"Same. Good-bye, Lorne. Your loyalty will not be forgotten."

Rexan hung up the phone and thought about what he had seen in Bogotá and smiled again. What a perfect couple of days for a future dictator.

Rexan moved to his computer and ran his chubby paws over the keyboard. The email he was drafting to Dr. Lyon described the details of a mutually rewarding exchange of products and services between him and her company, COBRA. Rexan's roadmap to victory, as he coined it, called on COBRA to prefect the mass production of implants and to insert them into Rexan's handpicked men and women. In return, Rexan would work with Lyon to provide her company with the funds necessary to perfect her work and market it worldwide. As if guided, Rexan's mind and fingers wove a web of semitruths and outright lies that needed to be irresistible to Lyon. What was truthful was his desire to become more involved with her. What was unclear was the nature of his desires.

It was time.

Dr. Lyon could see that unless she became implanted herself, her subordinates would become more capable than her. That was unacceptable. No one would ever beat her again. Her father's ghost would not allow that. His voice still haunted her.

Being implanted was still a risk, though. No real long-term studies had been done, but still it was time and she knew it. Dr. Lyon sat in the chair specially designed to aid the implantation process. The molded arms and back of the custom chair had grips and straps designed to hold the implantee. She refused them. Her head was inserted into a restraining device. Lyon felt vaguely claustrophobic and unusually helpless.

The nurse carefully cut and then shaved off a coin-sized area of her golden hair. A damp swab of cotton soaked in topical anesthetic touched her on the back of her head at the site. She closed her eyes and felt the cold steel of the implant injector resting on her skin.

"Are you ready, Dr. Lyon?" asked the surgeon.

"Do it!"

The surgeon reached down and applied the instrument to her lovely neck. He pressed the trigger. A quick clunk and a small piece of Lisa was driven into the base of the brain of Dr. Xavier Lyon.

It was over.

She couldn't believe how quickly it had happened. So much had already been learned in a few short weeks. The technique was virtually painless and very quick.

Lyon arose from the table, and waited for a bandage to be applied. As she stood up, she felt a little dizzy. On the way back to her office, she maintained her dignity, never stumbling, knowing all eyes were on her.

Once she entered her private domain, she rested at her desk for a few minutes, cupping her chin with her hands. When she was ready, she raised her head. It was then that it happened. Her innermost being began to fuse with the implant. It was a wonderful melding of technology and ambition. She leaned her head back and smiled as the flow of information and capabilities began to flood into her consciousness. Her central nervous system began to acquire and plot new pathways. Her cerebrum and cortex became immersed in a way that made her previous brain function seem timid and slow. Yet, for

Lyon, this was only the beginning of her personal evolution.

As she soaked in the power of the implant, occasional vague references of Lisa intruded, as if to insist that she lived. But Lyon quickly suppressed them, just as she repressed memories of her father. She was an expert at repression, something she had developed over years of hideous childhood events. In these circumstances the ability to repress feelings and innermost thoughts was tremendous psychological advantage.

Unfortunately for COBRA corporation, not all the implanted individuals were able to repress their inner selves, or even the manifestations of their donor, Lisa. Lisa was not dead, just living inside of them, and they didn't even completely realize it.

The first batch of volunteers was beginning to arrive in Colombian airspace. The chartered aircraft that held them had visited a scattering of cities throughout Europe. Most of these elite volunteers spoke several languages and they came from a variety of ethnic backgrounds. What they had in common was that they shared a common vision. The vision they shared was of the rebuilding of Europe, and they wanted to lead that rebuilding. They were the New Europeans, and they were soon to have portions of Lisa's extracted brain inserted into theirs.

For the volunteers, the drive from the airport to the research and implantation facilities of COBRA was quiet and uneventful, unlike what was about to befall them. The volunteers talked a little amongst themselves, once they found others they could communicate with. The buses they were riding in were comfortable enough and several of the passengers fell asleep until they arrived at the compound. As the buses passed the guard vans, several men noticed and commented to the others as they observed the armed guards casually sitting in lawn chairs, smoking.

"Such men would never survive in our New Germany," said one.

"Hopefully none will," replied his neighbors with a hearty, if not nervous, laugh.

The bus came to a halt beside the rear entrance of the building and the occupants were discharged from the vehicle. Several more professional and sterner looking security personnel held open the door to the compound the volunteers would call home for the next few weeks.

The men were moved into a gym-like part of the compound and told to line up. They stood nervously for several minutes and tried to imagine what the experience of being implanted would be like. They knew for the most part that each of them was to play an important and patriotic role in the reclaiming of their homelands. They just were not sure what the role was. These men were selected from thousands who had attended meetings of the New Europeans and had volunteered to be implanted and then placed as leaders. All were investigated and those showing the most promise physically and mentally were questioned further. Most were university educated, in their twenties or thirties and prime specimens. They also showed signs of being of acceptable temperament. The men waited.

Minutes later, Dr. Xavier Lyon entered the room followed by Jacko, who was strutting and making it clear he was the head of security at COBRA. Having just returned from her daily run, she was breathing heavily and still sweating profusely. These factors, though, did not detract, and many might argue, added to her appearance—at least in the eyes of one of the observers.

Several of the men stared at her and grinned as she marched in.

A tall dark-haired recruit in the front row whistled quietly in appreciation as much as anything else. Lyon said nothing as she started her inspection at one end and then proceeded down the line, inspecting each man briefly. Halfway down, she stopped in front of the man who had whistled at her.

"Do you know who I am?" she asked with a crystalline smile.

"I do, and you are even better looking this close, Dr. Lyon," said the handsome man who stood before her. She stood for a moment, admiring his green eyes and strong chin.

"Thank you," she said, smiled coyly, then turned, strolling further down the line. The man turned his face and grinned to the recruit who stood at attention beside him.

Lyon stepped back and, with the quickness of a viper, lifted and kicked her left foot at the face of the still grinning and completely unsuspecting victim. His peripheral vision caught a blur of motion and he instinctively turned his face towards her. The heel of her running shoe met his face. The force of the impact immediately crushed his jawbone and shattered several teeth, ripping them from their sockets. The new recruit was pushed backwards by the force of the blow.

Lyon took two steps towards him and this time her right foot swung in a deadly arc. The front of her Nike Air led the assault on his ribs and broke several on impact. The volunteer collapsed in pain and fell to the floor, holding his face with one hand and his chest with the other. No one else moved. He lay on the concrete floor, wheezing.

An insult that questioned her species hissed from the rapidly swelling and bloody mouth. His eyes, despite the pain, still glared in defiance.

Jacko walked over to the crumpled ball of manhood and, in one fast motion, withdrew his sidearm and shot the man in the face, killing him instantly. Jacko stood above the body, the hand carrying the pistol hanging still, the gun barrel pointed downwards as a wisp of smoke curled gently from it. He turned to face the remaining men in the line. Standing almost motionless, his dark eyes found the man who had only just recently rubbed shoulders with the unfortunate on the floor. He stared at him until the man was compelled to look to the ground. Jacko surveyed the group for any further signs of rebellion. Each pair of eyes he met affirmed his dominance, or perhaps more truthfully, the eyes told of their owner's submission to her.

Dr. Lyon stepped forward and wiped the blood from her runners onto the shirt of the body. She then completed her inspection of the line and moved front and center. There she stood, feet apart, and began to address her men. They looked straight ahead, spirits broken.

"Gentlemen, is there anyone else who would like to be disrespectful?"

Each remained at attention, eyes straight ahead. Not one moved. The only sound was Jacko's machete doing its grisly, yet traditional decapitation of the offender.

"Excellent. At ease," she commanded.

The men, although few had formal military training, assumed the correct posture and position.

6

It was early in the morning. A summer breeze wafted through the screen door, bringing the sharp taste of salt water with it. The sheer white curtains that covered the wire mesh intermittently caught the breezes and intruded deep into the bedroom, only to fall limp once the air stilled.

Seagulls far below the window cried as they fought for the scraps that the receding tide had left behind. The young of the flock often could not fight their way past the slashing beaks of the older, stronger birds. Many perished from starvation, unable to feed themselves once their mothers had abandoned them. Their cries were lonely, pathetic, and haunting.

Edward Calais was still weary from the trip back from the conference he had attended with his friend and business associate, Dr. Jerry Chen. As an entrepreneur and visionary, he reflected on Lyon's announcement of COBRA's success.

Indeed, Calais was entirely capable of picturing a world populated by creatures who had been implanted using Dr. Lyon's technology. He imagined the marketing and sales possibilities, to say nothing of the opportunity to invest in the company doing the implanting itself. He imagined the power of being able to insert ideas directly into the brains of people. It was certainly seductive.

Calais threw back the duvet that covered him, arose, and left the massive king-sized bed in which he had slept. He walked from the bedroom into the kitchen, where he poured a cup of coffee. He selected some fruit from the fridge, and as was his custom, returned to the bedroom. Wearing only his bathrobe and slippers against the coolness of the dawn, he stepped past the two warm bundles of flannelette and curls—his wife and daughter—who also occupied his bed. Edward silently slid open the screen door that led from their bedroom and onto the balcony.

Last night had not been a good one with Jane. He was weary from the trip, and what's more, good nights were becoming less and less frequent and the troubled nights more confrontational.

Edward stood up from the chair and stepped towards the rail of the balcony. He placed his hands on the iron railing and felt the cold metal drawing the warmth from his palms. The seagulls' cries resonated in his heart, but only briefly.

Edward Calais did not understand how this could come to be. He loved his wife, or at least he thought he did, if one could define love. He showed how much he cared for her by working long hours to build an immensely successful business in venture capital.

He smiled to himself as he thought of his prowess in the business world. He was a prospector of sorts, and not unlike the brave souls that had carved a province out of barren wilderness during the gold rush days of the past. He thrived on risk, and of potential. If he could find a great new idea, match it with the right investor, it was like striking a motherlode of high-grade gold ore. On the other hand, a poor investment could turn out to be worthless, and an investor could lose millions on a deal that Calais had put together. Like the gold prospector, the risks, dangers, and potentials were all huge. It was not a game for the weak or nervous.

While Calais didn't look for gold hidden amongst the black sands of British Columbia's creeks and river beds as the gold miners did, he instead focused on uncovering rare nuggets of intellectual achievement emerging from the new and innovative high-tech companies exploding in the Vancouver area. From hydrogen fuel cells created to power pollution-free cars, to the best video-gaming producers in the world, Vancouver was definitely growing as a modern-day high-tech gold rush town. He wondered if COBRA represented the mother of all investment opportunities.

In his early years, Calais had graduated in Electrical Engineering from the University of British Columbia, then supplemented that by getting a Law degree from the University of Victoria, followed by an MBA from the Queens School of Business. Despite these amazing academic credentials, typical office work did not appeal to him...even if he was offered high pay and phenomenal perks upon graduation. Instead of becoming a high-priced cog in a corporate wheel, he sought to start from scratch, to be in charge of his own destiny.

When he first joined the company as a venture capital broker, he devoted 16-hour days to making cold calls. He put on poorly attended seminars on cutting edge companies, and played golf with potential or new investors. His first five years were lean years that he described once as "basically begging and telemarketing." Gradually, though, his highly instinctive, yet profoundly intelligent approach to hunting for new companies and investments began to pay off. He began to accumulate clients with substantial holdings to manage and found complementary undervalued companies ripe for investment. Calais's "book" of clients and investments began to grow exponentially. He hired support staff and his business and commissions grew and, with time, began to take care of themselves. Most other venture capital brokers who had reached the point of a self-sustaining business would begin to leave the office early to play golf or visit a mistress. Not Edward. If anything, he worked harder and stayed at the office longer. He worked unceasingly to provide and protect his wife and daughter, sure that nothing would ever happen to them as long as he did his job well; sure that his efforts were appreciated by Jane.

He had been wrong, on all counts.

For her part, Jane Calais simply could not understand why Edward did what he did. She didn't see why he could be so passionate about his work, yet treat her as peripheral. It wasn't that she didn't understand the world of business or what it took to be successful. Jane Calais had worked her way up as a tax lawyer and sleuth for the Canadian government. She specialized in uncovering company attempts to hide income in foreign banks, countries, and in webs of numbered companies. She had an uncanny ability to uncover the most hidden corporate secrets. Her skills soon caught the eyes of numerous corporate law firms with huge clients who needed to find the edge of legality. If she could dig them up, she certainly knew how to bury them.

Unexpectedly, Jane discovered she was pregnant the same week she was offered a full partnership in a major Vancouver law firm. There was no doubt in her mind about the decision; she didn't even ask Edward about it. She simply came home from work, parked the Miata in the condo parking lot, and announced that she had taken maternity leave and that they needed to buy a house with a view of the ocean and several bedrooms.

The distraction of house hunting and preparing for the baby eased the tension between husband and wife temporarily. They even began to attend church services together on Sunday mornings, for the eventual good of the child. Things seemed to be going well, at least from the outside. Yet Jane began to feel her husband drift further from her and their baby, Leah. She couldn't understand why his eyes would light up at the prospect of a new business venture or a high profile client acquisition, yet those same eyes would dull at the dinner table.

She worried about those eyes.

Far below the Calais home, the waters of Deep Cove were being swept by the wind, with whitecaps dancing over the deep blueness of the choppy ocean. The Calais home was still quiet, and Edward left for work much earlier than he needed to. As he left, Jane rolled over in bed and touched the pillow on his side of the bed. She pulled it close to her face, her nose drawing in the faint smell of his cologne. She held the pillow close, her tears staining its cover. She was alone again, save for their one remaining common bond, their little girl, Leah.

Jane felt like she'd sacrificed so much for her family and for her husband. She'd left her legal practice and the prospects of full partnership to tend to him and their daughter.

But that was not all. The first two years of their marriage had been amazing. Obsessed with each other, every available minute had been spent together. While they each worked 14-16-hour days and many weekends, the remaining time was a vision of passion juxtaposed with quiet devotion.

He did all the right things and said all the right words. She felt safe in his arms and thought she saw love in her eyes.

But at the end of the third year she felt him changing. She had become a task, a project, a thing to be managed. He was spending more time at the office or on the golf course. Even when he was home, she sensed he still really wasn't with her; he was somewhere else.

She hated this new Edward.

7

The morning sun crept up and crawled over the dusty, smoggy hills of Bogotá. As her pure rays touched the atmosphere, they immediately entered the pollution of the city. The sun's progeny, blood red and hemorrhaging, soaked their way through the low-lying morning clouds like blood through an inadequate bandage. The carnage of Bogotá had claimed another innocent.

Dr. Lyon stood before the men. A cooler filled with party ice lay at her feet. In amongst the frigid crystals, pink vials of humanity floated.

Her eyes surveyed the assembled volunteers who stood at attention before her. "You," she began, "are about to become the *chosen* ones. Each of you was selected to fulfill the divine decree of the nation states that you represent. You are about to become the elite of the world. You will learn, however, that of your own power you are nothing. But tomorrow you will receive the greatest gift ever bestowed on humankind."

She bent down, picked up the cooler, and held it up, tilting it in the direction of the assembled men. "You will receive these, the COBRA implants. With it, you will transcend humanity itself. Think hard about what that means."

Lyon began to move down the line. "What you will give in return, both to me and to your country, is both respect and total obedience. You see, it is respect and obedience that allows humankind to progress, in fact, to evolve. It is respect and obedience that creates order in society. Without order, you are nothing. Without order, those who wish to delay and impede your glorious evolution will gain, and you and your native countries will lose. Losing is not an acceptable alternative for our kind."

She reached behind her head to the base of her skull and touched the small lump that rose from the top of her neck. The skin covering the wound was almost healed. Only a small scab remained, rough and a little sticky to the touch.

"Tomorrow gentlemen, you will become the implanted. In addition, a microchip will be embedded in your forehead. It contains your serial number. On the back of your hand you will each receive the mark of the COBRA. Wear it with pride!"

Dr. Lyon continued. "For tonight, find your bunks, get cleaned up, and then sleep. By this time tomorrow, you will be changed. You will be better. Tomorrow, history will be made and you are that history. You are dismissed."

"Follow me," Jacko ordered. The men obeyed without hesitation.

Werner Braun was the fourth in line as the group made their way to the part of the old warehouse that had been made into their quarters. He had attended a meeting of the New Europeans months ago after being invited by a coworker in the high technology equipment firm he worked for as an engineer. Henry Rexan had spoken at the meeting and had immediately captivated the imagination of Braun.

Rexan's vision of an economic and social community based on technological evolution seemed to be such a logical solution to the suffering and chaos permeating Eastern Europe. To Braun, it seemed the various factions and ethnic groups would be forever at war. Implants will cure all that, Rexan claimed. Werner Braun wanted to be a part of that cure.

Braun and the other men entered the sleeping area and found freshly made bunks, neatly set out in perfect rows. Khakis were laid out on each bunk, as well as several sets of high-quality civilian clothes, including an Armani suit made to measure. Also included were boots, a kit for shaving, and personal care items. The men were impressed.

Jacko ordered the men to shower and change. While they did so, all their personal items were removed, searched, and burned.

Braun changed, then rested on his bunk. He noticed that the others, from various other European communities, talked little amongst themselves. The cameras staring down from each corner of the large bunk area might have had something to do with that, he thought. He took several minutes to read through some of the material that was in a file folder on the small shelf beside each bunk. It described the implantation procedure and told them what to expect, including the crucial first few hours after the implant's installation.

"Are you afraid?" said the man in the bunk above him in a deeply Italian accent. His black hair and olive skinned face peered down from over the side of the bunk.

"I suppose I'm afraid that my brain might not accept the implant, and then I will fail," replied Braun.

"They say it never happens because the implants are treated with an antiallergic coating. It is our brains that grow into that material. They have found a way to get nerve cells to regenerate. It's quite remarkable."

"Why is it that you know so much?"

"I'm a medical doctor. I did much research into the whole process before I joined."

"Are you looking forward to it then?"

"I can hardly wait. When it's over, I'll be working to take Italy out of the pits we are in now. My people will finally be able to take their future into their own hands."

"I am German. Aren't you afraid our causes will collide?"

"My friend, these implants will overpower the manipulations that have been forced into the brains of the people by the past. We will become brothers, working and fighting together. That is the picture of our tomorrow. There will be enough for all, once waste and ineffi-ciency are conquered. We need not fear."

"I think you are correct, my friend," replied Braun.

The men continued to talk quietly until the signal came for lights out. Braun fell quickly into a heavy sleep.

At 5 a.m. the next day Jacko entered the room.

"Wake up, super heroes!" he shouted. "Time to get up. It's your day."

The men leaped out of bed and donned the casual khakis and T-shirts provided for them. After washing up, they were escorted to a room that reeked heavily of antiseptic cleaning solution.

Braun was nervous; he was third in line this time by coincidence and not by choice. He watched as the man in front of him had a small section of hair shaved from the back of his head. The orderly then swabbed a small area with alcohol. The doctor in charge picked up a device that looked like a cordless drill. He opened a cooler and took out a thin pink-colored object and attached it to the drill. Braun watched him place his hand on the man in line in front of him. Holding his head, he pressed the drill into the skin and pulled the trigger. A whirring was followed by the sound of a stapler. It was that fast. The new implantee moved ahead in line.

It was Braun's turn next. He waited in nervous anticipation, wondering what it would be like to be a new creation.

"Braun, you're next! Come and sit here!" barked the nurse.

He stepped forward and sat in the seat that awaited him. The nurse shaved the hair from the top of his vertebrae to near the middle of the back of his skull. He felt the coolness on his neck as she applied an alcohol-dampened cotton swab. The swab seemed to numb the skin. He tried to relax as the hand of the surgeon was placed on his head. He heard the whir of the implantation device and soon felt its touch. A warm sensation, followed quickly by a brief period of nausea overwhelmed him. It was finished.

He moved to the next chair, where a tiny barcoded chip was slipped under the skin of his forehead. It held his serial number, 666. He stood up and waited in line for the image of a red king cobra snake to be tattooed on his hand. It was tiny in its appearance, but monumental in its significance.

As Braun left the recovery room, the remaining nausea subsided, then disappeared entirely. He returned to his quarters.

That evening, each of the men who had been implanted made small talk but did not discuss at any depth how they were feeling. It seemed they were all hesitant to communicate with the others the strange thoughts beginning to intrude their minds. None of them had the innate strength their creator Dr. Lyon had. None of them were able to resist the slow infiltration of Lisa's consciousness into theirs. None, except Braun.

Braun lay quietly after lights out. Every time he closed his eyes, the room seemed to spin ever so slightly. At one point he fought the strangeness enough to fall asleep. It was then that the transformation began. Once the inhibitions of consciousness left him, the implant began to find nerve passageways through which it could interact with his brain. He began to dream as the infusion began. Images of his past in Germany appeared, then merged strangely with places he had never been.

Even in his dreams he knew he had never been in Brussels, yet the image of walking down an alley towards a van invaded his mind. He was in the dream, yet it wasn't him. It was as if another person, deep inside of him, was remembering an event that he had nothing to do with. Fear saturated him as images of men, a wooden box, and a steel knife that cut into his skull flashed through him. He fought back.

A few of the men cried out in their sleep that night, although none would share the experience with those around them. They seemed to know not to express their fears.

The next morning their training began.

Initially, the men were trained to handle weapons. The instructors were amazed at how quickly this group learned. Within the same day they covered unarmed combat, communications, and explosive techniques with a proficiency that normally wouldn't be expected of a Naval Seal until after several weeks of intense instruction. The same was true of all the other facets of training for the soldiers of the New Europe. They seemed invincible.

8

The combination of seeing the city of Vancouver on his right, the snowcapped Coast Mountains on his left, and the water before him took Edward Calais's mind off of his wife, and put it more properly on him. He owned it, this city, or at least, he planned to.

Turning his head, Edward peered through the glass of the door and watched his wife and daughter for a brief moment, all cuddled up to each other, fast asleep. A tinge of guilt crept past his usually resilient façade, but he wasn't really sure why it was there. Someday he'd get a handle on it. It was as if something was missing, but he couldn't describe it, never mind purchase it. He looked out again over the ocean and watched as the first rays of the morning sun hit the penthouses that crowned the massive buildings of downtown Vancouver. His pulse quickened as he anticipated another day at work. He loved his Vancouver and he loved his work.

It was in this city that Edward Calais had decided to put his remarkable talents to work. On this morning, like most others, his mind was shifting from concern for his family to what was really important: making money and, with it, buying prestige. The morning sun was just beginning to show its warmth. Edward loved getting an early start, mainly because he felt it gave him a headstart over the competition.

Calais smiled to himself, walked silently through the house, then stepped through the doorway and into the garage that was attached to his home. He carefully locked the outside door before entering the space that held the Calais family vehicles. His treasured vintage convertible sports car sat waiting for him. He loved the looks he got from those walking or jogging as the MGB passed by them with its convertible top down. The passersby, particularly those female, watched and often openly admired the combination of car and man.

He lovingly guided the car to the Sea Bus parking lot, put up the convertible top, and safely locked the doors. Carrying his laptop in a leather Gucci bag, he boarded the passenger ferry for the short trip into the downtown business district of Vancouver.

During the timespan of a trip that lasted half an hour, Calais had gone from a virtual country estate seemingly miles from the city into the core of the bustling city itself. Edward stood near the front of the line of passengers waiting to disembark, a little annoyed that he wasn't the very first. Once the ferry had come to rest, he strode briskly up the street that led from the landing.

Within the first few steps, huge modern steel and glass buildings reached upward and surrounded him, piercing the sky and blocking its daytime master, the sun. These were the buildings that housed the major Canadian and foreign banks, the national law firms, venture capital firms, and the corporate headquarters of the major multinational forestry and mining companies. This part of town contained the apartments and condominiums of those who chose to live in the trendy, and very expensive, city center. Within a few blocks, Edward could brush shoulders with those who billed out their minds at hundreds of dollars an hour, and then, only steps away, stroll by those who sold their bodies, also at an hourly rate.

A collage of fellow north-shore people that had left the Sea Bus along with Calais also proceeded to make their way through the network of streets and up into the offices that sat perched atop the business high rises.

Edward, unlike many of the others he walked with, looked forward to going to work each day. His walk was fast, and he put on a classic type A performance as he passed the others. Turning off the sidewalk, he strode up to and unlocked the main entrance door to the massive building that held his firm's offices. He entered the opulently decorated elevator and stabbed his finger at the number 27.

Edward Calais's luxurious private office had a view that captured the famous and well-appointed Waterfront Hotel and nearby Canada Place plaza. Out a corner window, he could see that the ocean was coming alive with the ships, helicopters, and planes of commerce that abounded in the harbor. He also enjoyed watching the abundance of sea life that comfortably coexisted with the many maritime showpieces of the extremely wealthy. Seals, bald eagles, and the occasional leaping salmon searched the water for food. The finest of Vancouver's watercraft lay before him. Live-aboard yachts, sleek sailing vessels, and boats designed simply to impress lined the docks. Above, on the horizon, the jagged mountains struck up towards the sky. Clean and crisp, the mountains beckoned many hikers, fishermen, and photographers. He watched with pride as the city came alive with the flocks of financial planners, lawyers, and accountants who hurried to beat their staff to their offices.

As a venture capital broker, being ahead was everything. He needed to be the first to find that new technology that was underfunded and looking for investors, desperate for cash and willing to part with equity. He needed to be first to that retiring CEO with a few hundred thousand dollars to play with and looking for something exciting and risky, but with large profit potential. He needed to be the first to match those two together and then create the kind of deal that neither could refuse. At this, Edward Calais was the ultimate prospector, deal-maker, and closer. He was "scary smart," as one of his many admirers and investors would say.

It was in Vancouver, miles from Bogotá, that temptation would greet Calais. Temptation in the form of the new Eve.

In Bogotá, the newly implanted volunteer lay on the examination table writhing in agony. He was screaming. His skin was a puffy mass of self-induced bruises. Foam dripped from his nose and mouth and ran down his chin. His eyes opened and closed rhythmatically with the convulsions, betraying a terror deep within.

"Dr. Black, how long has this been going on?"

"It began in the night, Dr. Lyon. He apparently had a nightmare and started crying out in his sleep. His comrades could not wake him, so they called us."

"Have you given him anything?"

"Absolutely not. We did not want to change anything in his body chemistry for fear of hiding or masking the root cause of the problem."

"Heeeelp me! " he screamed. "Pleease, Lorne. Heeeelp meeeeeee!"

"What is he talking about, do you think? Who is Lorne? He keeps asking for help from him," asked the orderly.

"This is interesting. Lorne Browne was the name of the man engaged to collect subjects for our initial studies. He kidnapped Lisa, the brain donor. He is one of Henry Rexan's point men."

"What does that have to do with this man?"

"For Lisa, the encounter with Lorne Browne was terrifying. Her brain slice must have somehow retained some of the memories."

"What? You mean that some of Lisa's consciousness is still alive, and living in the tissue that we harvested from her? How could that be? The tissue was from the base of the brain...surely no memory would exist that low!"

"We don't really know how the brain functions completely!" spat out Lyon. "How many are like this one?"

"Aaaaaaaa," screamed the man on the table.

His back arched and his hands clasped together so hard that his fingernails penetrated the palms of his hands. Blood oozed out from the nails as they sunk deep into his own flesh.

"Get her out of my head! Get her out of me..."

His body suddenly went limp. His head fell lifeless. Open eyes stared into space, then twitched momentarily as a small piece of Lisa died, finally. Her host died at the same time, emitting the telltale cackle of death from deep within his throat. The heart monitor flatlined. As they watched, the seemingly disinterested Columbian orderly began to disconnect the wires and monitors from the still warm carcass.

"Black, how many more are like this? How many are infected by Lisa?"

"Well, he is the first to die. But several implantees have had episodes of what we thought were flashbacks of their own lives, or perhaps implant-induced psychosis. We never thought of the implanted tissue itself having any influence on the conscious thought of the implantees. We considered the rejection problems and we believe we have defeated those. We have solved the issues around the growth of the implant into the brain itself. This is something entirely unexpected.

It's like she's fighting back...the donor, I mean."

"Do you think there are any others harboring her?"

"There could be."

"We will have to find out then, won't we?"

"Lisa's consciousness is certainly a threat to us."

"No one outside the company must know of her."

"Are there any implants you are sure of? That we can trust?" asked Lyon.

"There is a subgroup of those who have nightmares, but are able to control their minds while conscious. Some of those may prove to be useful eventually. The better news is that the majority of implantees seem to be very functional. They are in control and are successfully uploading the training programs and software we are using."

"Who is the best of the lot?"

"Clearly the best is a man named Werner Braun. He is amazing, and shows no outward sign of being infected by Lisa. He is implant number 666."

"That is good news. Send him to my office immediately." Lyon turned and headed towards her office.

Minutes after arriving at the office of Dr. Xavier Lyon, Werner Braun was led into Lyon's office. He stood at attention.

She arose and circled him slowly. She reached up and tenderly touched the back of his neck. He seemed to be very kind-looking, not hard and rough like the others she had inspected. He had blond, almost white hair that curled delicately around his ears. His skin was almost too white, and his complexion clear. He stood a full six-foot-two and weighed 220 pounds, exactly twice Lyons. His frame was lean and muscular, although not overtly so. His face was almost angelic in his nature.

"Does it hurt, Braun? Your implant, I mean?"

"Not really, Dr. Lyon. It's healing nicely."

"Do you like having an implant?"

"I love it. It's amazing. I can do things that would take ten men to do and in half the time. I fight and shoot better than any human should be able to. I feel so powerful, Dr. Lyon, and it's all because of you. I am forever in your debt."

"Fine. Braun, tomorrow I have a special mission for you. I hope you are up for it."

"I will do my duty, Doctor. I will do my duty."

"Dr. Black will brief you. We have to go on a little rabbit hunt. The rabbit's name is Lisa." Lyon studied his eyes closely as the name *Lisa* left her lips.

When Braun looked puzzled, she was relieved at his tepid response.

"Does that name mean anything to you?"

"No, other than it is an unusual name for a rabbit."

"Excellent," was her only reply.

Near the compound, and down several dusty streets, a local worker employed as an orderly at the COBRA facility arrived home and immediately went to his computer. He opened his email program and wrote a detailed summary of the day's activities, focusing on the death of the implantee and the reappearance of Lisa. He reached deep into his desk and pulled out an American 1000-dollar bill. He transcribed the email address written on it and doubleclicked the send button.

The next day, on the parade ground, the soldiers of the New Europe stood at attention. They were unarmed, except for Werner Braun, who stood behind the soldiers, at ease. His sidearm, a vintage German Army issued Luger, rested comfortably in an open holster on his belt.

In front of the men stood Xavier Lyon, still striking in appearance, despite the battle fatigues she chose to wear that day. Since she was working with Lexan on building an army, she chose to dress the part.

They stood at attention, none of the men venturing to look at her. They knew the risk.

"Men and Women of the New Europe, we are at a crossroads," she said.

"You are the beginnings of a mighty army, and you are the chosen leaders of that army. At the moment we have thousands of volunteers being covertly flown here to become implanted and trained. Our factory is being expanded to meet the demand we anticipate. Europe needs you to lead her out of the chaos that she finds herself in. The Americans are raping your mother countries, and the politicians of the day, polluted by the whore of a false democracy, are cheering them on. You are the only answer for your people. You are Europe's new guardian angels.

"It seems, though, that we are being attacked—from without, but also from within. On the outside, our resources are being dangerously stretched. You need not worry, though, we are developing a plan and we anticipate you will play a part in that plan. At this very moment we are constructing a strategy that will make our people and our vision for the future known throughout the world. This will surely bring those who wish to play a part in the salvation of our people to our doorstep, begging to participate.

"However, this is also a most dangerous time. You see, there are those who will try to block our progress. There are those who will not believe that sacrifice is necessary for progress, and since this progress is on a grand scale, so will be the sacrifice. That is where you come in. Your implants are beginning to reach their potential and are initiating processing and memory capabilities into your own brains. You are beginning to access that large portion of your brains that used to be deemed 'unnecessary.' As the software creates new neural pathways and avenues for processing, your capabilities will climb exponentially. You will truly become a master species. And what could be more natural than a master species evolving out of prime European stock such as ours!"

The men cheered spontaneously.

"But there is also danger. Our research staff has detected a vestige of evil, hidden in the recesses of some of you. This intrusion could be our undoing and will not be tolerated. It seems that the brain tissue used for the implants is tainted with a few random thoughts of its original owner. Some, the most feeble ones, are unable to control these impulses, so cannot be counted on. We must find these weak ones, and cull them."

She moved to the side of the rigid lines of soldiers, all facing forwards. Werner Braun moved restlessly behind them, pawing at his weapon in anxious anticipation.

"I am looking for a traitor." She paused for effect. "A traitor by the name of *Lisa.*"

The words were quietly spoken, yet two men, one in the front and the other near the rear of the group turned their heads at the mention of Lisa. Their wide eyes betrayed them. Lisa herself had inadvertently betrayed her presence in them.

A loud pop shattered the silence. The betrayer near the back collapsed. Blood slowly drained from a wound in his head and gathered in a shimmering, coagulating pool of crimson. Werner Braun's piston moved smoothly to the other offender and fixed its sight on his temple. He held his fire. The offender turned slowly and faced Lyon. Pure hate poured from his eyes.

"Take him!" she ordered.

Arms and hands immediately reached for the man and pinned him to the ground.

"Keep him alive. I want to examine his implant while he is still breathing to find out why he is a traitor!"

The men and women wrestled the unfortunate to his feet and led him off towards the lab.

"Bring the other, and I will personally dissect his brain. The rest of you, keep watch for any others who show any signs of this regression towards savagery."

Braun stood beside her and dismissed the remaining soldiers. Jacko approached the fallen soldier, machete in hand.

Dr. Lyon followed the prisoner and the body to the lab.

"Dr. Black, we need an immediate download from the dead one, and a complete physiological analysis from the live one. After you are done with this vermin, remove his implant and the surrounding tissue as well. If he is still alive after that, kill him."

"I'll do a complete workup, Doctor, and run the analysis through the software to see if we can pick up a pattern common to the two men."

"Excellent. Get your results to me as soon as possible. Email me the raw data too. I'd like to have a look at the growth patterns in the brain tissue anyway."

"As soon as I can, Dr. Lyon."

"We need a way to allow the implantees to filter out impulses arising from the donor brains; otherwise we will not be able to trust our people!" she shouted. "There must be a way."

Lyon returned to her office. She sat in her rather rigid office chair and placed her head in her hands. What was she going to tell Rexan? The implantees were clearly flawed. Suddenly she felt her own implant move in her consciousness.

An inaudible voice posed a question. *How can Lisa be suppressed?*

Immediately and of its own accord, the implant within Lyon's brain began a web search of databases throughout the world. Accessing the Internet via satellite, it hunted university websites, private and government facilities where brain research was being carried out. Within minutes, the research project centered at Simon Fraser University in Canada was cross-matched with the key words. The researcher was Dr. Jerry Chen, and the commercial contact was given as Edward Calais, of Vancouver Venture Capital. Dr. Lyon reasoned that since they had already met at the Zurich conference, it would be child's play to get the information, techniques, and procedures Chen had developed in his lab.

All of this was accomplished within her mind, the implant enabling it. While the work was being done, it was as if voices within her head were talking to her and each other. The voices she heard within her shaped and refined her own ideas in a perfect, sinister synergy. The technology was flawless, seamless, and entirely amoral.

9

Everyone has Voices inside their head. Some are quiet whispers that urge us toward good. Others hiss temptations, insults, and perversions. Some inner Voices cry out for attention; others demand it. For a few unfortunate ones, the Voices take over, the mind succumbing to their roar.

The sources of these Voices are debatable, many claim. The biologist speaks of their evolutionary heritage, promoting the survival of the species. A mother's inner Voice causes her to act instinctively to protect her young, risking her own life in the process, for example. Yet if that were the only source of the Voices, why would another mother's delusions demand that she take the lives of her children, in order to protect them from an invisible Satan?

The Christian clergy claim the Voices are the workings of God and His eternal enemy, Satan, battling for our souls. They say that which Voice we chose to listen to and act on determines our destiny. That we all share eternity, they tell us; however, it's a matter of geography where we spend it.

What is clear is that there are many Voices, both good and evil, and that they exist to fulfill a purpose and to exert their presence in our human lives. What might be called *coincidence* seldom is and at times only the Voices know why. In the unseen world of the hidden depths of the mind, the Voices do their work. It is there the battles are either won, or lost. It is there that Lisa lives.

For Lisa, her natural earthly voice was lost for all time when she was murdered. But hidden in the recesses of her dissected brain, in the fused matrix of brain and technology, lay her soul, and it would not surrender. Her soul chose to survive, and to avenge, however thinly sliced her brain became. She became one of the Voices by an act of her will.

Edward Calais leaned back into the soft Italian leather office chair. It gave way and wrapped itself around his body, not unlike a python wraps around its prey. He checked his emails and made a mental note of which ones needed his attention.

The morning editions of the *Globe* and *Mail* and *Financial Post* newspapers sat waiting on his desk. He picked them up, tucked them under his arm, and headed downstairs for the usual mocha at Starbucks with his partners George Miller and Jerry Chen. They had 30 minutes to talk before the T.S.E. opened in Toronto, announcing the start of another financial day in Canada.

Jerry arrived at the coffee bar, disheveled and nervous. He eyes betrayed a mood that Edward recognized as being both troublesome and inefficient. Chen held his head low, and his eyes flickered back and forth rapidly. His hands picked away at invisible fluff apparently stuck to his stained jeans.

"Are you ready for the reunion weekend? Jane is doing the breakfast again."

Jerry looked up and smiled. He did love breakfast, and strangely enough, that was enough of an emotional response to alter his thought pattern to a more positive one, for reasons quite unclear. These rapid changes of mood characterized the enigma of Jerry Chen. A practiced eye could see the difference wash over his face.

Edward recognized the change from years of experience and was pleased—not so much because of an innate caring for Jerry, but mainly because Jerry was one of Edward's most prolific sources of new software and hardware discoveries, and as a result, of revenue. He nurtured this relationship for somewhat selfish reasons.

Edward chose to prolong the positive conversation, in the hopes of keeping Jerry positively minded, and as a result, productive. "I'll pass that on to Jane! Do you realize it's been 10 years since we started getting together for the long weekend?"

"Yeah, I know. It doesn't seem like it should be that long."

"Do you think George will be okay this year?" said Edward.

Jerry replied, "I don't know. He sure hates it though, eh?"

"Yeah, he sure seems to. But Tara has a good time."

"Ah yes, I always look forward to seeing Tara on the beach. I love watching her."

Edward smiled. "Maybe things will be different this year, for George I mean."

"We can only hope."

The men nodded agreement, then each sipped at the excellent cup of coffee that sat before them.

Minutes later, George arrived at the men's table. He was quiet and seemed uncomfortable, which was nothing new for him. He grunted a hello, grabbed Edward's copies of the papers, and hungrily began to search the sports pages for the latest scores. Jerry and Edward carried on, allowing him time to complete his ritual.

George eventually closed the paper, his hands shaking almost imperceptibly. Something was wrong, but the other men knew better than to push.

The men's conversation shifted to the investment seminar they were going to present next week. One of Jerry Chen's new software inventions was the topic. Edward's job was to sell shares in the invention in order to fund Jerry's research and development phase. Edward had perfected a technique of prospecting for new investment business by giving entertaining and insightful one-hour presentations to invited potential clients. He was a master at the game now, after eight years of practice. George was a "closer" by nature. He had an uncanny ability to take a potential client from a probable no and change it into a definite yes.

After finishing their coffees, they separated. Jerry headed west to Simon Fraser University to check up on his research assistants, and Edward and George walked to their upscale offices. Edward checked in with his two assistants on the way and collected the most recent updates of stock market activity from the computer screens that sat on his desks. He then took a moment to straighten his hair and adjust his tie, then walked down the long hall that led to the conference room.

"Good morning, ladies and gentlemen," said the office manager of the investment firm he worked for. The other brokers selected their seats and settled into the deep luxurious leather and oak chairs that awaited them. The aroma of Italian leather, Colombian coffee, and freshly squeezed orange juice blended into a glorious perfume that was intoxicating to Edward. It was the smell of money, and of success.

The meeting was called to order and the manager began by listing new companies that were looking for capital investment. The list was supplied by the head office in Toronto, which apparently also thought itself the center of the universe.

"We've got a couple of hot prospects for you to consider. Toronto is recommending buys on the technology side. Take a look at these new entries into the market."

George leaned over and whispered to Edward, "Those guys in Toronto make 250K a year, and they are still wrong half the time. I could be wrong for half that amount of money."

Edward laughed loudly, making no effort to be either quiet, or respectful. Several young brokers smiled and looked their way. Several older ones stared disdainfully.

"Something you'd like to share with us, Edward?" said the manager in a schoolteacher-like tone.

"I never was very good at sharing, sorry," was the reply from Edward. "But you guys know that, don't you?"

Calais was a relatively new golden boy of the firm. The more seasoned veterans were lifers of 20 or more years with the company. He had started only eight years ago, but now earned as much as most of the older brokers that occupied chairs around the table. Their clients loved him, and what's more, they trusted him. It was an unbeatable combination. It was because of his ability to generate and develop rare finds, like the talents of his quirky friend Jerry Chen, that he had the ability to generate huge commissions for the firm, and management tolerated his cocky attitude and complete disregard for the rules.

"Well, let us continue then. One company in particular will push all the hot buttons. COBRA is researching and developing a secret new computing system that connects directly to the brain of the user. They call it COBRA for computer brain technology. It's an interface device I suppose."

Edward smiled. His attendance at the conference where COBRA

64

was introduced had, yet again, given him the edge. He had Jerry Chen to thank for that.

"Another virtual reality system?" queried one of the brokers.

"No, this one seems to be a two-way connection that allows the brain and computer to think together. I'm not sure how, but they intend to produce a marketable product any day now, although the components of it are top secret. They are very cash short right now, so are looking for some high risk money."

"Sounds a little crazy to me," said Edward.

The manager continued, "We're recommending you approach it as a soft buy on the venture capital side of your larger client's portfolios, and then hold it. It may be another Apple Computers."

"COBRA has operations in Vancouver, LA, and Bogotá," added one of brokers.

"It will qualify for Canadian content then," said another.

"Their CEO has a PhD," noted a third as they all viewed the glossy brochure in front of them. As they opened the brochure an audible sigh floated from their lips.

A photo of the chief executive officer, Dr. Xavier Lyon, gazed from the second page. The men's eyes were riveted at the photograph, although their jaws hung slack. Despite the laboratory coat and severely drawn back blond hair, she was stunning. Her muscular tanned leg was draped over an office desk. Her smile transcended classic beauty. Her eyes, although beautiful, were cold, if not emotionally vacant.

"Wow, get a load of the CEO," murmured one of the suits.

Calais remembered her well from the conference. He remembered his attraction to her as well. His mind wandered towards fantasy, and the white hot voice of guilt singed his soul yet again. Fortunately, or perhaps characteristically, a second inner voice offered a poisonous advice to him. "Looking never hurt anyone," it hissed. The first fought back, reminding him he was married. His personal battle continued for a moment, exchanging barrages like old-time battleships, the second voice gaining the lead with a couple well-placed shots. The manager's voice pierced through the din of battle and jolted him back to the conversation.

"Okay people, let's adjourn and go out there and make some calls, then make some money," encouraged the office manager.

Excellent idea, thought Edward, who was becoming jittery as the mocha's caffeine content was beginning to accelerate his mind.

Edward and George walked with a quickened pace as they left the meeting, Edward in the lead, as usual. The kill instinct was beginning to rise to the surface within them as they each intuitively made a list of clients who would be interested in buying into such a hot prospect as COBRA.

"I'm going to give Jerry a call first. He seemed a little unsure of the company. I don't really understand why, though."

"You're brilliant, partner. But you're not as brilliant as I am. I'm going to call some rich old people who won't know enough to ask me any hard questions."

"You're such slime, George," murmured Edward as they walked down the hall and strode by the reception area on the way to their private offices.

"At least I admit it, Edward," said his long-time acquaintance.

"Whatever, George, whatever," answered Calais as the two parted.

At his office once more, Edward Calais glanced at the latest Vancouver Venture Exchange stock quotes that flashed on the computer screen before him. The Asian market's most recent slump was beginning to take its toll on the North American markets.

Edward tapped the intercom. "Please get Jerry Chen on the phone for me."

He listened as the phone rang first momentarily and then an annoying synthetic voice told him that "this cell phone customer is unavailable at the moment, please try again later."

"Probably left the phone in the fridge again," Edward said to no one in particular. Then he left for home, vowing to remember to try Jerry's number again.

When Edward called, Jerry's cell phone was resting comfortably on the floor of his truck, turned off. This was typical for Jerry.

Despite Jerry's social ineptitude and moodiness, he did have a gift. He was a rare combination of creative spirit, technical expertise, and driven productivity. To look at him one would never guess that the unlikely Dr. Jerry Chen, university professor and professional freelance software writer, was one of Edward's more valuable assets. Even Jerry did not know how much a role he had played in Edward's success as a venture capital broker. It was for that reason Edward kept Jerry close at hand. But to be close to Edward was not enough to protect Jerry, especially from himself.

With few social skills, he had been able to maintain only a close relationship with a select and small group of high school friends. Edward Calais was one of those. Edward, in turn, valued the relationship because he had come to rely on Jerry's ability to predict quantum leaps in computer technology. These quantum leaps meant those companies with the technical know-how to place theory into practice went from penny stocks to blue chip in a matter of months. Jerry had picked Yahoo and eBay and had made Edward's clients millions. Along with the growth of expertise in the local Vancouver area, Jerry and Edward focused more locally and became Vancouver's unbeatable combination of brain power, creativity, and people savvy.

On his way by, Jerry stopped in at his university laboratory and confirmed his grad student was making little progress on their latest project. The sophisticated language of modern programming just did not seem complex enough to handle the complexities of conscious thought. Dr. Chen sensed there was some simple solution; he just could not resolve it at the moment. He didn't expect the search being conducted by his student to solve this one. He just knew that the answer was within him; he simply needed some time to sort things out.

Dr. Chen left the lab, in the middle of what should have been a work day, saying good-bye to no one. Jerry was as valuable to the university as he was quirky because the university shared in his developments and acquired a portion of the profit stream. As a result, they gave him a long leash, freeing him entirely from lecturing duties that plagued other less notable professors. Jerry often just took off to go fishing, and no one minded because often he would return to the lab with some brand-new idea or some old problem solved. One benefit of his brilliance was his ability to develop his fly-fishing techniques whenever he wanted to be unfettered by probing questions offered up by the powers-that-be.

Jerry Chen loved to fish the deep, cold, and haunting lakes of the Coast Mountain Range. They were within a few hours' drive of Vancouver, yet not heavily used. A fisherman could find a picture-perfect lake, stocked with plump and feisty rainbow trout...and no one else there. It was at these little-known lakes where Jerry sought solace; and, at times, the tragic solace of a fantasy; a murky, depressed fantasy of never returning at all. To just simply die and disappear into the depths.

Jerry was, at times, a severely troubled, depressed, and lonely little man. His mental illness was undiagnosed, and therefore especially dangerous, particularly to himself. Voices would flood into his consciousness from nowhere. The feelings of loneliness, coupled with a frantic need to escape that saw no obvious path at times, edged him closer to ending it all. The Voice loved that concept. The Voice wanted him dead.

Sometimes Jerry felt his life was simply a story of one bad, heart-sinking, uncontrollable emotion after another, with no sign of relief and seemingly only one tragic ending. He often found it difficult to get out of bed and he would spend hours either in bed or sitting in his tiny basement suite with all the lights out.

Then, again from out of nowhere, he would fly into a period of intense optimism and energy. He could work twenty hours a day and jump from one major discovery after another. This was his manic phase, and in it he was a genius.

In the times when he was neither depressed nor manic, when he was emotionally functional, his escapes were fishing and the day-to-day work routines at home or at the university. The fishing lakes he frequented afforded a brief respite from the down times, which could strike at any moment.

This afternoon he was on one of the lakes. He cast out a fly line and watched as it slowly sank.

Ironically, Chen already had what most other fellow yuppies could only dream of—in fact, he had more. He had a dream career that resided on the cutting edge of computer software development. His work on countering industrial computer espionage had led him to play key consulting roles for multinational corporations. As word of his abilities spread he began to get calls to assist government intelligence and counterterrorism agencies. While much of his work was secret by necessity, he still had more job offers on his email mailbox than others might see in a lifetime. His commercial software programs, marketed by his friend Edward, earned him more money than he could possibly spend. His hobby was inventing new devices to improve computer performance. He sold the patents to these as fast as he created them, again to companies whose growth was being facilitated by Calais.

Nevertheless he was not interested in the usual trappings of the "me generation." Cars, clothes, houses, and world travel had no real appeal to him. Embarrassingly shy, he avoided most social contacts.

As a result, not very many people could see through, or took the time to see through, the nervous, self-conscious, inept social façade that Chen presented. Jerry had spent most of his life immersed in a world of safe removal—the world of cyberspace. When Jerry entered into the realm of the computer, he was free from having to maintain relationships with real people, in real time. He could not be hurt, and if rejected, who cared? His conversations were typed, not spoken, so no bumbling, stuttering, and eventually devastating real conversations took place.

Not many were trusted enough to enter Jerry's black world. Chen had fought with depression for most of his adult life. And today, as he peered into the depths of the lake, he wondered what it might feel like to sink into those depths, never to return to the surface. He wondered about last moments, final moments. He thought briefly of what the first, and hopefully last, deluge of cold water filling his lungs might feel like. Would it be relief or agony? Would God forgive him?

A slight breeze quickened the wavelets on the surface of the lake and the sky began to blacken. Chen did not notice the change and the impending darkness. He was forcing himself to think of something more positive in his life, to quiet the Voice that was again urging him to slip off his life vest and enter the ice cold water one last time. He quelled the Voice and thought of Edward.

One of the few real relationships Chen had maintained over time and to a certain depth was with the Calais family. He had grown to trust them and, with time, had even shared his feelings of despair. Jane Calais was a good listener, and non-threatening because she was married. She had often encouraged him to seek out a girlfriend, but nothing ever seemed to work out. Sometimes he felt like nothing would ever work out.

He turned his head and consciously aimed a thought in the general direction of the laptop computer, nicknamed "Dinah," which was sitting on the boat seat beside him. Beside the computer were a large number of empty soft drink containers, candy bar wrappers, and empty coffee mugs stained by their last use. Popsicle sticks were stacked like trees downed by a hurricane. Jerry never cleaned his boat between outings and he loved Popsicles.

As Jerry thought, a small patch stuck to the skin of his neck picked up his brain's faint electromagnetic signals, analyzed them, and sent them via a small emitter to the computer. Recognizing the pattern, Dinah sprung mindlessly to life. The computer responded to, in a rudimentary manner, Jerry's thoughts. This was a little feature that Jerry himself had created and installed. It allowed him to fish and write program lines at the same time, with only the regulation two hands.

Although Jerry had solved the problem of transmitting brain waves to the computer, he was still stymied by the massive confusion of thought, translated into computer language, which tended to crash the computer, as had happened in the lab that afternoon. As a result, he still relied on a much slower, voice-activated feature to record programming lines that needed to be precise. This brainwave failure was another problem to solve—a computer technology package that worked with the brain in a seamless, error-free manner. It was just a matter of time, Jerry knew, before someone would be first to perfect such a thing. Perhaps it was the ultimate puzzle. Best to put it out of his mind for a moment, he concluded. Jerry found that programming solutions often came from unexpected sources, such as a dream or, at worst, a nightmare.

For Jerry, the solving of the puzzle was bittersweet. Once the task was completed, once he knew its secret, the thrill of the hunt was gone.

These times often preceded and even triggered bouts of oppressing misery. He found he could sometimes overcome these feelings by tackling a new problem, before the darkness grew and thoughts of the quietness of the bottom of a lake and the Voice began to permeate his mind.

Abruptly the calm of the lake was broken by the crash of thunder. Jerry looked up for the first time and saw the storm. Massive black clouds raced down the valley towards the tiny lake Jerry was fishing on. It was almost too late.

Jerry was caught out in the middle of the lake, near a shoal. The wind was blowing the boat towards the shoal and away from the boat launch. Jerry grabbed Dinah and placed her safely in her waterproof case.

The sky rocked with thunder and exploded with lightning. Rain peppered his face with bullets of icy droplets. Jerry rowed hard, battling the waves and wind. Waves crashed against the flat bow of the boat and emptied themselves into the boat itself. The craft was beginning to sink into the numbing cold water. Jerry's muscles began to ache as he battled with the waves. His lungs began to feel like each breath was scorching the linings. The rain soaked his clothes and drained energy from his body. As Jerry fought death with everything he had, he had never felt so alive.

Just before the boat filled with water, Jerry made the shore, carrying Dinah tenderly under his arm. He climbed out of the craft and collapsed onto the shore, exhausted. He heart took several minutes to return to a normal rate. As he lay there, panting, he noticed how fear had affected his body. He was sweating and his pulse was pounding because the adrenaline had turbocharged his nervous system. He felt inexplicably wonderful.

Dr. Chen's mind raced. He was on the verge of breaking through to something outstanding in the field of merging computer technology with human intelligence. Literally hundreds of researchers were trying to solve the puzzle of making the input from conscious thought to computer input seamless. Jerry wanted to be the first. But the answer eluded him.

Later, after bailing out the boat, Jerry loaded it into the back of his rusty 1987 Toyota 4-wheel-drive pickup. On the way he began to refine the basic constructs of the brain-activated computer system he was devising.

Then it came to him.

"Of course!" he yelled.

Chen pounded the steering wheel with pure childlike glee. It was almost too obvious, yet elegantly simple. "I'll build a filter, a suppressor, to control and remove unnecessary thoughts," he said out loud to himself. "One allows the user to set a level that works for them! Once the user can eliminate unwanted conscious thought it's easy. I can use a much simpler translation process and elementary computer languages. It will be a cleanser."

Jerry began to think the program lines to the computer as he drove home. His laptop helped keep him company as he read off instructions to it.

After several hours, he was home. It was well into the darkness of night—Jerry's favorite time to work. He sat, molelike, in the dark at his desk and began to create the magic he was known for. The faces of famous Toronto Maple and Vancouver Canuck hockey players peered down at him from posters he'd nailed up to cover the walls. The images of hockey stars also served to motivate him. He worked all night like a maniac.

By morning, he was finished. Jerry entered the word *Leviticus* as the code name of his new creation. It was, after all, about making the contaminated clean and so was the biblical Old Testament book of Leviticus. He grinned to himself and began the process of determining how best to test Leviticus and, better yet, to what ultimate purpose his creation would serve.

Jerry punched keys furiously and commanded the computer to create a security device in the program that would destroy the program and the computer hard drive of the thief if it was stolen. This would ensure the prototype version could not be used effectively without Jerry's disabling the safety device. He saved his work and closed the lid of the laptop. It was time for breakfast.

Jerry made some toast and applied copious amounts of butter and clumps of strawberry jam to its blackened surface. As he ate, drips of

72

the mixture fell from Chen's greasy fingers and landed on several envelopes containing uncashed checks from Edward Calais for software Chen had written. Other documents, carrying the logo of the Canadian Security Intelligence Service, sat unattended.

A coffee cup stain circled the middle of a letter enticing Chen to join Microsoft. Bill Gates had signed it. Mr. Gates wanted him to work exclusively for Microsoft, but Jerry just wanted to do research and to stay close to Edward.

Jerry looked up at his wall and stared at the high school pictures stapled to it. Edward Calais and girlfriend Jane, George, and Tara looked blankly back at him. He thought about the reunion, the next few days, and the time he would be spending with them. He wondered if George would be his usual temperamental self.

Jerry threw a few clothes into a hockey bag, placed Dinah carefully alongside them, and jumped into the Toyota. He headed towards the ferry that would take him to Hornby for the reunion.

10

Dr. Xavier Lyon picked up her ringing cell phone and looked at the call display screen. She saw that Henry Rexan was on the line. She shuddered to think of the fat hulk of a man, in spite of the fact that, at the moment anyway, she needed his particular expertise.

"Hello, Henry."

"Hello, Xavier. I hear you have some bad news for me."

"What bad news, Henry?"

"A little snake has told me that some of our men are failing. That they can't control themselves and that there are residues of brain matter sneaking through the COBRA membranes. These faulty products are tainted goods, Xavier, infected with that Lisa tart. I have already invested millions under your assurance that you could provide perfect specimens. What's more, we are spending tens of thousands daily air-freighting you converts for implantation. My suppliers are demanding to be paid. The cost of the aircraft alone—"

Furious, Lyon vowed to find the snake who had betrayed her and let the secret out. She'd probably have Jacko skin it once she had ripped it out of its den. The factory could use the fresh skin to produce interface units.

"Rexan, you are so thick. Unless I get more money, we are both out of this business. You will never have the army you need to create the New Europe you so love. Remember that, Henry. You need me as much as I need you."

"Yes, of course, my dear. But you do need more cash, if only for the short term. Perhaps you can use your beauty and your ways to appeal to some man who is really wealthy. Surely you could get cozy with a sheik or something."

"A non-European, Rexan? I'm shocked."

"I was just reminded of the term 'sleeping with the enemy.'"

"Shut up, you pig!"

"Watch your tongue, young lady. Remember that without my money, your company is no more! And without the implantees you promised me, in perfect working order, I will finish you personally. You must solve this, Xavier. *You must solve this.*"

She hung up. Then It came to her. She could sense its presence. The urging came from deep in her brain stem, from the implant that had grown into her brain itself. In some ways it seemed to have a mind of its own. Yet it needed her to exist at all, at least for now, in a strange symbiotic relationship. In the future it would be referred to by scientists as a classic parasite, unable to survive on its own. Others thought a virus was a better way to describe its place in the biological hierarchy. Either way, tomorrow could mean its death, and it knew better than to let the frailty of its human host undermine its chances for survival.

External to her will, the implant came to life and began to search. It knew that its future depended on finding an answer. Within the huge database of the worldwide web, it found a solution, and one that she was already familiar with: Dr. Jerry Chen. Most recent findings indicated he was getting close to a breakthrough. A software breakthrough that would exterminate the danger that Lisa was. Even more, it appeared that his work could make Lisa disappear from the implants already created.

Because some of the details were foggy, she would need some sort of confirmation before she placed her company in harm's way with some new and risky software. Yet, this timing was unbelievable, to all except the implant itself, which was beginning to acquire a mind of its own, feeding ravenously off Lyon's propensity to the dark side. Xavier was beginning to respond well to its work. She was learning to recognize the sound of its Voice. She loved it.

Prompted by the inaudible Voice that was growing with her, Dr. Xavier Lyon punched a cell phone number and spoke to her personal assistant. "Book me a flight to Vancouver, Canada."

Dr. Xavier Lyon left that evening. During the flight, she reviewed data provided by her staff. The latest findings were constantly being updated to her implant via a direct satellite feed and the implant passed them on to her.

The latest information indicated that her research and development team were being very successful in introducing DNA liposome mediated bimolecular computation architecture into implant interfaces. These findings indicated that the implants themselves could grow processing capability using the brain tissue of the recipient of the implanted "Lisa" material. As the tissue grew into the brain, new memory and processing abilities were being created, merging with the recipient's brain and nervous system faster than anticipated. In fact, they could evolve and self generate. Ironically, she didn't recognize that this process was already occurring in her personally. She didn't understand that the Voice that resided in her was becoming freer to do its will, even over hers. It was an easy evolution, an easy transition, because she was so inclined that way anyway.

"An implanted individual could evolve, perhaps within months, and into a new creation, a new species. And I would be the new Eve...no,not the new Eve," she said quietly to herself. The possibilities of Her new role leapt in her mind. A whole new species could be created and She would be the Creator.

"My God," She said, pondering the possibilities of Her future. If She could maintain control of COBRA over the next few weeks, and use Rexan to promote the New Europe, with Her ultimately in control of the multitude, Her conquest possibilities would be limitless.

She would outshine her father, the man she hated, and loved, more than any other living thing in the universe, including herself. But to do this she would need cash, and she knew Rexan was the key.

The results of the autopsies didn't indicate any physical difference between the two subjects who had shown signs of Lisa. She concluded that there must have been some physical predetermination or pre-existing condition that facilitated the growth of Lisa's influence. No obvious solution came to her mind, so she leaned her head back in the seat and let the implant process the new information into a form she could better comprehend. It was an unusual feeling.

Living on the edge of bankruptcy was dangerous and exhausting. As a result, George Miller's bowels were beginning to show signs of erupting. They reminded him that, as bowels go, his demanded respect and a certain degree of care. Too much stress and George would pay. The cramps and diarrhea could be crippling and ultimately completely disabling. Such was life when one suffers with inflammatory bowel disease. George reached for and quickly downed three codeine-laced painkillers in the hopes they would quell his rebellious intestines and provide some relief from the gripping cramps and pain. He followed this with 40 mg of Prednisone, an anti-inflammatory, known for its harsh side effects.

When he returned to work, his desk phone indicated a text message was waiting. He hit display to find what he dreaded, yet expected.

The message was only two words and left no ambiguity: *Two weeks, no more.*

As George read the message, he began to shake and get dizzy. The stress was so great that his chest felt like it had a huge weight resting on it. A searing pain shot across his gut as a cramp tortured his insides.

It was his loan shark who had sent the cryptic message. George was an Internet Gambler, and hopelessly in debt to a shark who was threatening all the classic punitive measures in order to get paid. The shark specialized in well-educated, high-earning, feeble-willed addicts such as him. George had used the easy credit of the last ten years to pay them off, only to bet more, lose more, and then to rack up even greater debts.

His credit cards were yet again approaching their maximums and his wife was shopping—a brutal combination. The thought of another long weekend with the Gang sickened him. He simply could not bear for them, the Gang, or his beloved Tara, to find out the truth. The stress would kill him, if his associates didn't get to him first.

George leaned back in his chair and let his eyes fall upon the wall that lay behind the computer screen. His oak-framed MBA degree mocked him from the wall of his office. With those credentials and his skills, he should be very wealthy. But he was, in fact, technically bankrupt. His debts exceeded his net worth, particularly since the downturn in the real estate market had temporarily collapsed the housing values of his posh White Rock neighborhood.

Today, George found himself again frantic for money, and worse yet, it was just before the infamous reunion weekend. For him, that was a time more than any other that he needed to appear to have things under control. He needed to feel wealthy, so he could act wealthy. Just once, he wished he could be free from the guilt and shame. Just once, he wanted to be able to buy an expensive meal for the whole Gang and not have to secretly phone one of the 1-800 credit card information numbers in order to check his balance before he felt safe to use the card to pay the bill. Just once, he wanted to be better than Edward Calais. Just once.

George Miller was a desperate man, and desperate men do despicable things.

Henry Rexan's empire was vast and well hidden. He had originally built his wealth arranging for immigrant families from the old Soviet Union to be brought to the United States via Canada. His thugs extracted thousands of dollars from people who were counting on North American to free them from the misery that was Eastern Europe. Needing a way to "launder" his earnings, Rexan invested in high-risk new companies, to make even higher profits. His business grew over the years to the point where he was able to invest his money in legitimate opportunities. The high-rolling hi-tech companies particularly caught his attention.

But Henry Rexan was a dangerous man, capable of anything. He also had a way of working his way into a company to the point where he could force a hostile takeover. These business skills and capabilities were indeed a powerful force. Indeed, Rexan planned to use Xavier Lyon's COBRA's implant technology to create an invincible army. Such an army could enable Rexan to infiltrate the European political system and remove any significant opposition. This would give Henry the political clout he needed to implant the whole population, less any deemed unworthy. Yet he needed to become politically mainstream in order to succeed and to properly feed his lust for power.

In his vision of New Europe, he would be adored by all. In his New Europe, those who opposed, those of less desirable genetic makeup, or those who vied for his power would simply be eliminated and therefore removed from the genetic pool. Rexan could use the New Europeans to accomplish his sinister goals of domination and conquest. Fortunately, there were many who lived in the "old country" and who shared his beliefs. They simply needed a strong, visionary leader. They sought such a leader and the time was right for one. This time was an imperative one in history.

For COBRA and Dr. Lyon, therefore, Rexan's sense of timing was also a massive concern. The whole project's future rested on the developments of the next few weeks, or even days. Everything had to work perfectly. If the authorities found out that the only way to create implants was to use brain matter extracted from kidnapped people, disaster would surely ensue for the company and its officers. Police forces and government authorities would raid the buildings and research centers, and kidnapping charges would be laid. Software would be destroyed and manufacturing would stop. Rexan and Lyon might even be returned to the United States since their companies had offices there. That would mean the death penalty.

Timing was everything. They needed the implantation process to have enough momentum to be unstoppable.

11

Tara Miller was worried about her husband. She knew nothing about George's gambling, and neither did anyone else. His intestinal disease was a constant problem, and stress seemed to exacerbate the symptoms. He seemed driven for reasons she did not understand and she wished he could just relax. But, at that moment, she was unknowingly raising her husband's stress level by preparing for the weekend by shopping.

Heads turned as she walked out of the shop on trendy Robson Street.

A woman, sitting on a wooden bench, whispered to her husband as Tara Miller approached, "She would be quite a fashion model, don't you think?"

A sharp elbow to the side delivered by his wife broke the elderly man's trance. "She already is," was his reply as he watched her stroll by.

She was tall and came fully equipped. She just didn't know it.

Tara had one more stop before showing off her new clothes to George. She was so proud of George's work with Edward. She wanted to look her best—something that he always appreciated. New shoes were necessary. Her Gold card flashed once more. *$198.00, on sale*, the tag read. She chose to wear them immediately to show them off to her husband. She stepped out onto the street from the shop.

Several young tax attorneys returning from lunch admired her as she headed towards the big brass doors that led into George's office building.

"She probably has a nice personality too," commented one as he admired the way her dark hair cascaded down in perfect curls onto her rich, Polynesian toned brown skin.

"Her eyes *have* to be a major contributor to global warming. Did you see them?" said another as she, in passing, smiled at them.

"Her husband must be one lucky man," added the third.

Tara Miller, amazingly enough, did not acknowledge, or even comprehend how truly beautiful she was. And she certainly did not know of the power she could wield over men.

When she reached her husband's office, the receptionist nodded that it was all right for her to enter the area where her husband George's office was. She came up behind him and tapped him on the shoulder.

He turned in his chair and beheld her. "Wow, you look incredible, Tara," he said softly.

"You always know just what to say!"

"Only the truth."

"Thanks honey. I hope it's okay. I picked up a few things."

"I guess if you need them, you need them."

"It was kind of expensive, George."

"Tara, don't worry. Just leave it up to me."

"Oh, George, I'm so proud of you."

Tara loved her husband and the way he showed her off.

Tara was anticipating the weekend. She felt great because she would enjoy seeing everyone, yet she felt some apprehension because of George's usual moody response to it. She wasn't sure why he hated those few days so much. It didn't make sense to her because the time was simply an opportunity to spend time with everyone all together.

"Well honey, I need to go home and pack us up."

"Thanks Tara, I'll see you at home about 6."

"See you then," she replied, blowing him a kiss.

George hated these long weekend reunions because he was a failure and failure was unbearable. He stared at the picture of the Gang. *Grad 1994* was the caption. He and Tara had a future then. Did they have one now? He wondered.

It seemed he was the only one who had not made it big. Jerry Chen was a genius who had more money than he knew what to do with. And of course Edward and Jane Calais's life was a particular source of envy for George. Not only was Edward successful, he was well liked and admired. Sickening. Soon the torture of pretending to be something he was not would begin. It was going to be the death of him yet.

The Gang was filling up the rustic old lodge that was set on the shore of Hornby Island. Edward Calais, his wife, Jane, and their child, Leah, George and Tara, arrived together at the rambling fishing lodge known as Georgia Chimes. It was named firstly after the body of water it was built on—the Georgia Straight—and secondly after the musical sounds of the ocean that serenaded the lodge occupants. The lodge had been built in the early 1950s, during the post War boom that boosted British Columbia into a major lumber and paper products manufacturer. Over the years the lodge had hosted thousands of wealthy guests who sought to do battle with the various runs of scrappy coho or mighty spring salmon that abounded just off shore.

Little of the building itself or its furnishings had been changed since the original construction. The outside was cedar shingled both on the roof and the walls. The main entrance was from a deck that held classic wooden outdoor furniture that had long since lost its paint. The wooden armrests of the chairs were worn smooth by the hands of many guests over a period of decades. Stepping inside the door, one's eyes were immediately drawn to the massive fireplace. It was constructed of river stones that had been handpicked and shipped over by barge. Around the fireplace were several large and immensely comfortable overstuffed armchairs, which also highlighted the living room. The upstairs held five bedrooms and one bathroom. The old style bathtub was placed in such a manner that one could lie back in it and enjoy a remarkable view of the ocean through one well-placed window.

When Jerry Chen arrived, little Leah Calais giggled in delight as he handed her a large, bulging bag. Jerry had raided the gift shop on the large Horseshoe Bay to Nanaimo ferry for candy, comic books, and toys, and had paid outrageous prices for them all. After she had opened her presents, Chen lifted Leah on his shoulders and headed out to the beach. For hours he devoted himself to playing with her, ignoring the adults. They built sand castles, played tag, frolicked in the waves, and tossed giant plastic beachballs back and forth. When it was time to return to the cabin, Leah cuddled into Jerry, her eyes taking longer and longer blinks.

"I love you Uncle Jerry" were her last words before she fell asleep.

That night, as the earlier warmth of day kept gentle summer breezes flowing, the group sat on the large porch surrounded both by patio lanterns and the music of the seventies. The gang stayed up well into the night, enjoying each other's company.

Jane's remarkable breakfast began early the next day. The gang awoke to smells of fresh hot coffee, bacon, eggs, and toast heaping with butter and jam.

In the late morning, George and Edward sat relaxing on the beach, admiring the new ski boat of Edward's and the fishing craft of Jerry's. George spoke highly of both new water toys.

Chen came down to the water and opened up a lawn chair, sat on it, and opened up his laptop. "I think I solved the problem, guys."

"Great Chen. Wanna Coke?" said Edward as he reached into a cooler of ice and soft drinks that lay nestled in the shade beside his chair.

"Thanks." Chen took the drink.

"What problem?" asked Edward.

"The problem of the software crashing."

Edward's eyebrows perked up with interest.

"What did you do?" queried George, grinning ever so slightly as he glanced at the other two.

"I used a far less sophisticated computer language to solve the problem of the computer being overwhelmed by the brain's input to it. Because the language is so simple, it naturally allowed the user to filter out unintentional components of the EKG signals. The software is so insensitive that it is able to avoid getting caught up with random thoughts emitted by the brain. It puts the user in full control and it works great. The hardware patch is cheap to build and to mass produce and the system should be easy to learn how to use. The next step is a computer that thinks for you!"

Jerry was entering a manic phase of his illness. He was showing all the signs. He was talkative, optimistic, and energetic.

Edward and George, although somewhat used to Jerry's mood swings, stopped and looked at Jerry Chen. They knew of his genius, as well as his propensity for understatement.

"What do you mean, Jerry?" Edward asked intently. "Are you saying your software is ready to go to market?"

"Exactly…well, give or take a few more trials. But I am confident."

"That's amazing. Go on."

"Using Leviticus means no more typing."

"Leviticus?" questioned George.

"That's the name I gave the system. It purifies and cleanses the signals from your head, just like in the Old Testament book of Leviticus, where the priests had these rituals to cleanse the people…"

"Save us the Bible crap, Jerry."

"Back off, George!" snapped Edward.

"Who are you going to sell your work to, Jerry?" asked Edward.

"How about you? Why don't you take the software and make it into a company or something? I hate all that corporate stuff. Maybe I can explain next week at the new investors' meeting. It could be like a 'what's new' segment."

George shifted uncomfortably in his chair. He shook his head slowly, back and forth. The grin was still there, as was the emotional facade.

"Would you like to come in, George, as a partner?" said Jerry.

George leaned forward in and looked out over the beach. "No thanks. I've got some other good things on the go, and frankly, this one doesn't seem to add up."

"Are you nuts?" said Edward. "Remember, this is the guy who wrote the program that reads emails for NATO's antiterrorist capabilities. It made a fortune when we sold it!"

"Echelon isn't as foolproof as Leviticus is, Edward," commented Jerry. "This one is much better, with more potential for the average user. Within a few years, everyone will attach a little patch to the back of their neck…"

"Are they still using it?" interrupted George.

"What?"

"Echelon, you idiot!"

"Well, yes!"

"Who's using it?" questioned George.

"The CIA, the FBI, and CSIS," answered Edward emphatically.

"Yes, all of them. But it's a little bit of a secret, the finetuning I did," was Jerry's modest reply.

Edward turned his head and looked out at the ocean. "Point made. George, get a grip. Jump in with us."

George rose slowly from the lawn chair. He knew Edward would yet again make a killing, but his stubborn pride was preventing him from participating in this seemingly last opportunity to dig himself out of financial ruin.

"Okay guys, let's leave the business talk and get out on the ocean. We'll figure stuff out later," said Edward, sensing it was time to move on.

"I just want to show you guys," said Jerry as he brought out Dinah.

"Fine," said George, sitting down quickly and somewhat impatiently.

Jerry reached into Dinah's computer bag and brought out a small sticky patch that seemed to have a device within it, held there with duct tape. He carefully placed the patch just behind his ear. He took Dinah and placed her carefully on George's lap, then returned to his chair.

"Open it up, George."

George reluctantly obeyed. As soon as the screen was lifted, Dinah came to life.

Jerry reached over and typed a password when requested by Dinah.

"Ask me to do something, Edward," said Jerry gleefully.

"Open a document and print Edward Calais is going to be rich."

Jerry leaned back and closed his eyes.

Dinah's screen first displayed a blank document. Moments later, the words *Edward Calais is going to be rich* appeared in the document, one letter at a time.

"See? Cool eh?" cackled Chen.

Both Edward and George were astonished. What lay before them was incomprehensible. The profit potential was almost unfathomable. If everyone who owned a computer purchased the Leviticus system, the company would make hundreds of millions.

"Let's go for a boat ride, guys. We need to talk this through together," offered Calais.

"I'm staying here," grunted George.

Jerry peeled off the patch and offered it to George. He waved it off.

Jerry and Edward left George and walked to Edward's craft that lay bobbing in the waves.

As they climbed aboard, Jerry turned back and yelled, "George, shut down Dinah for me, will you?"

George nodded and looked down at Dinah. He looked up at his best friends getting into the boat. Edward used an oar to push the boat into deeper water and Jerry fired up its engine. He turned the boat around to face the open ocean and gunned its engine.

George watched them from his chair until they disappeared around the corner of the bay. Then he reached into the carrying case that Dinah lived in. His fingers probed into its dark recesses. They felt something soft and he pulled out a half-consumed O'Henry bar. Cursing, he tossed it aside. He reached back in and removed a blank CD. George activated the appropriate software and, within minutes, had made a copy of Leviticus, left vulnerable by the trusting Jerry Chen. George slipped the copy into his shorts and closed up Dinah and placed her in the case. He carried the case up the beach.

At the cabin he placed Dinah in Jerry's room and put his stolen copy of Leviticus into his luggage. He had no idea about the cyber bobby trap that Jerry had installed. All he could think about was the value of the program, and who he might sell it to. He wasn't worried about being caught. In the high-tech industry simultaneous discoveries were often made, and sometimes cutting-edge "discoveries" had their genesis in espionage.

For the first time in years, George was able to relax on the Hornby weekend. While fishing with the boys, he uncharacteristically hooted with indignation when Chen caught a 17-pound spring salmon. The golf round that followed went well. George even won the skins game. Later that night he tolerated the obligatory singing around the campfire. For the first time in many reunions, George felt like he had a future.

The packing-up process on Monday of the long weekend was the usual ritual that had gone on since high school. This time, though, George didn't mind admiring the Calais's latest acquisition. It was Jane's newest Lincoln Navigator SUV.

"I have been looking at the new Volvo all-wheel drive," feigned George as he stroked the leather on the Lincoln's interior.

"Really, George?" said Tara, glowing with pride. Her breezy sundress was both tasteful and captivating as usual.

"Why not? The van's getting old. What do you think, Tara?"

"I've always loved Volvos," cooed Tara as she hugged her husband.

As Tara turned away, she glanced for a moment at the back of the shirtless Edward. He was lifting some of the wake boards to the roof rack of the Navigator. Edward's back was tanned and muscular.

George happened to catch the direction of Tara's gaze as her eyes hesitated just a moment too long on Edward's muscular and tanned back. A Voice told George to hate Edward, and he obliged.

12

Rexan leaned back in the chair and looked out over the ocean that glimmered in front of his house. A marauding harbor seal was feeding on herring several hundred yards offshore. The seal's technique was very simple. He dove down deep, far enough from the herring so as not to break up the school. Rising up from the depths he herded the school towards the natural barrier of the surface of the ocean. As he rose, he moved to and fro in order to force the fish into a panicky ball. Each fish would be trying to force its way into the middle of the ball for its own protection. Some would leap into the air, only to fall back into the ocean. Finally, the seal would accelerate, then drive up through the ball, snapping its mouth open and closed on the fish mass and devouring pounds at a time.

The herring would then momentarily scatter, only to immediately seek comfort in the presence of others. A new, somewhat depleted, school would form, and the process could then be repeated as if for the sake of the seal alone. Soon the seal was full, and the remaining survivors continued on their way, presumably happy to have lived. The wounded fish the seal missed floated towards the bottom, often meeting their final moments in the jaws of a salmon or mud shark.

"Watch this, Monika," said Rexan as his servant girl entered his office, bearing a tray of Earl Grey tea and fresh scones. "Watch the seal hunt for his dinner. It says a great deal about the ways of the world. The seal is successful because the fish feel safer as a group, even though it means death to stay together. If the herring school scattered, the seal could only catch one or two at a time. The seal could never catch enough and would surely go hungry. But the stupid fish insist on grouping together."

"They don't learn, do they, sir?" said Monika as she set down the tray and watched.

"Fortunately for the seal, they never will."

The phone rang and Monika answered. "Henry Rexan's office...Yes, he's here, Dr. Lyon. I'll see if he is available."

He nodded and took the phone from her hand. His fingers slightly caressed the soft young skin of her hand as the phone was passed between them.

"Rexan here," he barked.

"Henry, I think I've found a way to rid our implants of the scourge of Lisa, that cursed girl. I've gained access to a prototype software program that could neutralize her impact."

"This is very timely."

"The program is written by Jerry Chen, a real genius. He's the best."

Rexan's heart rate increased and his blood pressure rose dangerously high. It was like an answer to a sinister prayer.

"Can you arrange to acquire this precious program, Henry?" she said sweetly. "You are so good at getting what seems impossible."

"Absolutely," said Rexan, relishing the flattery as well as the opportunity to play the role of the hunter, much like what was happening with the seal in the water below.

"I'll prepare a little backup plan, in case some pressure is needed. Perhaps I can use one of the implanted."

"Excellent idea, Henry!" replied Lyon.

For the next two days, Rexan's men researched Dr. Jerry Chen. A psychological profile was developed. They soon found he had few personal vices. As a matter of fact, he was frustratingly pure. He did have a weak link, though. It was the Calais family, especially their little girl. He'd clearly do anything for her.

Their focus soon shifted to Edward Calais. His home, family, and schedule were videotaped and recorded. Next, Rexan placed a call to the COBRA laboratory and spoke to a Dr. Black. At the end of the conversation, Black went to her laptop and typed in some precise instructions to be transmitted to Werner Braun by way of his implant. It was a bit of an experiment, because direct communication with the implanted was only in the initial stages of research. The message was sent.

Braun lay on his cot, resting. Suddenly, as if drawn by some inner voice, he rose from his bed. He stood for several seconds, as if in a trance, then his mind returned to him. He knew what to do, but did not know why he was doing it. When he arrived at Dr. Black's reception area, there was a puzzled look on his face.

"We've been expecting you," the receptionist said, motioning him towards Black's office.

Braun cautiously opened the door.

"I see the implant is taking nicely," said Black.

"I don't remember you asking me here. How did I know to come?"

"Your implant is downloading from a satellite continuously. As the implanted tissue advances into your brain, you will find that you are able to sense what to do and how to do it. Your orders will come directly from me."

Braun smiled. "Wonderful, Doctor! I will be able to serve you even better!" he exclaimed enthusiastically.

"You will at that, Braun, you will at that. We have a crucial job for your special skills. I want you to sit down and relax. We are attempting to download a set of orders for you. You will sense faces, directions, and instructions. Just relax and let the information flow into your brain."

Braun sat and closed his eyes. Suddenly he became aware of a strange floating feeling. His hands gripped the arms of the chairs. He vaguely heard Dr. Black's voice urging him to relax. He obeyed.

Images of a city he had never seen and of streets he had never driven began to appear deep in the recesses of his subconscious. Video began streaming into the vast memory space of his brain. He noticed street signs and bridges and other landmarks that would serve to guide him to his destination. An image of Edward Calais's home appeared, along with flashing images of its floor plan. A bedroom window materialized. As if in virtual reality, a baby's bed emerged from his consciousness, and pictures of a sweet young girl danced before his closed eyes. The name *Leah* appeared in his thoughts. His arms reached out to grab her. His hand covered her mouth. Her eyes opened and widened in fear.

At the sight of her eyes Braun's mind fractured and then split. One side screamed, "No, let me go! Who are you! Lorne, help me please."

Yet, it wasn't his voice that penetrated the silence. It was the voice of a young college student named Lisa. She was being attacked. Lisa was taking over his brain, at least for the moment. She took his eyes and observed the surroundings, taking in as much as possible. It didn't last long, though.

"Braun, are you all right?"

At the sound of Black's voice, Braun's eyes became his own again—steely, vacant, and black. "I am fine, Doctor."

"Do you understand your mission?"

"Completely, Dr. Black."

"So our downloading process is a success?"

"I know exactly what you want me to do, and how to do it."

"Do you have any problems with your task? If you are ordered, will you hesitate to steal a little girl from her family?"

"Dr. Black, you know I will follow orders. It is not my business what they are. I will always follow orders."

"I know, Braun, I know. You are dismissed. You leave this afternoon."

Braun left the office somewhat bewildered by the occurrences that had just taken place. However, he had a mission to perform, and of that, there was no doubt. Nothing could be allowed to interfere with him kidnapping the Calais's child, even Lisa. He hoped he was up to the task.

The city of Vancouver was making the transition from day into night. The day shift workers were scurrying back home, perhaps after having had a drink or two with coworkers. The night occupants of the streets were beginning to show themselves on the sidewalks and street corners, urging men to partake of their wares. Others, those better dressed, made their way to a civilized evening of music at the Queen Elizabeth

Theater.

In front of the Waterfront Hotel, Edward and Jerry were unloading their laptops, projectors, and screens. They were setting up for the hot prospects seminar that they were about to host. Only a few days had passed since the reunion long weekend at Hornby where Jerry Chen had told them about the Leviticus program. They really hadn't had time to process the information.

From the rear of the room, a tall blond in a black business suit entered the seminar. Edward looked up and was shocked to see Dr. Xavier Lyon purposely striding in. She took a seat at the back. Lorne Browne accompanied her. Calais's eyes widened at the sight of her. She was even more attractive than he remembered.

Lyon smiled as their eyes locked. Calais hesitated for a moment, smiled, then continued to set up the laptop as if nothing had happened. He was not often disconcerted by beauty.

When he was ready, Calais moved towards the podium and signaled George to dim the lights.

"Thank you for coming everyone," Edward said. "We'd like to introduce ourselves by way of a little video clip."

At that moment the sound system began to play, and a five-minute video clip appeared on the screen. It started by showing Jane, Leah, and Edward participating in a community fundraising drive. Edward was announcing the amount of money that had been raised for the local women's shelter. The video production then moved to George and Tara, frolicking in the park with a rented golden retriever. An image of Jerry appeared, in a white lab coat, working away in his research facilities. He appeared to be attaching computer equipment to a child in a wheel chair. The last scene was of the Calais family, playing baseball in front of their million-dollar home.

The video wasn't really about venture capital; it was about creating an image. It was an image of family, of community, of compassion, of trust, and of success.

When the video was over, Edward told some very funny jokes, then introduced Jerry, whose role was that of an eccentric genius. He easily was able to get into character. Jerry opened up Dinah and did a brief demonstration of Leviticus. It was just enough to pique interest, but disclosed little. Edward was not ready for too much information on the program to become public.

Edward then enhanced the mood for the evening by being a warm, confident, and keen host. He interviewed Jerry about his other creations, and Jerry obliged by describing his work using incomprehensible jargon while only disclosing the vaguest details. A question and answer session followed with Edward heading off any trouble at the pass.

George's role was to size up potential new money, so he lay low and listened carefully. In the back of his mind, he also sized up potential purchasers for his pirated version of Leviticus. Various attendees selected brochures as they snacked on butter tarts and drank coffee or iced tea. Clearly many of those attending were very wealthy and pleased with what they saw. Calais's Armani suit matched his *Gentlemen Quarterly* looks and made a good impression on all those in attendance. People began to leave, often depositing their business cards in a little basket as a way of indicating they were interested in investing with Calais. The basket was nearly full.

Near the end of the evening, when most attendees had left, Dr. Lyon and Lorne Browne approached Calais. She extended her hand, which Edward took gently. Her handshake was firm, yet her skin was exquisitely soft. It was Calais who pulled his hand away first, though not without some hesitation.

George Miller left his post and joined them, sensing opportunity.

"Mr. Calais, I'm Dr. Xavier Lyon, and this is my associate, Lorne Browne. We met at the Fusion conference. Thanks for the excellent presentation."

"You're welcome. I do recognize you from the conference. But tell me, are you interested in investments?"

"Well, in a manner of speaking. I have a small company that is in need of some venture capital. You remember COBRA. "

"Indeed I do. Your company looks very promising. The technology breakthrough such as you are working on would be phenomenal. But how could I help you?"

"Edward...ah, I hope you don't mind me calling you that."

"Of course not."

"What I am looking for is someone to market our company, and its potential. We need some working capital. What's more, I don't have much time."

"Go on, Dr. Lyon."

"Call me Xavier, please."

"All right, Xavier, but you understand there are no guarantees, don't you? Raising capital has no guarantees."

"I understand. But will you try anyway? It will be worth your while."

"Yes, that I could do. Just send me some details about your current financial position, your products, and where you are intending to go and I'll have a look."

"I'll have the material tomorrow." She cast her eyes down his silk tie and whispered, "And I'll show you everything you'll want to see. Oh yes, one more thing. Now this part is rather private and has to deal with my companies need to continue to grow. I understand you have a program that could help us with our technology. It's the work of your friend, Dr. Chen. His software may compliment our COBRA technology. My sources tell me it's almost ready and may help with a little glitch we have encountered. I hear it's a kind of filtering device."

Calais stopped dead. "What??"

"Don't be so surprised, Edward. We play in the big leagues. Information is everything in our business. Be flattered that we know about your little secret. And, well, be thankful that we are asking. The big leagues can be kind of scary, if you know what I mean. By the way, it will make you very rich, trust me. I'll meet with you tomorrow, so you have some time to think about a price."

Edward, still in shock, did not know what to say. He responded warily. "I guess so. How about the Pacific Cafe at noon?"

"Excellent. I'll make the arrangements," said Lyon on her way out of the room.

Edward shivered; the room suddenly seemed to grow cold. He needed to think. How did Lyon learn about Leviticus?

Edward turned to George, who was just finishing packing up the equipment. "I can't believe the gall of those people."

"Do you think you'll sell to them?"

"She gives me the creeps, and Jerry told me at the conference that he thought she wasn't giving the whole story. So I don't think so."

"Probably wise, Edward. See you tomorrow."

Edward finished packing and left the hotel through the main lobby. Jerry had already vacated the premises apparently. A busboy had the Navigator brought around.

The trip home allowed Calais to begin to collect his thoughts...that is, until the cell phone rang.

He answered, "Hello."

"Hi, honey, I looooove you soooo much." It was Jane.

"I love you too, honey," said Edward, "but why the warm and fuzzy?"

"Well, Leah and I just got a beautiful bouquet of flowers, a new outfit for her, and a seasons dinner theater package for the Queen Elizabeth Theater with our names on it. This Dr Lyon's card was so sweet. Who is he? Is he one of your clients? Let me read the card to you: *Looking forward to doing business with Edward. We know the supportive role you and Leah must play and want you to know much we appreciate it.*"

"I'll be home in a bit, Jane. I've got to go now...heavy traffic. There has been an accident, I think. Love you!"

Edward stabbed the end button and immediately speed-dialed Jerry's cell. For once Jerry answered.

"Jerry, it's Edward. Did you mention Leviticus to anyone before tonight?"

"Just you two. I'm not that much of an idiot."

"Jerry, listen. Make sure you secure the program and lock your door tonight, okay?"

"Sure, Edward, but are you turning paranoid or something? That's my territory. I have all the key algorithms in my head anyway."

"No, Chen, it's just that someone has to look after our interests," said Edward before he hung up.

Edward then hit the button for George's number.

"Hello."

"George, tell me you didn't approach anyone with the Leviticus stuff," said Calais.

"I have no idea how she came to know about Jerry's stuff...honestly."

"Okay, George. Sorry, but I had to ask. Right now we just aren't entirely sure how to handle this. I'm thinking Microsoft is our first stop."

"Good idea, Edward" monotoned George.

Edward was nowhere near ready to offer Leviticus up for the business world to see. There were intellectual property patents and copyrights to develop and obtain. There was a bidding war to set up. Contacts to make. Bill Gates to phone. Edward was furious that he was being forced to speed up such a potentially profitable business deal.

At his home, Chen was working on tidying up loose ends on the latest version of Leviticus. Suddenly his computer beeped a warning and *Intruder Alert* appeared on the screen. A few passes at the keyboard enabled him to watch the alien invader try to access the information on his hard drive. This was not unusual for Chen. Industrial computer espionage was rampant in an industry where competition was so keen, and the competitors so skilled. The screen flashed images of computer code that Chen watched and was able to decipher as quickly as it appeared. His mind was traveling virtually as fast as the computer worked.

This intruder was clearly professional, fast, and its work was directed towards Chen's Leviticus software. Chen's phone rang and as he answered it, he watched the cyberspace intruder probe and prod his hard drive.

"Hi, Jerry, it's Edward. This is important. Are you sure Leviticus is secure?"

"I told you—only you two and I know, as far as I'm concerned anyway. On the other hand, someone else must have found out because, as we speak, a very professional hacker is trying to break in."

"Okay, I'm not surprised. I need to do some tracking down. Have you copied the program and left it somewhere weird?" asked Edward.

"Look Edward, have no fear. It's me you're talking to. Me, remember? There is no way this baby is going anywhere. No one can get in but me."

"You're positive no one could get in?"

"I'd bet my life on it."

"Great. And Jerry? Be careful."

"Sure thing. Keep me posted."

Jerry sat back in his chair and watched as his security system watched, waited, then blocked the electronic trespasser. Jerry smiled and saved the changes he'd made to Leviticus. He then encrypted the program, effectively locking it away in an electronic vault.

Jerry flopped on his unmade bed and was asleep within minutes. An unheard summer breeze quietly opened the unlocked door of the basement suite Jerry occupied. Anyone could have walked right in.

13

The next morning, Edward Calais entered his office and found a note from the branch manager of his firm sitting on his desk. He was to report to his office immediately. Edward walked down the oak-paneled hallway and into his manager's office. Stewart Griffin jumped up from his leather chair and offered a firm handshake.

"Congratulations, Edward! I had no idea you were working on getting the COBRA account."

"What? I have the COBRA account?"

"Don't be coy, Calais. The other brokers are going nuts trying to figure out how you grabbed their R and D portfolio so fast."

"Yeah, I guess I recall talking to Lyon at the Waterfront presentation."

"It's another banner month for you, Edward. We are all very proud. Any ideas about raising capital for them?"

"Nope."

Edward was in shock and worried. Something was seriously wrong with the whole process. His instincts warned of danger…and not just from an investor's perspective. Something else was wrong. He couldn't put his finger on it, though. It just felt wrong, and dangerous.

On the other hand, the commission on the portfolio work would be significant both for Edward and his firm.

"Thanks, Stewart. By the way, I have a lunch meeting today and may miss my turn covering the front desk. Is that okay?"

"Edward, I'll cover for you personally. Have a great day."

The Pacific Cafe served the best fish chowder and hot bread on the West Coast of North America. The delicious mixtures of aromas emanating from it drew crowds of tourists, especially in the summer months. Usually, there were no seats available during the lunch rush, but today there was more than the regular luncheon crowd.

When Calais arrived, two rather serious looking men wearing dark suits met him at the entrance. They escorted him to a private room in the back, off the kitchen. Dr. Xavier Lyon and another gentleman sat awaiting his arrival.

"Edward! Thanks so much for seeing us. This is Mr. Henry Rexan, who is, shall we say, in an excellent position to purchase this exciting program we've been hearing of."

Calais shook hands and sized up Mr. Henry Rexan. He was a large and fat man. Balding, Had the ruddy cheeks of a heavy drinker. The stench of cigarette smoke filled the room. Edward noticed the yellow fingers of his adversary as the enormous man drummed on the expensive Irish linen tablecloth. Ashes from the offending cigarette fell and landed beside his hand.

"Mr. Calais, I'll get right to the point. We need something from you, and we are prepared to pay well for it."

"What do you want from me?"

"We need the program Dr. Chen has created." The huge man's eyes never left Calais's.

"It's not ready to be sold yet, and besides, it's not mine to sell."

"Mr. Calais, we are prepared to take the program as is, and adapt it for our purposes. And as for it being not for you to sell, we know full well Dr. Chen relies on your judgment completely."

At that moment the chowder and hot bread arrived. Rexan began to eat immediately, not waiting for others to be served. The room fell silent, except for the loud sounds of his sloppy eating. The others picked at their food, having lost their appetite beholding his terrible lack of manners or decorum.

When he was finished, he immediately lit a cigarette, blowing the smoke across the table. "You won't disappoint me, will you Calais?"

"There is not a chance in—"

"I'm sure Edward won't, Henry," Lyon interjected at a timely moment.

"Edward," Lyon went on, "we not only wish to do business with you in a traditional sense, but we also want to make sure your family is provided for as well."

"Jane mentioned that," said Edward coldly. He didn't move a muscle.

"Calais," droned Rexan, "get us the software from Chen, and five million dollars will come your way."

Five million dollars was a lot of money. Edward hesitated momentarily, then looked straight into Rexan's black eyes. "If such a program existed and was in my hands, it would not be for sale to you. Microsoft will pay far more. "

Mr. Rexan's head turned and he stared icily at Lyon for a moment. He turned again, then smiled at Edward. His yellow teeth, filled with bits of clam, poked out at all angles from his cracked lips.

"Mr. Calais, if you accept our very generous proposal, our company will make sure that you and your family are very well taken care of. We will ensure their financial and *personal* security for an indefinite period. If you don't, I guarantee nothing."

Cigarette smoke left the ember that had spawned it and weaved its way like a snake through Rexan's yellow-stained, immensely chubby fingers. He spoke again, choosing his words carefully. "I believe our business is done, Mr. Calais. As you can see, you really have little choice, facing such a fine offer. Xavier, my sweet, please wrap up the arrangements with our friend. Call me if there is a need for further discussions. I know we'll be seeing you again, Mr. Calais, to sign a deal."

"I doubt it," said Edward Calais.

Rexan pushed the table away from his massive gut, dropped his cigarette into a crystal water glass, and walked away, leaving by the back door. Calais watched him exit the restaurant and enter a large black Mercedes that was waiting for him in the back lane behind the restaurant.

Edward turned to face Lyon.

"Edward, think this through. We are offering you the kind of money that frees a man to do whatever he wants." She reached over the table and touched his hand. "And I must tell you that Rexan is a savage. Who knows what he might do?"

"I'll need to think more about it."

Her tone softened. "Can we meet later for drinks? We have so much in common and so much to gain."

"I'll get back to you," he replied and got up swiftly from his chair.

"Don't go, Edward!" she exclaimed, following him.

Ignoring her, Calais briskly walked through the public part of the restaurant, out the front door, past the line of waiting people, and headed directly down the street and towards a nearby police station, not even knowing what he would do when he got there. As he approached the door of the station, his cell phone rang.

He stopped, pushed the receive button, and said "hello."

"Hello, Mr. Calais. I can see from here where you are, and can see also where you are going," said a man with a German accent.

"Who are you?" Edward exclaimed into the phone as he looked around for the owner of the voice.

Across the street, he could see a man standing by a black BMW. He was holding two cell phones, one to each of his ears. He smiled and spoke into one of the phones. "Here I am." The man waved at Calais.

"Oh no," whispered Lyon, who was standing behind Calais. Her shoulders touched him, as did her hip.

"What?" he said, startled by her sudden appearance.

"It's one of Rexan's men. Edward—" she reached for his arm, clinging to him—"he is very ruthless. And capable of anything."

"Why are you with him then?"

"Because we need the money. Please help me, Edward, I'm afraid."

"I'll call you tomorrow. Just go, please."

As if on queue, Edward's cell phone jumped to life. Edward listened.

"Mister Calais, I am an associate of Mister Henry Rexan. One of my associates is parked in front of your house. He is watching over things, shall we say, making sure nothing tragic happens. You'll be pleased to know that the new outfit fits your little girl perfectly. The flowers? They are set on your kitchen table, in a beautiful white porcelain vase apparently. Jane looks very beautiful this morning. She seems so happy too, but so alone. It's almost dangerous, such a beautiful woman by herself. Anyone nearby could just go and get her and your little girl. And who knows what might happen?"

Calais turned towards the door to the police station.

"Don't be an idiot, Calais," added the voice.

Calais took the phone from his ear and pressed the end button. Then he turned away from the police station and walked away from it and in the direction of his office.

The phone rang again.

"Hello."

"Well done, Mr. Calais. Oh my, there goes your wife and child now, in that beautiful white truck. We'll make sure they can go on their way, safe and secure. As a matter of fact, my man is following safely behind. You know what? If you ever have need of someone to keep an eye on them for you, just let us know. Any friend of Henry Rexan is a friend of ours. Oh, and if you don't know, any enemy of Rexan's ends up dead. "

Calais pressed the end button and continued walking. He strode at a steady pace until he reached his own office. He went inside, closed the door, and just he sat for a while, catching his breath and trying to calm down. Once he had stopped shaking, he got up and went to the basement car park where his MGB awaited him. He climbed in and fired the car up.

Edward speed-dialed George's cell phone number, and amazingly, he answered.

"I've got big problems, George."

Edward went on to describe in detail what had happened, including the five-million-dollar offer to his business partner.

George knew exactly how to solve Edward's problems. After ending his call with Calais, he reached into his desk and took out the Leviticus CD and held it in his hands. He phoned Dr. Lyon's number and explained how she could obtain the CD and they confirmed the price. As hot property, its value was significantly less than what Rexan had offered Calais. Still, Miller was desperate. Not only that, it was just in time for online Texas hold 'em, and George felt lucky.

The courier delivering the Leviticus software arrived at Lexan's home and was greeted at the door by Monika. She signed for the small package and delivered it to the office where Lexan sat waiting. He took the package and used his long, dirty fingernails to rip open the tape that held the seals in place. He carefully opened the case and tenderly placed the CD into the laptop. The name *Leviticus* appeared on the screen and he clicked on it. A pop-up appeared and asked if he wanted to load the contents of the CD onto his hard drive. He clicked on the yes button.

That was his mistake.

Jerry Chen had placed a loop in the program that began to erase the contents of both the CD and the hard drive of the recipient computer if the person said yes to the computer's query.

Initially the screen of the computer appeared to show the loading of Leviticus. In reality, Jerry's virus was blasting through Rexan's hard drive. In front of his eyes it destroyed everything, including the secret recordings from his bedroom of him and Monika, in addition to other members of his personal pornography collection. As the files were destroyed, Rexan screamed, "No, No!" and pushed every button on the keyboard.

Minutes later, the screen just went blank.

Rexan sat astonished. He tried to reboot and failed. He turned the computer off and then on again and failed to get a response. His anger grew. His face turned crimson and his heart raced. His blood pressure rose and his chest ached. He was not the kind of person to be fooled, and he had been.

He reached for his phone and called Lorne Browne.

"What is it, Henry?"

"I tried to load the program we bought off of that puke George. My computer has gone blank. He must have sabotaged it!"

"Did you try restarting it?"

"Of course, you idiot! There is nothing left. He destroyed my computer, that swine!"

"That's Jerry Chen for you, he's a pro. George probably didn't even know about the virus. What do you want me to do?"

"I want the real program. I want my money back. I want Chen

dead."

"I'll do what I can."

"You'll do what I tell you to do, Browne." Rexan hung up.

Lorne immediately dialed George's cell number.

"Hello."

"Hello, George. This is Lorne Browne. You have delivered bad goods."

This was very bad timing. George has just lost over $50,000 playing poker online.

"Rexan is a very unhappy man."

"What do you mean 'bad goods'?"

"Not only did the program you sold to us not give us Chen's software, it also destroyed Henry's computer. You have taken his money and then made a fool of him. You are a dead man."

"I didn't know. I swear, I didn't know," cried George.

"It doesn't matter. You delivered the goods and took his money. That's all that counts with men like Henry Rexan."

"What do I do?"

"Get us the program. And it needs to be a clean one, guaranteed. Make sure Chen goes nowhere near it! These people are serious. You'll be lucky to get through this alive. You'll need to put yourself first, George. You'll need to make sure you get done what Rexan wants, then maybe he'll forget about you and your minelayer partner."

"You mean Jerry?"

"Think of yourself, George, and your wife. Thinking about anyone else will get you killed."

The phone went dead.

George placed his head in his hands and wept. Did he have it in him to betray Jerry and perhaps cost him his life?

14

It was finally time, and he knew it. Dr. Jerry Chen packed up his stuff and left for his fishing trailer on the rugged West Coast of Vancouver Island. He caught the first ferry from the terminal in Horseshoe Bay. Once aboard he consumed a breakfast of greasy fried eggs, bacon, toast heaped with jam, and the infamous ferry coffee. When the boat reached Naniamo, he followed the Island Highway as it wound its way up the coast of Vancouver Island. The summer cities of Parksville and Qualicum were alive with beach dwellers that were in the process of spreading blankets on the vast gray sands and unpacking picnic lunches.

A turn towards the middle of the island at Parksville and Jerry was driving through the vast forests of the northwest rain forest. An hour or so later and he bumped up the old logging road that took him to the West Coast recreational community called Salmon Beach. It was there that Jerry maintained a small property. Jerry parked the truck and unloaded one small bag into the trailer that served as his cottage. He turned on the radio and listened to the weather forecast for the next day. A storm was coming. He fired up the propane heater and sat with Dinah, occasionally thinking notes into her memory.

Jerry Chen needed some time alone to work on the program, and he did much of his best work at his trailer on the shore of the ocean. He loved the open waters of the Pacific but respected their power.

The next morning, Jerry wolfed down two muffins and made some horrible instant coffee. He packed his fishing kit, survival suit, and hooked up his boat to the truck. As the sun rose, Jerry drove the few hundred yards to the boat launch and parked for a moment, then backed the trailer into the water. Chene opened the door of the truck, stepped out, and surveyed the waves. Shivering in the grey gloom, he moved to the trailer and unclipped the boat. The boat moved down the trailer wheels and into the sea of her own volition, with help from gravity.

As Jerry watched the boat bob up and down with the swell, he felt the inner call that was becoming so hideously familiar. A moment later, the insistent hiss of a Voice slithered into his consciousness. It told him that if he had not created Leviticus, none of this would have happened. It told him that without him in the picture, Edward and Jane and Leah would be safe again. He listened as he watched the waves surge up to his rubber boots and then pull away, tugging relentlessly at him. He held the boat tight, waiting for the right moment. The salty drops that drifted down his cheek were a mixture of the spray of the ocean and his tears. This was nothing new to Jerry Chen. He knew sorrow and unrelenting pain.

Over the years, many lives had been lost to the vicious currents, raging surf, and icy waters of the West Coast. The small open boat Jerry used to pursue salmon and cod slipped easily away from the concrete ramp, carried along by a descending wave. Almost immediately a groundswell of rushing water threatened to take the boat with it. A fellow angler waiting his turn at the ramp offered to help.

"Looks like there is some weather coming!" commented his drafted assistant as he held the boat steady for Jerry. "I'm staying inshore today."

"I hear there is some big fish out past The Fin," said Jerry as he pointed to the big rock that marked the opening to the Pacific.

Huge waves crashed into the small islands that sheltered the larger island. Over the years, the waves had carved the outermost one into the shape of a shark's fin.

Jerry left the boat in his helper's hands while he parked the truck. Then he thanked his helper and started up his motor. He headed deliberately towards the "Fin" and the open ocean.

As Jerry fought the waves, the wind whipped at his unzipped maritime survival suit. The seas began to get even more violent. A lone commercial halibut fishing boat plowed past Jerry's small boat, waves

106

crashing over her bow. A crewmember ran out on deck and waved furiously, pointing at the oncoming storm and then the channel through which they could both pass to safety.

The fishing boat continued on, alone.

Jerry fought the surf, the wind, the currents, the rain, and the Voice. As the boat approached the rocky shore, a particularly violent surge spun the little boat sideways. Exposed to the full force of the sea, and broadside, the boat was completely vulnerable. The next wave toppled over the boat, filling it with ice-cold salt water. It was over quickly, and for that Jerry was thankful.

Waves pounded the boat onto the rocky shore, tearing it to pieces throughout the rest of the day.

Night fell. Crabs began their relentless search for the carrion that the storms of the Pacific often produce.

Jerry's helper at the boat dock reported him missing when he came across Jerry's truck. The Coast Guard sent out a lookout request by radio and the halibut boat responded by reporting seeing a small boat near the shore past the "Fin." Search and Rescue found the empty boat the next day. A Coast Guard cutter plucked an empty survival suit with the name and address of Jerry Chen from the surging waters.

The halibut boat had cruised throughout the night, outrunning the storm. It docked the next day in Vancouver and unloaded its most recent catch.

"Computer Genius Missing: Presumed Dead" read the headline. The story went on to describe Jerry Chen in an obituary like style. He was described as one of the people most responsible for recent breakthroughs in computer security systems. The picture of him was an old blurry version.

Computer programmers throughout North America paid silent

tribute to a person they had revered but never met face to face. Such was their life.

Financial markets recoiled at the loss. Companies who used Jerry Chen's services reported losses at the close of trading. Microsoft and IBM were particularly hard hit as they both used Jerry on a freelance basis. He was that well known. His skills were particularly valuable where large amounts of information needed to be accessible to the right people but safely locked away from the wrong people.

Edward Calais was deeply shocked by the news. It was not fair. He'd lost a terrific resource. He'd also lost someone who had consistently denied wealth and its relationship to happiness. Edward could never understand that.

Jerry had always taken joy from the simple things. His love for the Calais children, respect for all people, and his unending compassion was so evident in his life, despite his emotional troubles. Then it happened. Something moved in Edward as he thought about his friend. Something he hadn't felt before. Something spoke to him, from deep inside. It wasn't audible, but it was clear nonetheless. The Voice told him to look for his friend.

15

The news of Chen's death struck Henry Rexan like a gift from above, or perhaps, from down below. He was thrilled at his unexpected good fortune. The elimination of Jerry increased the secrecy of the Leviticus program tenfold...once he had it in his hands, of course. And like a great work of art, its value would increase at the death of the artist. His death would also dispel any fear of the talented Jerry Chen using his skills against COBRA and the new COBRA implants.

For Rexan, the next step was simple. He would get the program from Calais—whether by brute force, fear, or manipulation mattered little to him. Edward Calais had already shown himself to love his family, so fear of them "having an accident" would probably motivate him. Rexan's prey also clearly enjoyed the material side of life, so that might be used productively as well. Of course there were always women and other such vices. *So much to work with and so little time,* thought Rexan, as he nodded to himself. Getting the program itself was child's play. Once the program had proven its value, however, anyone outside his organization with knowledge of it had to be eliminated. Rexan could not risk government authorities finding out about his plan too early. He would therefore need to get rid of the "Gang," as they sometimes called themselves.

Rexan's spy, Werner Braun, had mentioned the tightly knit group of Calais's friends. Assuming their wives also knew of Leviticus, it meant five people would have to be disposed of. If only they were at the same place at the same time, it would be so easy, he reasoned. Perhaps a funeral of a friend might be just the occasion. He hoped they would find the body soon. Not so soon that the delicacies of the sea didn't have a chance to feast on it, though. Not that soon.

Being drowned in the ocean was such an awful death.

In his earlier days, when Rexan was more of a "hands on" kind of murderer, he'd personally witnessed the effect of a living ocean on a dead human body. Crabs and shrimp were particularly adept at dismembering and consuming flesh, starting within minutes of the body coming to rest on the bottom. Initially he'd been repulsed at the thought of eating such animals, once he realized what their diet might have consisted of. However, he now relished their meat. Perhaps it was because he had disposed of so many of his past enemies in the ocean surrounding Vancouver. It was as if he was consuming their human souls as he dined on the animal's flesh. It was this that he was evolving into.

Rexan peered through the big view window of his waterfront mansion. He was looking west, towards where Jerry Chen had gone missing. While he could not see the actual place—it was too far away— he could imagine Chen's body being dragged along the bottom by the tidal currents. He could picture the crabs and shrimp catching the scent of the beginning of decay and clamoring towards the body. He smacked his lips and reached for the intercom button and called the kitchen.

"Monika, make sure we have some fresh shrimp and crab for supper Friday. I want them brought in from the West Coast, near Salmon Beach. Have them flown in, if needed. I have an urge for fresh seafood. I understand they are particularly flavorful this week. Perhaps done in a Chinese style would be...appropriate."

"Yes sir," replied Monika, shuddering at the implications. She'd experienced her employer's special requests before. She'd also overheard too many conversions. "Why did I ever leave home?" she whispered to herself.

Jerry Chen chuckled as he listened to the news of his disappearance that was being broadcast on the radio. The ploy must have worked. Being dead allowed him the luxury of working on defeating the COBRA creators in secrecy, without worrying about them being overly protective. A virus as simple as the one that George had passed on would not work a second time, at least without fear of immediate retaliation.

He sat, warm and safe, in the cabin of the halibut boat that had been hired to pick him up from the relative calm of the lee side of the "Fin." Once Jerry was safely aboard, the fish boat towed Jerry's sinking craft out and released it to be ripped apart by the raw surf on the windward side of the little island. Deck hands had thrown his survival suit into the water to make his death seem certain. Once Jerry's simulated death was complete, Jerry changed his clothes and was given some hot coffee and a ham sandwich. Nothing tasted as good as that combination to the cunning Jerry Chen. Jerry then took some time as the boat rounded the North Island to begin the much calmer run down to Vancouver to survey his future abode. As planned by Jane, the halibut boat had been quickly converted into a temporary office for him. She and Tara had taken turns supplying the boat's cabin with the computer hardware and software he required. A mini satellite dish, cell phone, and a fax machine were all he needed to complete his work. The boat's crew was sworn to secrecy, paid well, and sent to get Jerry and bring him back to Deep Cove.

Initially, Chen felt somewhat energetic as he surveyed his temporary domain. Before long, however, the fatigue created by the stress and the work of the last hours began to take its toll. Jerry headed for his berth and climbed into the bunk. He slept well that night, a rarity in his life.

Early the next morning, as the boat slipped quickly into Deep Cove and docked, Jerry began to work using Dinah. His fingers reached out to the Leviticus patch, and he placed it gently on the proper spot behind his left ear. It immediately and automatically synchronized itself to the laptop's software. While Leviticus was working perfectly, it did take some getting used to. Jerry leaned back in his chair, closed his eyes, and began to think in programming lines. Leviticus immediately added the lines to his laptop's screen. It was amazingly efficient, as long as he was focused on the program. Letting his mind wander slowed things down somewhat as Leviticus worked to separate what Jerry intended to think from what he actually was thinking. Leviticus was learning, though, and getting faster exponentially.

His job today was to modify a parasitic virus program that he'd created previously under a secret government contract. Its sole function was to seek out and steal information from the host it was inserted into. In common terms it was an electronic spy. Ironically, Jerry had developed the virus in order to test the fallibility of a new security system he was developing for the Canadian version of the CIA, CSIS.

What made the parasite program interesting was that Chen himself had been unable to defeat its ability to hide and replicate itself once it had gained access to the host computer. Every time an email was sent, the virus was attached to it. It could not be destroyed, either, unless one was willing to destroy all of the records of the whole system. It was very frustrating not to be able to defeat one's own creation. The virus, however, was almost perfect for his new use.

Jerry Chen worked on the program, commanding it to send copies of files, email messages, voice mail, secret access codes, and any other information that might be of value. It must be completely hidden, once installed. The work was long and hard, but he was in hyper drive mode.

As lunchtime approached, Jerry scratched his unshaven face and put on a baseball hat and tinted glasses. It was the entire disguise he needed, as so few people knew the face of the recently deceased Jerry Chen, despite the fact he was internationally known. It was one of the advantages of being a computer geek: few people cared what you looked like. He stepped onto the wharf from the boat and went up to the small restaurant that was attached to the marina. On his way in he purchased a local newspaper and tucked it under his arm. A newspaper made it less awkward for Jerry to eat alone. Jerry entered the diner and picked a table looking over the water and off in a corner. He sat down and was immediately served a glass of water by the waitress who worked his section.

"Can I get you a coffee or something else to drink?"

He looked up from the paper and beheld the most amazing smile he had ever seen. She was not a classic beauty, but one that would stop most men in their tracks. Her brunette hair was pulled up into a messy bun that only made her perfect complexion more outstanding. As she waited, she began to blush because Jerry could not take his eyes off her. This was very awkward for Jerry, who was quite unnerved by most people, never mind an attractive woman. Rachel was the name on her nametag. She finally looked at him directly, and when he looked into her eyes, his knees quivered.

"I'll have tea, please."

"Sure—are you ready to order?"

"Anything you'd recommend?"

"Our fish and chips are fantastic, especially with the coleslaw we make. It's amazing!"

"Sounds great, thank you."

"Are you new around here?"

"I just arrived. I'm living on that fish boat. It's got a little office for me right on board."

"What do you do?"

"Computer program development."

"No kidding! I'm working on my Masters in Computer Science. My thesis is on enhancing the interface between users and their computers."

"Really?"

While Rachel Kennedy did have to take care of other customers, every chance she got she came to Jerry's table. Their conversation was completely natural. They laughed and shared expertise and stories that only geeks could relate to. Too soon for Jerry, it was time to go back to work. He collected the check and went to pay at the till.

As he turned to leave, he said, "Thank you. See you later."

It was an innocent-enough statement, to which she replied with a broad grin and a quiet, "I hope so."

Jerry was so astonished that such a beautiful woman was actually speaking to him that he felt compelled to hurry away, somewhat panicked. Halfway down the steps from the restaurant to the boat, he realized he hadn't left a tip. He was mortified, but couldn't bring himself to return that day.

The next day arrived, and Jerry determined his response would be different this time, when he returned to the restaurant. In the early morning hours, he tried to work on the parasite program. Things went even slower this time. Leviticus kept writing program lines with Rachel inserted in them, because the name *Rachel* kept popping into his head and Leviticus was, after all, reading his mind. Fortunately, Leviticus recognized that there seemed to be a pattern here and often asked if he meant what he was thinking. After a while Jerry gave up on the programming and focused on the upcoming lunch with Rachel as his waitress.

How should I act? he asked his image in the mirror as he shaved. Perhaps he'd be the confident, almost arrogant man women seemed to like. That's it—he'd be Edward Calais! He could not conceive of the fact that she might just like him the way he was. It was too much to dream of, that a woman who shared his interests, who was so much fun and so full of life, and so beautiful, could ever be interested in a romantic way to the likes of him.

Oh, she probably didn't even remember him, he thought. And if she did, it would be as the guy who didn't tip and couldn't look her in the eyes without getting pale, and that was quite a feat for a man of Asian descent.

As Jerry approached the restaurant, he saw her. Unfortunately for him, her allotted section was already full of diners. As he reached the hostess standing by the cash register, she asked if he preferred the smoking or nonsmoking section. He said he preferred whatever section Rachel was working. She smiled and asked if he'd like to wait in the lounge area and she would return for him as soon as a table became available. He grinned like a teenager and walked into the bar and ordered a club soda. It seemed forever for a table to be ready. Would it be worth the wait? He wondered....

The plan was coming together. George and Tara sat beside each other on the loveseat in their living room. Jane sat across from them in an antique chair, her petite frame scarcely depressing the ornate cushion.

"George, thanks for all the help with getting Jerry set up on the boat."

"It's the least I could do, especially after getting you into this mess with that scumbag Rexan."

"Apology accepted, George. We understand the pressure you were under, and everyone makes mistakes."

Tara's eyes welled with tears. She gave Jane a hug.

"I can't believe that you forgive me, and that you trust me to work the plan," George told Jane.

"Well, to be honest, it's Tara we need." Jane laughed nervously, as did the others.

"Why don't we just go to the police?" asked Tara.

"First of all, we have no proof of anything, and secondly, if what I believe is true about Rexan, he'll kill us unless we have something on him. We have to do this thing first. Then we can go to the police. So let's get updated on 'the plan,' as George calls it. I am working on researching the legal ramifications of whatever information might be gained from COBRA by using Jerry's virus. Lorne insists we all come to their office. Probably to let us know that if something goes wrong, we are all toast. But I know it's worth the risk.

There is no chance that they are clean. Clean companies don't have hit men and muscle like Rexan uses. That's our key. Once we have some proof of illegal activities, we can use it against them, and we stand a chance of getting some protection. If we can't, or it takes too long, they will come after us and we will have no protection. They are very fragile right now. Any bad press would kill their chances of getting legitimate financing, which they need. The trick will be getting the parasite virus onto their computing system without them knowing it. We will need a mule, a tremendous distraction, and great bait. Edward is going to act as our mule."

"What is a mule?" asked Tara.

"It's someone who unknowingly carries a package, usually drugs. But in this case, it's a virus. The bait is Leviticus, and the distraction is

Tara. We'll need to be careful because if they catch on...well, I don't know what might happen. But I have learned one thing about scum like Rexan. You cannot run. Once they have something on you, it becomes a matter of pride. Rexan wants revenge for being humiliated, and he is irrational. This is our only hope. Having Jerry dead should lower their guard because they won't suspect we have any computer expertise of any significance. The other key is that our 'mule' is Edward, and he must believe Jerry is dead or they will suspect something is wrong by his behavior. He is a terrible actor. He could never pull it off otherwise.

"Right now Edward is off the West Coast and headed to Jerry's cabin. It's awful having him believe that Jerry is dead, but it is necessary. Rexan cannot even consider the fact that Jerry may be alive and able to help, and we can't let anything tip him off. We have to catch them off their guards. Jerry is holed up on the boat. He is set up and online. He's in geek heaven, trust me. He has a big program to corrupt, and a huge system to hack into. What could be better?"

The three of them shared a laugh as they pictured Jerry. Despite the fear of Rexan, they needed to release some of their nervous energy and laughter was a way to do that.

"How is the virus work going for Jerry?" queried George.

"It's a little scary. The main problem is time," said Tara. "He is modifying an old virus program he created for the Echelon Project—you know, the one that inserts itself into emails and then sends the files of the owner back to the government. He's modifying that one and restructuring it so it can be attached to the Leviticus program. The problem is the original virus wasn't meant to be secretly loaded. Jerry is afraid it will show up as a corrupt file or a virus. Also, currently it takes 10 minutes to load, and during that time at least three warnings appear on the screen."

Jane added, somewhat coyly, "On the other hand, Jerry is quite focused...for now anyway."

"What do you mean, for now?" questioned George.

"It seems he's met someone—a waitress at the marina."

"Great. The computer nerd turns human...perfect timing." George shrugged.

"I think he'll still do the job, but he might be a little less single-minded, excuse the pun," said Tara.

"The virus," Jane added, "will do exactly what Jerry wants. It will be passed on through emails and account transfers. It is also able to replicate itself, once it's loaded into the main network. Even if they find one copy and delete it, another one will take its place. It will also send back names, addresses, messages, account balances, transfers, etc. I'm positive we'll find something dirty."

Tara looked concerned. "How will we get the program onto Lorne's computer with him seeing the screen and the warnings?"

"That is where you come in," said Jane. "We need something very powerful to take his mind off of the computer. Who else could be a better distraction for a creep like Lorne?"

"Okay, I get it. Who's going to load the program while Tara works her magic?" asked George.

"Edward."

"Is he up to it?" questioned Tara.

"Let's hope so."

The meeting went on and several remaining details were cleaned up. Time was running out.

The chartered helicopter that was searching for the remains of Jerry Chen passed quickly over the cold and damp Pacific rainforest. The woods were lush with growth. Edward Calais looked down to see two black bear cubs lumbering up a dry riverbed. Their mother plodded patiently along behind them.

The chopper he was riding in banked quickly and dropped as it passed from flying over the land to skimming over the sea. The pilot maneuvered the craft so it was traveling parallel to the shore. A huge, thick, gray blanket of low cloud lay offshore, resting on the surface of the ocean.

"The fog bank is only a few miles out, sir. I can't go anywhere near it or I could lose my license," crackled the pilot's voice over the intercom.

Calais adjusted his headphones and replied, "Just do the best you can. I'll watch the beach side and you watch the water."

He could not bear to watch the icy water. He knew if he saw his friend, Jerry would be floating facedown. The water was far too cold for someone to survive the several days since the disappearance, even if they had a survival suit on. As the aircraft passed over the "Fin," they checked the craggy rocks where an injured man might have climbed. The Coast Guard had already been over this area several times. The professional searchers had even used a Hercules aircraft equipped with infrared cameras. They had found nothing human. There was really no hope.

After two hours of skimming back and forth along the shore, Edward noticed that the margin between the shoreline and the fog back had narrowed. Edward dropped his head and said quietly into the headset, "It's time to call it quits. Let's go back to Tofino."

"You're right sir, it's time to go. But don't lose hope. He still might be alive. I've seen stranger things happen out this way."

The pilot banked the chopper and in minutes was carefully hovering over a small landing pad near the RCMP station in Tofino. The chopper gently set down on the pad. Calais climbed out of the craft, ducked his head under the rotating blades, and jogged to the police station. He opened the door to the small office and was greeted by the officer on duty.

"Any sign of Jerry Chen?" Calais asked.

"Not since we found the boat and the survival suit. I'm very sorry, sir," responded the officer.

"Thanks. I'm going back to the hotel. You'll give me a call if you find anything?" Edward asked.

"Of course. Want a lift? I have to go downtown anyway."

"Sure, thanks."

Edward and the officer left the building together and drove in a police cruiser through the beautiful little town and to a nearby hotel.

Calais entered the lobby and checked in. He asked the clerk to arrange that a rental truck be delivered. Finding his room, he cleaned himself up and went for supper at the Fisherman's Diner, which was attached to the hotel. He ordered a coffee, a bowl of clam chowder, and

118

a clubhouse sandwich. The coffee was hot and strong. Drinking it helped to clear his mind.

After eating, Edward sat back in his seat, looked out the diner window, and watched the fog roll in. It was thick, cold, damp, and foreboding. Edward thought about his friend, and about the past, and then how he would miss the innocent brilliance of Jerry Chen. Edward's thoughts turned to Jane, and to Leah, and to Henry Rexan and Lorne Browne.

Jerry was dead. The Leviticus program was sitting on his computer. He could send it over to Browne, as is, and hope for the best. At this stage in the game he didn't care about the money or Browne benefiting from the program. He just wanted it to be over.

When he returned to Vancouver, he knew he would have to start making arrangements for Jerry's funeral. He would probably be asked to speak at it. The large church Jerry attended in Burnaby would be a good place, although it might be too large. Jerry was kind, but had few friends, to Edward's knowledge anyway. He didn't think there would be enough to appropriately fill such a large auditorium.

He thought again about the times he and Jerry had shared together as they were growing up and going to high school. There were times in those days when Edward could have had several girls who would be hoping that he might ask them to a dance. On the other hand, Jerry would be left at home, alone. Edward had gone on to the dance and joined the other couples, usually leaving Jerry to be on his own. He regretted leaving Jerry now.

Calais finished his coffee, and went back to his room. He phoned Jane and explained his plans. He started talking about Jerry, but his voice left him.

"Edward, are you alright?" Jane asked.

"Yeah, I'm okay. I guess he really is dead, isn't he?"

"You're going to miss him, aren't you, Edward?"

"More than I ever imagined."

Edward asked about Leah, and they made small talk for a while, neither wanting to hang up. Eventually, they said their good-byes.

He slipped into a hot bath and let the soothing water relax his tense neck and back muscles. After drying off, he turned on the sports channel and watched the beginning of a Toronto Blue Jays versus Boston Red Sox game. Seeing the Jays take a comfortable lead, he set the sleep timer on the TV and promptly fell asleep. His sleep, however, was fitful.

The sounds of ocean were all around him and intruded into his consciousness. The roar of the waves penetrated inside his mind; they became a part of his dreams and of his nightmares that long night. Images of Jerry reaching up from the black waters, crying for help appeared. Images of Leah crying out for him, and he couldn't get to her. A Voice was calling to him, but he couldn't make out the words. He screamed out to the Voice to stop.

Edward woke up in a cold sweat. He had never felt so alone. *If you are really there, God,* he thought, *please help me.* He drifted back to sleep, tossing and turning.

16

At precisely 7 a.m., country music erupted from the clock radio beside Edward's bed. He woke from yet another nightmare and tapped the snooze tab. He lay back in his bed and listened to the rain and wind. It was as if the dreams had never ended.

He showered, rinsing off the sticky, salty sweat that had covered his body during the night. He dressed and left for the restaurant next door. His head was throbbing so he dry-swallowed a few pain tablets that he'd thrown into his pocket on his way out the door.

At 7 a.m., the restaurant was crowded with loggers and fishermen. He ordered bacon, eggs, and toast, and washed down the grease with bitingly bitter and acidic grapefruit juice. As he paid his bill, he ordered a large coffee with double cream and sugar—to go.

Climbing into the rented four-wheel-drive truck, Edward put the coffee into the drink holder near the gearshift. He drove out of town and turned off the pavement and onto the logging road that would take him deep into the woods.

The big new four-by-four rental truck intruded into the heavy rain forest, thick with hemlock, fir, and cedar. Some of the biggest trees were over a thousand years old. The truck bumped and jarred over the gravel and rock that made up the roadbed. The massive heavy branches of the forest trees were leaning over the road, producing a dark, wet, and musty tunnel of tree and branch. A mist of rain wafted from the low clouds constantly wetting the windshield.

Edward leaned over to open the coffee cup that sat nestled neatly in the cup holder mounted in the dash. Once open, steam rose from the opening of the disposable cup. Calais then reached in the paper bag containing the small cream containers. He was steering with his left hand and reaching with his right. The truck veered slightly while he poured the cream into the waiting black hot coffee. Finally, he reached for the cup and took an ever-so-satisfactory drink. At fifty miles an hour, Edward was doing well performing a delicate balancing act of controlling a vehicle while drinking coffee.

Suddenly, from the right of the roadside, a huge buck mule deer leapt into the road in front of the truck. Calais reached for the steering wheel with his right hand, and in doing this, dropped the coffee, spilling its contents onto his thigh. Searing pain from the super-heated coffee penetrated his panicked brain.

Instinctively he looked down at his leg, taking his eye off the road. The truck's right front wheel drifted onto and caught the edge of the soft shoulder of the narrow and rough road. Calais immediately looked back up and saw the forest approaching, and with great speed. His reflexes cut in and he ripped the wheel left, but it was too late. The soft shoulder of the road caught the right rear tire. The rest was physics. As he swung left, the momentum of the truck leaned the vehicle to the right and as a result, the wheels slid further towards the forest. The mass of the heavy truck carried it over the shoulder of the road. It rolled down the bank, tumbling.

Calais's head was flung into the driver's side window, which shattered into hundreds of pieces on impact. Many of the pieces were coated in his blood.

The truck came to rest upside down, hidden deep in the forest, its wheels continuing to turn slowly. The engine ran for a while, then stalled of its own accord. Various fluids drained from the engine block and gas tank, staining the thick rich green moss where the truck had come to rest. The smell of leaking gasoline was everywhere.

The big deer on the road initially stood still, and then, thankful for the renewal of silence, continued carefully into the woods. All was quiet.

The halibut boat bobbed gently as the wake of a passing boat reached the wharf where it was moored. The motion caused Chen to stop his work on the computer and peer outside. He watched a dozen sea gulls diving and feeding on garbage that had been thrown out by the passing pleasure craft.

Idiots, Chen thought to himself.

Jerry Chen was on the verge of completing the virus attachment process he planned to use to infect and search the computing systems of the COBRA creators. Trial runs had proven the virus's ability to find and ferret out information. He was still unable to bypass some warning systems on the test computer he was trying to infect, but it was the best he could do. Once the program was successfully loaded onto a network hard drive, however, he felt that it was unstoppable.

Chen made final copies, backed them up and proceeded to burn them onto CDs. Once finished, he left everything running.

Chen then shifted his thinking. He needed to prepare for the special evening that lay before him. Now, with programming lines temporarily purged from his mind, all he could think about was Rachel.

Jerry showered using the small stall situated near the bow of the boat. Opening the soaps and shampoos provided by Tara and Jane, he scrubbed and lathered every inch of himself. Once out of the shower, he trimmed his nails and cut any hair that was growing where it ought not to grow.

Oral hygiene was the next event. He brushed his teeth, flossed them, brushed again, then used copious amounts of mouthwash. For good measure, he repeated the process. His gums were very pink by the end and they served nicely to show the newly whitened teeth.

Jerry applied several layers of a lightly scented, yet apparently effective antiperspirant. A light splash of Givenchy cologne completed the effect.

Reaching into the closet, he took out the new clothes that had been bought and delivered by the women. The clothes had been washed, pressed, and looked great. He put on the Polo shirt and the khakis and slipped on the Rockport walkers. A navy cashmere sweater completed the outfit.

A mere twenty minutes later his hair was acceptable. Looking into the mirror, he said to himself, "Hi Rachel, so glad to see you."

He thought he sounded stupid and he was right. He wondered what a man like Edward would say by way of introduction. Checking his watch, Chen realized he needed to hurry in order to be at the restaurant on time.

Hurrying out of the boat, he climbed the ramp that led from the docked boat and towards the restaurant where Rachel was on duty. He had left the door to the boat open and the computer was still running. Such was Jerry Chen's inability to deal with important, but small, details. Someday it would be the death of him, went the saying.

Chen walked through the big oak doors that formed the entrance to the dining hall where Rachel was just beginning her shift. From the way the other staff was acting when they saw him arrive, one could tell something unusual was in the air. Rachel hoped it might have something to do with the funny little computer man who had been frequenting her section of the restaurant.

She delivered salads to the group of business people who were the only occupants of her section. On her way back to the kitchen, she noticed a table for two with the word *Reserved* written on the card resting on its surface. Checking the reservation book at the desk, she found no name written on the space. *That's strange,* she thought to herself. It was her favorite table because it was secluded and overlooked the water. She had often thought it would be a very romantic place to have dinner.

Glancing up at the ornate mirror behind the bar, she watched Jerry approach. The funny little computer man looked fantastic. Her heart rate jumped as she ducked into the staff ladies' room to make some quick adjustments to her hair. She stood before the mirror and surveyed herself. She was petite, barely five feet tall, and perfectly proportioned. Her shoulder-length hair was brown but streaked blond by the summer sun. Needing little makeup to show her beauty, she simply dusted a light powder over her delicate face. Both her eye shape and their corresponding color were that of almonds. A tiny nose and perfect skin highlighted her chiseled cheekbones.

As she left the washroom, her stomach quivered. She was used to the attention of many men. Very few, though, knew how to reach her. She sought depth of character. Most of those types were too intimidated by her looks to even approach her. If only this Jerry character would ask her out, she thought as she rounded the corner to the dining room.

Their eyes met immediately.

"Hello," she said. "Can I, like, help you?"

She winced inwardly at her words. She had a university degree in computer science. She didn't speak like a seventeen-year-old prom queen. She blushed.

That blush only highlighted her beauty to the admiring Chen. Her stumbling made him feel more confident, knowing she was real and not an illusion of perfection.

"I am a reservation. Errr, I mean, I *have* a reservation. That table over in the corner. I'm meeting someone for dinner."

"Oh," she said, disappointed. *He must have a date,* she assumed. She led him to the table, where a bouquet of roses had appeared. As he stopped beside her, an unfamiliar scent wafted to her perfect nose. He looked and smelled wonderful.

Once they were at the table, Jerry pulled out one of the chairs, looked her in her eyes, and said, "Would you care to join me for dinner?"

Placing his hand in the small of her back he gently pushed her towards and into the chair. She resisted momentarily, then moved with him.

"But I'm working tonight," she said, sighing at the same time as she sat down lightly in the dining room chair.

"It's all been taken care of, Rachel," said Jerry as a waiter appeared with menus. The waiter winked at her knowingly, and the penny dropped. She understood finally that she was being courted in a most unusual, yet entirely endearing manner.

She smiled the smile of a won, if not slightly confused, woman.

As their eyes met, Jerry felt instantly at ease and confident, especially when she looked out over the water and almost whispered out loud, "This has never happened to me."

He smiled and took her hand in his. Time slowed and accelerated all at the same time. They began to talk and kept on talking for hours. So intense was their conversation that the wonderful meal that was delivered seemed only to be a distraction. After everyone had left the restaurant, late in the night, he escorted her to her car. Neither of them wanted to part, yet they knew they must.

Jerry Chen opened the door to her car. She stood close to him, not wanting to get in without him. She wanted so badly for him to come home with her.

Chen knew too that desire was beginning to cloud his thinking. A man of virtue, he gently kissed her cheek, eased her into the driver's seat, and said, "I'll call you tomorrow."

"I can't wait all the way until tomorrow," she said, smiling enchantingly.

"You'll have to," he replied. He knelt down and kissed her other cheek. Then he closed the car door and watched as she started the car.

The front driver's side window opened at the touch of a button.

"You sure?" she said.

"I've never felt so sure, Rachel."

She smiled and drove away. He watched until the light disappeared, then walked towards the dock that held his boat. The wonderful scent of her perfume clung to his sweater, and he drank it in.

The truck was still, as was the forest that surrounded the wreck. Edward Calais awoke partially inverted and suspended by his seat belt. Warm liquid was steadily dripping from a two-inch gash on the left side of his skull and was splashing down on the overturned roof of the truck. He looked down and found that a pool of his own blood lay congealed near the smashed dome light. As he turned his head, a drop of cold rainwater splashed down his chin. He felt strangely warm and comfortable. He turned his head again and looked to the sky. He could see the stars. For some reason he was thrown back in his mind to the words of a science teacher who told him and the other students that eternity was just beyond the stars. He had never really understood what that meant coming from such a person, until now.

He thought about his place in the universe and his place in his home. He knew he needed to change. He knew he needed something more than money. He thought of his friend Jerry and of his faith. He prayed to a God he could not see and asked for help, promising that if he could see his family again....

As he finished, a face appeared in front of his eyes. Unafraid, he said, "You must be the angel."

"Not likely, buddy," was the reply of a very real and very large and muscular man, "but I am going to help you. Take it easy and don't move. I'll call for help."

The Native American man reached into the cab and took out the cell phone lying on the seat and dialed the local Royal Canadian Mounted Police number. Soon an ambulance and the police arrived to free Calais from the truck and take him to the local hospital. A thorough examination and X-rays showed no serious damage, although he was sporting one ugly gash and was very bruised, strained, and sore. He was forced to stay overnight in order for the medical staff to be convinced his concussion was relatively minor.

The next morning he awoke in some pain, but feeling very hungry. The hospital breakfast left him in more pain, and still hungry. He had one final examination to endure, given by an intern who looked so young that his mother probably drove him to work, Edward thought. At last he was free to leave.

By that afternoon, Edward Calais was in the helicopter and on his way home.

Jane and Leah met Edward at the south terminal of the Vancouver airport.

"Daddy, Daddy you're home!" his little girl said as she leaped into his arms. "What happened to your head?"

"I was in an accident, honey, but I'm okay now."

"Edward, are you sure you should be lifting her?"

"I'm okay, Jane, thanks." Calais reached for his wife and hugged her, ignoring pains emanating from various parts of his frame.

The drive home was bittersweet for Edward. He was so glad to have survived the accident, but he missed his friend Jerry greatly.

"Edward," said Jane, "I've made the arrangements to transfer the

Leviticus program to Rexan via Lorne Browne. We'll go tomorrow with everyone. It's the only way."

"I don't care about the stupid program anymore. Let's get rid of it. Let's just email it to him. No charge."

"What? You don't care about giving it up? It'll cost you a fortune in potential profits."

"I know, and I don't care."

"It's already set up, Edward; we may as well see it through. We do it tonight."

They drove the rest of way in relative silence, with the exception of Leah singing "Jesus Loves Me" quietly in the back.

"Jerry taught her that," said Jane.

"I know." Edward stifled the tears welling from his bruised eyes.

17

Tara selected her clothes very carefully that evening. They would play an important role in the mission she was about to perform. The navy dress she had selected disclosed her remarkable figure while maintaining her dignity. The tightly woven curls of her ebony colored hair plunged onto her bare shoulders. A solid gold locket embossed with diamonds fell from her neck and down, stopping just in time near her fullness and against her mahogany-hued skin.

A spray of perfume sprayed from the bottle and into the air. She stepped into its mist. The delicate fragrance fell evenly onto her hair and neck. Her delicately manicured nails adjusted her hair one last time. She was ready. She and George went outside and saw the Calais vehicle approach.

Edward Calais opened the door, and George and Tara climbed into the Navigator. No one spoke during the drive to Lorne's office. Edward still had not come to terms with the death of Jerry, and his head was still pounding from the effects of the crash. He felt strangely compelled, yet unsure, of the feelings he'd experienced that morning. Selling the Leviticus program seemed like the right thing to do to protect his family; the men he'd be dealing with were both dangerous and evil. But Edward was also troubled about the decision to sell; it didn't seem fair, especially with Jerry gone. Yet Edward was resigned to end it, regardless of the danger.

The exterior of the building was steel and glass, the entrance was overly ornate, and the inside reeked of stale smoke masked by an overly ambitious air-freshening system. The office was cold—not a welcoming place.

Lorne Browne met Edward, George, Jane, and Tara at the reception desk and showed them into his office.

"Any news of Jerry's body being found, Edward?" asked Lorne sympathetically.

"No, no sign of it," replied Edward sadly.

Watching Edward's reaction to the question confirmed to Lorne that they didn't need to fear either Edward or the power of Jerry Chen. Chen was obviously dead; Edward's little trip to the West Coast to look for his friend had been fruitless. He appeared to be a beaten man.

"Well, let us move on to business," said Lorne. "We have the papers here for you to sign. There will be only one copy, and we will keep it, as agreed. The money will be transferred to your personal account as soon as we find out that Leviticus works."

At that point, Tara began to turn it on. She turned around and smiled at Lorne. He looked into her eyes, and he couldn't help it. His eyes began to stray lower.

Tara remained almost motionless, save some rather deep breathing. She allowed Lorne to examine her. While her skin crawled at the thought of his disgusting leering, she remained focused on her task. It was time for phase two. She glanced at the wall that was festooned with pictures.

"Is this you?" she said to Lorne, pointing to a picture of a snowboarder. A team of some sort surrounded the person in the picture.

"It was taken in Switzerland. I was training with the Canadian snowboard team."

"You trained with the gold medalists?" she said softly.

"Yes, they needed a little help," he said, evidently captivated with all that was Tara. He approached closer to her.

"Lorne, could you boot up your computer and sign on to the net? I will load Leviticus once you're in," said Edward.

"Oh, sure. I have a special access code only used by senior management," said Lorne, smiling at Tara. His fingers worked quickly, ensuring no one would be able to follow his keystrokes. Once he was done, Lorne quickly moved back to Tara's side. She knew he was close enough to smell her hair as he pointed to a picture of him and Ron Howard at Planet Hollywood in Vancouver.

"We own a part of that little dive," he murmured, his lips only inches from her ear. His thigh brushed up against her hip. She remained close, turned, and carefully removed a nonexistent piece of lint from the shoulder of his Armani suit, then tenderly smoothed the area. She glanced in the direction of the computer and then into his face. She smiled, toyed with her hair momentarily, then just remained still as he drank her in all over again. Several more minutes were gained in distraction.

The computer hummed in the background, then suddenly beeped a warning. *You are about to load a file that has not been screened for viruses. Do you wish to scan the CD or abort loading?* flashed on the screen.

At the sound of the beep, Lorne looked towards Edward. Edward looked up and their eyes locked. With his back to Tara, Lorne raised his index finger to his own throat and slid it across slowly, mouthing the word *Leah* as he did so.

Edward closed his eyes and nodded, almost imperceptibly. His eyes opened and he returned to his work. He clicked on the yes button. He did this fearlessly because he had no knowledge of the virus Jerry had attached to it. For all he knew, Jerry was dead and this was a clean copy of the program. As a result, Edward was utterly convincing and Lorne suspected nothing. Yet something inside Lorne made him consider watching the program loading procedure more closely. He moved toward the computer to get a clear look at the screen.

The words *Are you sure you want to load the program with scanning?* appeared.

Tara reached down to Lorne's hand and whispered, "Let the nerds do their thing, Lorne." Pulling on his hand, she turned him around, reached up, and adjusted his silk tie and smoothed his lapel. Her fingers lingered on his chest.

Lorne's eyes met her gaze and he was lost again in "Tara land." His back was to the computer being worked on by George and Edward.

Edward clicked on the "yes" button once again.

The screen cleared as the instructions caused the computer to bypass its protective programs, then begin to absorb the invasive and tenacious virus.

Once completely absorbed into the system, the virus began to probe its way into the hard drive of Lorne's computer. It replicated itself immediately, then quickly hid several copies in several electronic dark holes. Next it began the process of gathering account numbers, amounts, and names. All of this information was stored away to a time when it could automatically be downloaded to Jerry's waiting system. The next time Lorne sent an email, the process would repeat itself in the computer of the unfortunate receiver. Only this time there would be no warning to appear on the screen.

"The job is done, Browne," said Edward.

"Excellent work, boys. Now, why don't you head off? I'll give Tara a ride home. I want to show her around."

Lorne was standing by the window. He opened the drapes and pretended to admire the view. He secretly nodded to two dark figures waiting impatiently in the alley beside the office, fingering Uzis. They moved into position and watched the window for further instructions.

Tara approached Lorne and whispered into his ear, "I can't tonight, Lorne, but maybe an afternoon might be worth your while."

"Really?" he said.

Lorne thought for a moment, considered Tara's offer, then once again signaled to the assassins posted outside, waving them off. They immediately disappeared into the darkness.

Calais and the others left the building safely. Lorne Browne went to his computer and wrote an email to Henry Rexan. He was gloating in his success. He explained how it was too dangerous to eliminate the group right then, but that he would take care of it himself later. His message further confirmed that Leviticus was in their hands, and there was no sign of any problems with the program.

Rexan was waiting at home, where his real office was. He received Lorne's email immediately and opened it. It seemed to take a long time to download. However, it was good news, so well worth the wait. He immediately sent a similar message to the one that he'd received to Lyon and her R and D team. He gave no details, just confirmed the ability of Leviticus to interpret and translate brain signals into computer language. This technological breakthrough would ensure Lisa was no longer a problem and his militia was clean.

Carried with the email to COBRA was the hidden virus that Jerry had created. The virus opportunistically began to cruise through multitudes of electronic paths. It opened files, reproduced itself, then hid again, always secreting away information for its master.

Back on the street, near Lorne's office, George, Tara, Edward, and Jane climbed into the Navigator. Tara felt like she wanted to take a shower and wash off the nearness of Lorne Browne.

When the last door closed, and Edward had driven over a block away, Jane made a quick call to ensure Leah was safe. Then she took Edward's hand. "Honey, I have some wonderful news. Jerry is alive."

"What? They found him alive! How is he?"

"He's fine, and he was never lost."

"What? What do you mean he was never lost?"

"We figured out a way to fake his death. We hired a boat to pick him up from the water at Salmon Beach, and left his boat and survival suit to make it seem like he had drowned."

Edward looked stunned. "Why?"

"Because we wanted Browne and Rexan to think he was dead, so they wouldn't suspect anything when we loaded Jerry's program.

Edward, the program carried a virus that Jerry created. It will break into their system and send us the information. We think we will get enough information to call the police."

"Why didn't you tell me before?"

"Because we didn't think you could act like Jerry was dead, otherwise, and you needed to pull that off to bring this all to an end."

"What if they discover the virus?"

"Jerry is sure that once we got into the computer and past the warnings without being scanned, no one could find it."

"He threatened Leah."

"We have to trust Jerry."

Edward looked at Jane, marveling at her courage. "You're right...of course you are right. I can't believe he's okay!"

Jane added, "And there is more news. While Jerry was in Vancouver, he met the most amazing woman. Her name is Rachel, and she is a computer geek too! The best part is...they're getting married tomorrow!"

"Married," questioned Edward. "Are you kidding me?"

"No. She is beautiful, wonderful, and loves him just the way he is."

"Does she know...well...about him being sick sometimes?"

"Her brother has schizophrenia. She knows all about it and loves him anyway. She can't wait for tomorrow."

The rest of the drive was full of questions and explanations as Edward was filled in with the details of both the wedding and the "plan."

18

Jerry and Rachel's wedding was simple and beautiful. The small chapel was occupied by the Gang, and several dozen CSIS security agents. For the engaged couple, it was an opportunity to confirm to themselves, and to share with others, their very spiritual nature.

Meeting with the clergy who performed the ceremony had crystallized their belief in an alive, caring, and compassionate God. Their relationship was to model the intimate, inclusive, and forgiving nature of the One with whom their faith would reside. The words they chose to use as their vows spoke of patience, kindness, and the desire to bear all for each other. They vowed to be together until death; and they meant their vows.

The reception was well-planned—quite unlike Jerry, but very much like Rachel. Edward spoke briefly and made tasteful jokes about Jerry's tendency to use "geek-speak." The staff she worked with panned Rachel. They clearly loved and respected her.

The couple took their honeymoon in Disneyland. Jerry's childlike behavior and his passion for "one more ride" made the time together seem too short for Rachel. Soon the week was up and they were on their way home.

A few hours in the plane, and they were landing at Vancouver International Airport. Jerry had made arrangements to be picked up by limo and off they went. As they drove down the road leading to the marina where they had first met, Jerry asked his new bride to close her eyes.

"I have a surprise for you, Mrs. Chen. Keep your eyes closed. Remember when we were on the beach and you said you'd always wanted to live on a boat?"

"Yes, I do."

"Open your eyes and see what you think."

When Rachel opened her eyes they beheld a new, white, 86-foot yacht docked at a private wharf. It was immense, with clean modern lines. Near amidships was a giant red ribbon with a sign below it that read, *To Rachel, with love, your Jerry.* On board were the whole Gang, cheering and waving.

"I can't believe it! That's our home?"

"Yep. I hope you like it."

"How did you pay for it?"

"I cashed some checks that I'd sort of forgotten about. There was also a few stock options that came up as well."

"You're amazing!"

Jerry and Rachel spent a few days moving into the massive yacht.

Jerry felt so great after his honeymoon trip to Disneyland. Unfortunately, he felt so great that he began to fall into one of the most dangerous traps of the mentally ill. He no longer felt sick and wondered if he should begin to taper off the medications. They seemed to slow his abilities, and Jerry knew that once they returned home, he would have to be in peak mental condition. Jerry only had a few days left in his honeymoon vacation. It would be so wonderful to be mentally acute again.

As part two of their honeymoon time, Jerry and Rachel took some days to pursue one of Jerry's favorite ways of relaxing. Jerry had arranged for the two of them to make a trip to Rivers Inlet to go salmon fishing. They flew by twin otter floatplane up the rugged coast and landed in an isolated bay. As the plane touched down and the first float caught the glassy water, the usual drizzle gave way to the warmth of sunshine. The pilot cut one of the engines and used the second to carefully maneuver the craft towards the small dock that jutted out from the lodge. Several men came down to meet the couple and carry their luggage up to the oceanfront cabin they would share. They entered the room to find a beautiful sunroom with old comfortable couches and chairs and accompanying bookshelves of well-worn paperback novels. The main room of the cabin contained a stone fireplace that was burning brightly, having been previously set and lit by the resort staff. A private Jacuzzi and king-size bed completed the abode. It was perfect, and Jerry felt such a place was a wonderful spot to ease off the medications he was taking. He didn't tell Rachel. He was going to surprise her.

The young couple got settled and then walked to the main lodge where the restaurant awaited their attention. The menu tonight began with starters of alder-smoked salmon, a wild mushroom and leek soup, and three beautifully presented local giant prawns. Mozart played softly in the background as the pair dreamed and spoke of their future together. A beautiful prime rib dinner, served the English way with overcooked vegetables, mashed potatoes and rich gravy, and Yorkshire pudding followed the appetizers. Finally Jerry ordered apple pie served with a slice of aged cheddar cheese. Rachel ordered a small selection of fresh fruit, sliced and served with one rich, beautiful chocolate truffle.

The two returned to their cabin and spent the rest of the evening watching old movies and playing scrabble. Jerry never could win at scrabble.

The next morning, after a small breakfast of coffee, fresh juice, and toasted bagels, Jerry and Rachel were shown to the open boat that would take them to the best fishing British Columbia has to offer. Their guide carefully set up their gear for them as they boarded the open Boston Whaler type craft. Jerry had chills of excitement as the guide started up the powerful outboard motor. He and Rachel cuddled together in the seats directly in front of the raised platform where the guide opened the throttle of the motor and steered the boat down the narrow inlet.

Bald eagles, seals, and a variety of birds dotted the ocean, shore, and sky around the boat. The tide began to show its power by producing small ripples and whirlpools that the boat initially easily cut through. Rounding the corner of the narrows the guide directed the boat into the lee side of a small island.

Jerry baited his salmon rod with a cut plug of herring and let it drop to the bottom. He reeled it up several feet, then let the natural flow of tide and eddy move the bait. Rachel simply covered herself with a warm comforter provided by the lodge and put her feet up and pulled out a novel she was reading at the time. She didn't feel like fishing today, but would rather just enjoy the sight and smell of the ocean and the company of the man she loved.

The sun warmed them both as the morning wore on to afternoon. Jerry had not even had a small bite of his bait, but the time seemed to go quickly as they laughed, talked, and shared the small lunch packed for them by the kitchen staff. The guide had a perfect way of taking part in the day in a nonintrusive way, yet he seemed to add to the good time they were having when it was appropriate.

Spring salmon are the largest of the Pacific salmon. Occasionally one will grow up to 60 or 70 pounds. Such was the case with the fish that was lurking 80 feet below the boat that held Jerry and his new wife. This salmon was shrewd. Several times she had darted out from the cover of the kelp bed only to veer away at the last moment when something seemed wrong. Her instincts had saved her life many times over the years.

Unaware of the beautiful and hungry fish waiting below them, Rachel began to tease Jerry. "I bet I can catch a fish," she said, taking the rod from its holder.

"Go ahead, Rachel. Make my day," said Jerry in a resigned manner.

As Rachel lifted the rod from the holder, the bait below shot from the bottom towards the surface. As she returned to her seat, she jiggled the rod in a most unfisherman like way, taunting her Jerry.

The combination of tide movement and her sudden actions produced an action on the herring bait that appeared to the giant salmon to be a wounded herring, his favorite food. The giant moved out from the safety of the big broad-leafed kelp forest and inhaled the bait. She began to swim into the current unsuspecting of the hook that lay deep within the tasty baitfish.

Rachel suddenly realized that she could not feel the weight of the line on the fishing rod anymore. "Oh Jerry, I must have caught bottom or something. The line has gone limp."

The guide immediately suspected the truth. "Rachel, reel in quickly, and as soon as you feel any pressure, lift the rod tip up. You might have a fish!"

Rachel reeled the line up, then felt and saw the rod tip dip down into the ocean. She immediately, yet carefully lifted the tip against the weight of the line. This caused the hook to penetrate the big spring salmon's mouth. She immediately turned and swept her powerful tail back and forth, propelling her through the water and setting the hook deep in her jaw.

The rod tip plunged into the ocean and Rachel's reel screamed as the line peeled off it. The spring was making the first of three major runs. Rachel fought that fish, helped by the guide and the bewildered Jerry until it came near to the surface 35 minutes later. Not willing to hand the rod off, Jerry and the guide were forced by Rachel to watch and shout advice until finally Jerry was able to net it. The fish was 65 pounds of silver muscle. Rachel would never let Jerry forget who caught one of the biggest fish to leave Rivers Inlet Fishing Lodge.

They celebrated with hot chocolate and left for home.

On the ride home, Jerry felt a growing uneasiness, deep within.

By the time they had returned to the room, it happened again. The Voice returned. Jerry looked at his new wife and said, "I have to go to the hospital right away."

By the time he had finished the sentence, the Voices were becoming louder and more insistent. Without the new medication to bind them, the Voices had returned.

"Rachel, if I get much worse, call the police."

She understood and at her insistence, they were flying back to Vancouver in the float plane of the owner of the lodge. She took him immediately to the Emergency Room of Vancouver General Hospital.

19

Edward and Jane knocked softly on the door of the private room deep within the psychiatric ward of the hospital that held Jerry Chen.

"Come in," said Jerry.

As they entered, Jerry turned his head lethargically towards them. Edward saw his tears, as well as the leather straps that bit into his wrists. Edward sat down in a chair beside his friend and awkwardly reached out to playfully punch him in the shoulder. Jane moved to the other side of the bed and held Jerry's bound hand. Her tears could not be stopped, nor should they have been.

After a few minutes of quiet, Jerry looked towards Edward and smiled. An unspoken message that the sadness had ended, at least for the moment, was in his eyes. Edward smiled, then laughed. Jane began to giggle. Jerry's eyes brightened at their somewhat inappropriate responses.

"We love you, Jerry," said Jane.

"Yeah, we really do," added Edward.

Jerry's eyes affirmed his appreciation and love for these two. He was still too sedated to speak coherently.

The door to the room opened. A youngish doctor carrying a clipboard peered in, then entered. "I'm sorry to interrupt you folks, but I have something here Dr. Chen might want to look at and consider."

"What is it?" queried Edward.

"I've just pulled some interesting news off the Internet on his condition. An innovative approach to treatment has been approved down south, and they're looking for trial subjects. He would be perfect."

"What is it, Doctor? What does it involve?" asked Jane excitedly.

"A brain implant. A group of doctors in South America have been experimenting with a computer chip implant that seems to be able to modify brain function directly. It is actually meant to be applied to healthy individuals in order to expand their brain function. One of the medical staff herself has had an implant installed and the results are incredible. She's a genius. Their research seems to conclude that implants could have far-reaching positive impacts on neurodisorders, yours being one of them."

Both Edward and Jane sat quietly.

"The name of the Medical research group is COBRA. If you want, I can contact them and set up an appointment. They have a hotline and are looking to implant as many people as possible."

Jane and Edward looked at each other.

"He'll want to think about it," said Jerry.

"Of course, but remember, the earlier the better. The results are quite remarkable. He could live a perfectly normal life and have no symptoms at all. Not only that, his brain would probably function better than ever. I'll leave you alone now. Dr Chen will be sent home tomorrow. He'll be in much better shape once the meds are working again."

"Thank you, Doctor. We'll be by to pick him up."

At that same time, the Calais home phone was ringing. Because no one was there, their voicemail machine cut in. "Please leave your message after the tone," said the synthetic voice of the machine.

The caller replied in a throaty, guttural voice, "Mr. Calais, this is Henry Rexan. I'm so sorry to hear about your friend Dr. Chen's illness. He must be suffering a great deal. Mental illness is so tragic, and now, it seems, so unnecessary. I have a proposition for you. I am wondering if Jerry's life is more important than your hateful crusade against COBRA. If you really value his health, and want to help him, I'm sure our COBRA staff would provide Jerry's implant and postoperative care. We now have scientific proof that our COBRA implantation will effectively cure him. No more depression, no more suicide attempts. As a matter of fact, anyone you wanted could be implanted for free. Perhaps your little girl, Leah, might receive some of the advantages of an instant education? If you are not ready for that, I understand, but please let me help Dr. Chen. Call me, Calais. Call me."

The message ended and the machine duly saved it, a blinking red light indicating its presence.

Edward and Jane left Jerry and went home to think about what the doctor had recommended.

Flopping down on the couch of his home, Edward Calais absent-mindedly turned on the answering machine. He listened to Rexan's voice, offering the chance for Jerry to get an implant that would cure him. It was all too much for Edward. He reached for the remote and turned on the television news while he waited for Jane to finish putting Leah to bed.

CNN headline news flashed across the screen. A serious-looking young woman read studiously from her teleprompter.

"News of a major computer breakthrough has shocked the technological world. COBRA, the multinational computing software and chip manufacturer, has just announced that a computer chip implanted directly into the brain has finished its European and South American trials and is being prepared to be introduced to the North American market. Test trials on the latest and most advanced model of the implant have confirmed that a whole new world is about to come into being. The new model A total of 666 clinical trials has been held and all have been successful. The owners of this new technology are looking forward to being able to offer free implants for all who are interested. For news of the impact this might have on our world, we have gathered a panel of experts. First, let's hear from Dr. Harold Taylor of Harvard University. Dr. Taylor, what is your take on the situation?"

Jane entered the room and joined her husband on the couch.

"Well, Nancy," started Dr. Taylor as his image appeared on the screens of millions of American, Mexican, and Canadian viewers, "this research is very gratifying for the intellectual community. It means that we no longer need to be bound by mechanical devices such as keyboards. A person's thoughts can immediately be processed. It is truly wonderful."

"Dr. Green, what are your feelings?" interjected the announcer.

"I agree wholeheartedly with Dr. Taylor. While it is somewhat painful to admit that the discoveries have come from South America and not from us, we at MIT applaud the fine work. To think that everyone will have access to these systems free of charge is incredible. In the American West, the last century saw cowboys calling the six-shooter the great equalizer. In the third millennium, computer implants will have the same reputation."

"Dr. Graham, you have some concerns I understand."

"Yes we do, Nancy. The implants have been derived from human brain tissue for one thing. This has serious moral and ethical implications. Secondly, how do we know people will be able to control their own minds with this kind of input?"

"Dr. Taylor, how do you respond to these concerns?"

"We've heard similar opinions when radio became popular, when TV was first broadcast, and then when video games, personal computers, and the Internet became accessible to most of society. The cultures and countries where these technologies are not available are the poorest in the world. Technology will march on regardless; we must get on board."

"The tissue problem," added Dr. Green, "is similar to transplant debates, blood issues, and fetal tissue research problems. Technology is advancing faster than our ability to debate each one of these concepts over and over again. We owe it to our human race to encourage this sort of progress. Humankind will surely be able to deal with and react prudently to such advancement. It is what we have evolved to become. That is, we are becoming greater than we have ever imagined. Mother Nature has deemed us to be our best, and this will surely move us along."

"There we have it, Roger; by the way, interested people can access the website of COBRA in order to get more information on the next round of test subjects. The address is www.COBRA.com. The phone number is 1-800-COBRA 66."

The screen of Calais's television showed the trademark COBRA logo, *Creating Your Future.*

"Thank you, Nancy. And now for news from Europe as we hear of a new awakening of European traditions. A group calling itself the New Europeans is rallying in Germany this weekend in order to spread its message of unity and prosperity for old world cultures."

Henry Rexan's image appeared on the screen. He was standing near the old Berlin Wall giving a speech. Hundreds of thousands of his newfound supporters listened and cheered as he gave his message of unity and progress.

20

Edward and Jane sat quietly watching the speech Rexan was giving. Finally, Edward broke the silence.

"We need to consider in an unbiased way what the doctor said about getting Jerry an implant. Right now he isn't in any condition to think for himself, so we are going to have to help him. I want you to listen to this; it was on the machine when we got home."

Edward reached over to the answering machine and played the message Rexan had left.

Jane listened quietly, then spoke. "I cannot have anything to do with that that...*slime*." She stared out the window at the ocean below. She seemed puzzled by something.

"What are you thinking?" asked Edward.

She closed her eyes for a moment, then opened them widely. "Rexan *must* be scared to death of us if he phoned us personally."

"You might be right, Jane, but even if you are, it's Jerry's life we are talking about. The implant may override his disease. Not only might he live happier, he might regain his productivity and control. As his brain learns to use the power of the implant, he could become normal, even better than normal. He could have a chance for a great life."

"But he was doing fine on the medication; he just stopped taking it."

"I know, but think of him becoming cured—not simply under treatment."

"Don't you think I have thought of that!" shouted Jane. "It is all I can think of."

"Medicine has used transplants for years."

"It isn't just that," Jane went on, "it's that we know people were murdered to make the implants. What's going on is wrong."

Edward sighed. "But we haven't proven that in court."

Her eyes narrowed. "It's still a fact. A fact that will likely get buried."

"Think of Jerry...he has a mind that is quitting. It's killing him to be in the blur that the meds cause. He needs to be at his best. Think of him. Think of Rachel. Rexan may not be that bad. Maybe our facts are wrong...."

"That's it!" Jane replied. "I know exactly what Rexan wants. He wants us to back off the investigation and the referendum. He's figured out that we have the evidence that will sway the vote. They have so much momentum now that if they can stop us from disclosing now, nothing will stop them later. Jerry is their trump card. They are using him against us."

Edward stared at her. "You're right," he said slowly. "We need to talk to Jerry."

Joe Logan had watched the news as well. As he listened to Rexan, he was amazed at how quickly things were happening. The latest data on the rise of COBRA was resting on his laptop. It showed that the inserting of implants was growing rapidly. Someone had taken the time to create an image of the world using red dots to represent where implantation was currently taking place, and then forecasting its spread. To Logan, the spread looked liked blood creeping in all directions across a hemorrhaging map of the world. Only North America seemed immune, as if protected by some unknown force. Yet, although no implantations seemed to be taking place there didn't mean people with COBRA implants were not crossing its borders. In fact, sources confirmed that many had.

We have to stop it now, he thought, *before it's too late.*

Logan was receiving emails from CSIS headquarters almost on an hourly basis. Researchers there had collated information on COBRA's attempt to avoid prosecution, as well as their compelling marketing campaign designed to ultimately implant or eliminate everyone. Messages offering hope to people by way of their implants were being sent worldwide using technological vehicles such as the Internet, cable and satellite TV, talk shows, and the news.

Modern communication was being used in every conceivable manner to get the message to the people that not only would implants make them better people, but also, in fact, anyone without one would be left behind. Millions around the world were stirring to the call, spellbound by the possibilities. Greed and/or fear seemed to be the most common drivers of desire for getting implants. Many were waiting anxiously for a children's version to be made available for testing. He had even received messages from concerned members of the federal cabinet. What puzzled him was that they did not want to complain about Canada's role in the development of this infamous product, they wanted to find out how quickly implants could be introduced into Canadian society after a successful yes vote.

Logan reached for the phone and called the team together to meet on Jerry and Rachel's boat for a strategy session. He set up a meeting for a few days after Jerry's release from hospital.

After what seemed like an eternity, Jerry, Edward, Jane, and Tara were all sitting in the cramped halibut boat in a joyful reunion. It was 9:58 p.m. Pacific Time. Jerry had selected that time as the least likely to cause concern for computer owners whose machines had been infected. At that moment, several dozen computers around the world sprang to life under the direction of the virus Jerry had created that had been inserted into their systems. The computers were commanded to search their files and create a list of most recent activities, passwords, and other information. Lorne's contacts were beginning to yield their darkest secrets.

The group waited as 10 o'clock arrived. Nothing happened.

"What's going on?" Edward said.

"Relax. It'll take a few minutes for the files to arrive."

"I knew that."

Just then the sound of a duck quacking made them all jump a little.

It was Jerry's alert signal that he'd directed his computer to use. He opened the email that had arrived and downloaded the files.

"I need to see one," urged Jane.

Jerry selected the first one and Jane read it.

What she said astonished them all. It showed millions of dollars moving around the world: hidden accounts, foreign currencies, and names, lots of names.

"It appears to me the movement of funds is tax fraud. Open another."

This one was an email with a description of a young woman who was to be sent to Bolivia from a small university in Paris. "No food or water" during transportation was added as a comment. A strange ending was attached. "Please dispose of M. Dubois in the usual area. I plan to visit the area soon and wish to order some seafood."

The group continued to view various files.

"We have to call CSIS," said Jerry.

"Why them, and not the RCMP?" wondered Tara.

"This is big, really big, and international. They'll want to involve the FBI and the RCMP."

"Aren't we in danger too?"

"Yes, and we'll have to do something about that."

"Rexan will react at a gut level and probably send a hit squad. We have to make that a risk he won't want to take."

Edward described a simple, yet effective modification of the plan to the group. It would take effect only once Jerry had all the information from the virus. It would take several days for the computer system to sort and analyze all the data using the Echelon programming.

The Gang left the boat and went home exhausted. There was nothing they could do at the moment, and they needed to relax for a few days.

The Sea to Sky highway that ran along the coast from Vancouver to Whistler was busy with weekend traffic. The road was littered with expensive cars and expensive people driving to the posh ski chalets and hotels in the Whistler Blackcomb area. The BMW, Volvo, Mercedes, Lexus, and Jaguar automobile companies were well represented, as were the various brands of Sport Utility Vehicles such as Range Rover and Lexus. At this time of the year, many drove the highway to mountain bike, ride horses, or play golf at several fabulous, albeit pricey, golf courses.

Henry Rexan had chosen a rented Hummer to make the drive, and to make his entrance. The truck, regardless of its military origin, was perhaps the most profound statement of wealth in the world of mountain trendiness.

Pulling up to the Chateau, a young doorman in full dress uniform received Rexan's keys with gratitude. He was thankful to be able to park the truck, never mind drive it. He was also grateful to receive an American ten-dollar bill as a tip.

Rexan slipped into the lobby and was greeted with exceptional regard when he gave his name. His room was the best available. The arrangements for his care had all been handled in advance. Particular requests, such as all-cotton sheets and a goose-down duvet were made on his behalf by his ample staff. His reputation as a big spender had preceded him, and the hotel staff was ready to make sure all his needs were met. Chilled mineral water was waiting, as was a secure phone line.

Henry Rexan checked out his room, set up the computer system, and took a quick bath. The meeting was set for 8 a.m. the next day, so Rexan ordered room service for dinner and reviewed the latest company data while he ate. He went to bed early that night. He reached for the remote and turned to CNN. There was breaking news.

"It's a major breakthrough," the newscaster said. "The recent and tragic loss of Canadian software entrepreneur Jerry Chen took a bizarre twist today when upstart COBRA Corporation announced that they had obtained his most recent software innovation. The deal was apparently struck just before his disappearance.

"The Leviticus software allows a PC user to enter data, text, and spreadsheets and to surf the web all without the need for a keyboard or microphone. A patch placed on the user's neck picks up the brain's signals, processes them, and converts them into usable input. Bill Gates of Microsoft is quoted as saying, 'This software is to new computers what Windows was to PCs. Jerry Chen's legacy will live on forever.'

"Let's hear from COBRA's CEO, Dr. Xavier Lyon, who is at this moment attending an international meeting of investors in Whistler, British Columbia."

Her image appeared on the screen, surrounded by reporters.

"Look for us to launch Leviticus in the very near future. What's more, COBRA is set to deliver an even more exciting technology in the very near future. We are going to change the world."

The news announcer reappeared. "COBRA stocks have doubled and are predicted to do the same tomorrow."

Rexan smiled. Things were proceeding as planned.

The next morning, Rexan ordered a room service breakfast and checked his email before he left for the meeting. He had a message from Lorne Browne, a congratulatory message, and he was thrilled to get it. It was a bit strange how long it took to download, but Rexan just attributed it to being in the Canadian North, where electrical transmissions probably took longer. Neither he nor his computer knew that a little bit of the amazing work of the very much alive Jerry Chen had contaminated his computer and was beginning to do its clandestine duty.

Rexan left his room and dropped off at the lobby for a quick coffee. He worked his way to the Blackcomb conference room. Two very large men stood at the door. While they recognized him and let him pass, it was very clear that no one who was unknown to them would be allowed anywhere near the room. Inside a technician was sweeping the room for bugs. He declared it was all clear as Rexan found his seat.

Sitting around the room were the leaders of the New European movement. All were well-placed scientists, businessmen, politicians, judges, or clergy. Each looked to have a bee-sting-sized lump on the back of the neck, the sign of the newly implanted.

At the head of the table, Henry Rexan called the meeting to order.

He was flushed with excitement and perspiring heavily. He began to describe how the market was responding to COBRA's acquisition of the Leviticus technology. Share prices were rocketing.

Xavier Lyon provided an update on the software developments that allowed the brain tissue implant and inserted computer chips to self-generate new program loops together. Finally, she reviewed the emerging process of creating the newest version of Cobra implants using robotics. She described how donors were kept conscious in order to have as many neuron firings as possible. The newest engineering procedures were proving to be the most productive and efficient yet. A thin slice of brain was removed, then immediately sprayed with a micro-thin layer of gold and silicon on one side and a layer of oxygen-rich mesh on the other. The resulting section could then be used in conjunction with a computer processor. Recently, as many as 1000 implants had been sliced from one living human brain. The latest implants were also much more sophisticated that the earlier models. When connected to a traditional processor, each slice was able to process information as fast as the human brain, and as accurately as the computer to which it was attached. It also appeared to be far more creative in solving problems.

"Our research indicates each section has its own, well, *personality*. Some are weak in certain areas and strong in others. We've also found that by increasing the filtering power of Leviticus, in order to reduce intrusive thoughts, the subjects became less creative and more machine-like. We are looking for a combination of slices from various subjects plus adjusting the screening power of Leviticus in order to produce a more rounded, useful product line. However, the present models are fine for the moment."

"How many donor subjects are you using?"

"We have used about a dozen—mainly university students that have 'disappeared.' Lorne is particularly helpful at finding our 'volunteers.'"

"What does the future hold?" queried one of the visitors.

"Global implantation," replied Lyon.

"What do you mean?"

"We need to start mass implantation as soon as we can. We are set and ready to go. We will have a little social barrier to cross, though. People will need to accept the fact that some people are more useful in certain roles—as donors of brain tissue, for example. Once society realizes the benefit to remaining individuals, they will soon agree it is justifiable. People have always been willing to sacrifice others for the sake of the greater common good. Think about the advances to science and medicine that could be made if a genius's brain could be augmented by one of our little processors."

"Diseases might be cured. Creative solutions to starvation and war might be found. It could save the world," replied Rexan.

"We might even be able to insert our own little preferences into the chips," slowly offered Dr. Lyon.

"My sense is that whoever programs the mainframe, which will be networked via satellite, controls the people," responded a PhD.

"You mean to say that one person, or one group, would be able to influence the thought patterns of all who carry an implant?" questioned a minister.

"Yes," said Rexan and Lyon simultaneously.

"Quite a responsibility, I suppose," commented a politician.

"Definitely," said Dr. Xavier Lyon, "but who better to use the product than its creators and manufacturers."

"I suppose we have an obligation to bring as many people online as possible," said businessman.

"It will certainly make things easier for them, as well as everyone else," added Rexan.

"Those who resist...," queried a chief of police.

"Will need to be encouraged, or 'removed from the payroll,' as the need may be," Lyon said.

"Excellent. We share a common philosophy then, do we?" asked Rexan of the gathering.

They all nodded in agreement.

"The next few weeks will be crucial. We need to introduce the whole concept delicately, yet speedily," commented Rexan.

"Time is very critical; my people in Europe are ready to be led right now. Implants will be seen as their salvation. Hungry people will be excellent supporters of such a renaissance in human thinking," added a general.

"It might be good to start quietly, but as soon as possible, Henry."

"Agreed. Let's make sure nothing gets in our way," said Lyon.

"Raise a glass to the beginning of our New Europe, and ultimately a new world. A world of peace and tranquility. A world where the hungry are fed, the homeless are housed, and the sick made well!" said a member of the clergy.

"Amen!" said Rexan, nodding in approval.

All stood and drank.

Henry left the meeting of the New European leadership to enjoy a quick cigarette in the cool summer air of the spectacular resort area. Mountain bikers, hikers, and golfers abounded. Many casual visitors were slowly enjoying cappuccinos at one of the many trendy coffee bars. Rexan ripped off the filter, lit up, and headed for a newsstand. His eyes caught the headlines of the *Vancouver Sun*.

"Computer Genius Survives" screamed the headline.

Taken aback, Rexan threw $5 at the newsstand girl and grabbed the paper. He returned to the meeting, pushing the security men aside, and stormed into the room, holding the paper up for all to see.

"I have bad news! It seems Jerry Chen is alive. He apparently survived his little incident in the ocean and took his time returning."

"What do we have to fear from this Chen?" said a military leader.

"Everything."

"Then he will have to be neutralized and very soon."

"Agreed."

"Agreed."

"I'll see to it, then. My New European militia are ready for such a mission," said Rexan.

"And I'd like to help," added Lyon.

Lyon and Rexan went on line with their wireless laptops, courtesy of the hotel's technology. They fired up their email software.

Each had received the very long-loading transmission from Lorne, thus ensuring that Chen's virus compromised their work. They sent emails to their offices, warning them to be particularly careful of Internet usage. It was ironic since, at that very moment, their own computers were being searched and pillaged vicariously by Jerry Chen.

21

At her home in North Vancouver, Jane Calais was pouring over the latest email transmissions received from Jerry. After doing some research, she had discovered that several prominent university research professors had received funds from COBRA or its subsidiary companies. Most of these were experts in either the human brain or in computer hardware. One's area of expertise was neuro-electrode transmission. He was involved in the search for methods of transmitting messages from the brain directly to computers, much like Jerry's work. Another was doing research into the maintenance of brain tissue after the death of "the owner." Individually, none of this was particularly significant. In whole, however, it was enormous. Not only was it clear that humans were being used as research subjects, but that the research was well beyond the tolerance of society and law.

"Brilliant," she said.

"What's brilliant?" asked Edward.

"COBRA is a group of people associated with some weird political group called the New Europeans. They work through a hugely complex arrangement of international companies so fluid in nature that no one could connect them to anything. COBRA is a front company, well hidden in Columbia, where few would look for research ethics. Jerry's virus hit on their only Achilles' heel—the need to use computers to manage the chaos. By infecting their system at its heart, we have access to everything. It's like one huge, complicated onion. Each layer gets more interesting, and more sinister. The material from South America is awful. People's living brain tissue is being used to develop better computer hardware. No one will believe this. I have to call Jerry. "

" *We* have to call Jerry," said Edward.

Jane needed reminding occasionally that they worked as a team. Before she had time to reach for the phone, it rang of its own accord.

Edward answered.

"Edward, it's Lorne."

"Yes, Lorne."

"Wonderful to hear about Jerry. When did you find out?"

"Just recently," replied Edward suspiciously. "What can I do for you?" He put the phone on speaker so Jane could hear.

"The Leviticus program we bought from you...Our engineers have looked at it and decided it needs a little touch-up from Dr. Chen. Can you tell us where he is? We can't seem to locate him."

"I'm not going to tell you anything, Browne."

"You have no idea what you have done. No idea at all," Browne said in an icy tone. The phone went dead.

Edward immediately dialed Jerry. "We need to call everyone together," he said as soon as Jerry answered. "I just got off the phone with Lorne, and he is making threats."

"I think it would be wise for you to take Leah and Jane out of the house. Drop off the Navigator and get a taxi. Meet me at the Vancouver CSIS office. It's in the towers at Metrotown. I'll make some calls to my connections at CSIS and see what they suggest."

"We're on our way. Call George and Tara, and have them do the same."

Xavier Lyon left the COBRA directors' meeting agitated. Her dream of incorporating and fusing—in fact, merging—the human brain with hardware technology in a direct way was going to be realized, yet she sensed a danger that this Chen person could wreck havoc on her plans. She entered her suite, sat down on the huge bed, and entered the trance-like state that enabled her new implant to work at maximum efficiency. She lowered her intellectual guard in order to allow it to have full access to her cognitive capabilities. Within moments she was one with the implant, or rather, the implant eclipsed her.

Suddenly a knock on the door of her suite startled her. She was momentarily disconnected with the world around her. A cold chill ran down her spine as a memory intruded into her consciousness. She could not stop it, though she desperately wanted to. The Voice was fighting back, intruding into her consciousness.

"I am still here, and so is your father," the Voice of Lisa said.

Another knock jolted her back to consciousness.

"Miss, your helicopter is waiting," called a bellboy through the closed door and into her reality.

Lyon stumbled, confused, to the door. She stopped and consciously repressed the Voice of Lisa. "I must have been dreaming," she murmured to herself. Then, "Thank you, Hans," she said, opening the door.

He grabbed her bags and followed as she left the room.

When Edward and Jane arrived at the CSIS headquarters, their SUV was immediately surrounded by black Suburbans. Agents poured out, weapons drawn, surrounded them, and escorted them into the building. In the agency office they were rushed into a conference room. Two agents guarded the doors. No one unauthorized was allowed in, or out.

The guards let Jerry and Rachel in when they arrived and soon allowed George and Tara to pass through.

Chen phoned his friend Joe Logan, the Canadian Security Intelligence Service director in Ottawa. Jerry's conversation with the director of CSIS was relatively short, given the enormity of the situation. He handed the phone to Jane, who described the COBRA companies and the movements of cash and securities over international borders. Chen then took the phone and explained the illegal brain research and the transportation and subsequent murder of test subjects.

Logan respected Jerry's opinion in part because of the long-term relationship they had had. Jerry had played key roles in Logan's reinventing CSIS as a modern intelligence-gathering agency, particularly after 9/11. With many years' experience as a field agent, Logan was able to grasp quickly that he must allow Chen to continue his work. Clearly his support system, his group of friends, was both effective and necessary, albeit lacking experience.

Once informed of the situation, Logan called the Canadian Minister of Justice, whom he briefed orally and promised a written summation within 48 hours. Next, Logan made a call to his friend and colleague, Elizabeth Brooke, the director of the Central Intelligence Agency of the United States. Once Liz understood the enormity of the situation and its implications for the United States, she promised the full cooperation of the CIA and confirmed CSIS as the lead agency. She immediately ordered a support team to be sent to Vancouver. Logan would meet them there.

Joe Logan then hurried out of his office and to the airport, where a government jet was warmed, prepped, and ready. The four-hour flight to Vancouver went quickly. As Logan was pouring over the data provided by Chen and interpreted by Jane Calais, he shuddered when he realized how much Dr. Chen was able to do and find out without the help of CSIS. He was also sickened as he read the rhetoric held within the email transmissions of the inventors of COBRA, and of the groups who intended to use COBRA technology. The written minutes of the COBRA meetings were particularly informative, if not repulsive. What seemed to him to be especially dangerous were the cell groups that were forming at the instigation of Henry Rexan. These groups represented the genuinely held belief that the sacrifice of innocent lives to achieve heinous goals was not only justified, but a necessity in order for humankind to meaningfully involve.

Logan's eyes were riveted to one particular testimony given by Henry Rexan.

"Today's modern medical technology is largely misused. The sick, the weak, and the genetically inferior are kept alive at great cost, while the workers of Europe go poor and hungry. Why does this happen? Because the false god of democracy dictates that all are equal. We are not equal! We never have been and never will be. The only thing that prevents you from honest work, good food, and a free life is lying, weak-kneed governments. COBRA is your only hope to evolve into where your true destiny lies. COBRA implants will allow you to know what is truly good, and what is truly evil. It is this knowledge and wisdom that will set you free!"

22

The small Canadian-made Challenger jet Logan was riding in banked over Horseshoe Bay in preparation for landing at Vancouver International Airport. Logan peered out the window and admired the ocean. Over the years of doing government security work in Vancouver, he had acquired a liking for the most beautiful city in Canada.

The plane landed and a member of the RCMP greeted Logan. Several unmarked police cars accompanied the vehicle he rode in. They passed through nearby Richmond neighborhoods and over the mighty muddy Fraser River.

As they approached CSIS headquarters, he noticed several armored government-black Suburbans. These had been rushed to CSIS on loan from the US government. The motors were running, and they were parked in a position that would allow them to change position in order to block traffic if needed. The vehicle they were riding in had already been spotted and tracked as soon as it approached the building. Its license plate number had been checked and confirmed for identity. Regardless of that, several hidden snipers were following the car through their scopes, in case a quick and accurate shot was needed to stop someone from assaulting the mini-convoy. Logan hoped the surveillance and security net would eventually become less obvious.

When his vehicle came to a stop, agents surrounded it, opened the door, and whisked Logan into the building. As he walked towards the room that held Chen and the others, Logan slowed his steps to prepare his mind for the meeting that was about to take place. His study of the file on the case was not complete, but he was beginning to form a picture of what they were facing. The talent of the operation was his friend Jerry Chen. The CSIS file on Jerry had been begun when he had envisioned and then developed the Canadian version of the Echelon software for them years ago. Chen was a genius with a particular bent for hacking into computer systems in order to test their fallibility. He loved to outsmart systems designed to frustrate people like him.

The latest entries to the file revealed a very wealthy individual self-employed as a freelance computer consultant. Chen had, in the past anyway, had little use for material goods. A deeply religious man, he attended church regularly. He was a bit of an enigma in an age where intellectuals largely denied the existence of a God. There was also mention of mental instability. He had missed some of his university classes and some project deadlines as a result of "antisocial behavior."

Logan's files on the other members of the Gang were largely run-of-the-mill. All seemed successful. George had serious financial problems, and that was worth further investigation. Jane was a lawyer who was especially tenacious in corporate research and case preparation, and Edward was a venture capital broker. Logan finished reviewing the files as his driver parked the vehicle. He showed his ID, quickly gained access to the well-guarded building, and walked down the hall to the meeting room where the impromptu team were waiting.

Once in the room, Logan introduced himself, then announced that the whole group was going to be moved to a luxury yacht moored in Vancouver harbor. He told them that someone in security had decided the boat was safe, easy to guard, and a little less obvious than CSIS regional headquarters.

The group was then moved to the parking garage, where they boarded a plain white van with smoked-glass windows. The van was as unnoticeable as the black Suburbans had been obvious. Logan liked the sleight-of-hand that he hoped might just be enough to fool potential attackers into believing the group was still in the CSIS building. He assumed the group itself was no threat to themselves.

The white van left the underground parking and was followed by several varieties of cars and trucks, all of them carrying armed CSIS agents. After a 30-minute drive, the Gang arrived under escort to the docks. It was there they beheld the beautiful craft that was to be their safehouse for the near future.

Logan boarded the boat and was impressed by its luxury. The cry of the sea gulls and cool sea breeze was a welcome relief from the city noise and stale air of Logan's existence. *I could grow to like this,* thought Logan, as the aura and ambiance of the West Coast settled over him like a warm goose-down comforter on a chilly Ontario evening.

The weather in Bogotá was hot and humid. Dr. Lyon spent the morning in her office poring over the latest research findings and experimental results on the latest round of implants. She was very pleased as mass production was proceeding well. Even in the large-scale operation that COBRA was becoming, Xavier shivered with anticipation as she read the papers on her desk. She was God, she thought to herself.

Some of the psychiatrists' results were disturbing, however. Despite the Leviticus software, recipients appeared to have difficulty with the floods of thoughts that invaded their brains, somehow bypassing the filtering mechanism. It was as if the implants were evolving ways of becoming a functioning vestige of their origin. The implantees spoke of intrusive memories that they were sure had never happened to them. They spoke of hearing voices, both audible and not. *Probably the result of the donor tissue expressing itself,* she thought. A cold chill permeated her psyche. It was as if someone inside her was listening to her thoughts, and disapproved. She repressed the intrusive thoughts and carried on reading.

Further on in the reports she read that some of the implantees became suicidal and delusional as they fought to deal with their multifaceted personalities and abilities. Dr. Black, of all the experimenters, felt that many facets of the depression of the recipients were caused by the nature of the donors and what their brain tissue had been through immediately before its removal. Perhaps the tissue remembered its original owner's terror.

On the brighter side, the recipient's emotions were beginning to show signs of being able to be highly manipulated. Even their sense of hunger and thirst could be modified via input from the silicon wafers. *Imagine the commercial implications of this technology,* she thought. *Every person with an implant could be programmed to crave a certain breakfast cereal, and we would sell it.* She laughed to herself at the triteness of her thoughts. There would be no need for advertising. Competition would vanish. Whoever controlled the programming of the implants controlled the people.

Her brain raced. The COBRA implants were being provided free of charge. She thought of the future, on a grand scale. Implants guaranteed to increase intellectual ability were only a beginning. Computer interfaces would allow those implanted to buy or sell goods and services without the aid of cards or cash. *By direct input into the brain, we could sell drugless highs, virtual vacations, and who knows what else.*

Think of the efficiency of society, she pondered. Particular groups could be programmed for specific tasks, and what is more, they could be programmed to like it. One of the foundational truths of the COBRA philosophy was that to control information was to control people. What better way to influence people than to give them what they really desired—or at least the sensation of getting what they really desired?

People worldwide are already flocking to acquire implants. A whole new economy will arise. Even the desire to eat a better diet and to exercise could be introduced as a costly option. Disease caused by drug use, poor habits, or poor judgments would be eliminated.

Those that remained implant free would be dangerous to society and would have to be eliminated. This would occur by a sort of accelerated evolution that society would be induced to support. People like her would determine social conscience.

At this point Xavier Lyon's thinking changed. Up until now she had been viewing the use of the implants as essentially self-serving. It would be profitable and that was enough. All actions were deemed to be acceptable as long as the business grew. Now, however, she began to believe that the implanting of society with her philosophy would, in fact, change it for the better. She began to see that the New World they were creating would produce a place where no one need be hurt like she had been hurt.

This perspective began to permeate the updates she sent to her partners.

Jerry Chen, of course, was receiving all of this information.

The boat was beautiful, but its beauty floated in stark opposition to the darkness that was enveloping those inside…especially the mentally fragile Jerry Chen.

CSIS agents had set up the most up-to-date computing and security equipment available. Chen was working at a fever pitch and, unfortunately, the medication that served to repress his delusions was wearing off. He was too distracted to keep track of when they needed to be taken. The vast amount of data was overwhelming, even for him. He hadn't eaten all day. Large takeout coffee cups from the restaurant lined his desk like gravestones in an oversubscribed cemetery. Even Rachel was helpless to stop it.

The caffeine and low blood sugar alone could cause symptoms of overstimulation and perhaps mild paranoia. Most normal individuals could recognize that their physical and mental condition was dangerously close to collapse and take action; but not Jerry Chen.

His abnormal body chemistry, aided and abetted by too much coffee, too little food, and no sleep produced the Voices. This Voice was never subtle. It was unrelenting and vicious. It warned Jerry of non-existent evils. It urgently insisted that Jerry act. He had to. He had no choice.

This time the Voice told him that Rachel was the evil one. Rachel was the one who was reading his thoughts. She had planted the microphones in his mind. She was going to steal his thoughts and pervert his ideas. She had to die.

As these horrible thoughts cascaded into his mind, Jerry's brain felt like it would explode. Suddenly the Voice became audible. Its high-pitched hiss screamed at him: *Kill her, Kill her!*

Chen could barely hear the voice of his wife calling him for dinner over the inner Voice that was shrieking for her death, demanding that he take action. His face was white, and covered in drops of sweat. His eyes were wide and showed his terror. While he knew it was wrong, the Voice was undeniable. He had to act. He silently moved towards her.

Standing at the stove in the galley singing, Rachel didn't hear him approaching her from behind. The sound of the butcher knife being pulled from its block was masked by her own sweet voice humming the chorus of the old hymn "Amazing Grace."

"I once was lost but now am found, was blind but now I see…"

Something told her to turn around.

There he was, knife in hand.

"Jerry, what are you doing?" she whispered. Her hands rose and assumed the classic defensive posture.

In Jerry's mind, her gentle voice penetrated through the screaming that was urging him to kill her. For a moment he hesitated, but only for a moment. He raised the knife and walked slowly toward her.

"Jerry, noooo…!" she cried.

For reasons unknown to his tortured, delusional mind, Jerry stopped and dropped the knife. It clattered to the floor. He looked at her in horror at what he had done, or was about to do. Pivoting swiftly, he crashed through the outside gallery door and fell to the deck of the boat. Glass shattered and landed all around him. He arose, gave her one last look, then ran up the gangway and disappeared into the darkness.

Rachel fell into a galley chair and began to sob, holding her head in her hands. In a moment, she reached for her cell phone and dialed Edward's number. He answered immediately.

"Hello."

"Jerry's sick again, Edward! I thought he was going to kill me."

Edward drew in his breath. "Where is he now?"

"I don't know!" she whimpered.

"Rachel, listen to me. Do exactly what I tell you to do."

"Okay. I'm so scared."

"It's going to be okay, Rachel. But you must lock the door."

"He broke it."

"Then go to your bedroom and lock yourself in. Don't open it for him. Do *not* open it!"

"I understand."

She did as she was told.

Edward ran to the Navigator and headed for the boat. On the way he phoned 911.

As he approached the massive stone statues guarding the entrances to the Lions Gate Bridge, he saw the flickering of the bright blue and red lights of police vehicles. Through pelting rain a man stood on the bridge rail, surrounded by the lights and dangerously close to falling to his death in the ocean below.

Edward pushed his way past the uniformed police. "Jerry! Don't do it!"

Jerry looked over at his friend. As he turned his head, he lost his balance and teetered momentarily.

"Hang on!"

Jerry steadied himself. He looked down at the water. The waves called to him to join them. It looked so inviting; such a nice way to end the pain.

"Jerry!" called Edward. "Rachel loves you! We love you! Leah loves you so much. Stay there, and I'll come and get you."

"Leah loves me," Chen murmured to himself.

The Voice inside him told him to jump.

Jerry leaned towards the waves far below.

"Jerry!" Edward screamed. "Jane will be so mad at you if you do this!"

Jerry steadied himself. He began to laugh. It was as if a spell was broken. "You're right, Edward, she'd never forgive me."

Jerry leaned back and hopped off the railing. The police jumped on him and made sure he was safe. The trip to the hospital was a fast one.

23

In the posh ballroom of the Hotel Vancouver, Henry Rexan was speaking to a group of COBRA-friendly political and business leaders. Confident in the new technology Xavier was working on, Henry was setting the stage for its initiation to North America.

Attendees had been carefully screened, for security reasons. Most were well-educated, successful and natural leaders. They all shared a desire to see North America keep up with what was occurring in Europe. Without COBRA implants, North America was already falling behind economically. Rexan reported to the audience that implant technology was already an incredible force in Eastern Europe. As fast as the factory in South America could produce them, they were being implanted into anxious volunteers. Implanted leaders were growing and taking control of many key political positions. They were successfully changing the world for the people of Eastern Europe. The masses were seeing for themselves the amazing powers of those who carried the telltale small lump at the base of their skull.

Rexan went on to explain that in the recent past, the poor classes were suffering and often starving in countries that made up the old USSR. Particularly in Russia and Germany, many citizens felt as if they were being ruled by foreigners, that the United States was using them for their own economic growth. As well, their heritage as a nation was being diluted by other recently imported "ethnics." Others, with opposite views, were repulsed by the ethnic cleansings that were occurring intermittently and sought an end to the conflicts, even if it meant the sacrifice of personal autonomy. For both of these viewpoints, implantation could be seen as a form of salvation. Many were gladly submitting to authority and allowing implantation.

Rexan, with the help of an implant, was becoming a very persuasive speaker. His voice permeated the ballroom. "Soon there will be no fear of the political right wing, the middle, or the left in the future. Politics don't need to exist in a post-implant society. As long as a person can be convinced to sacrifice a little to gain a lot, they will have no quarrel with us. The implanted never sit in opposition.

"Our real opposition comes from those in power who refuse to support the efficiency of the rapid evolution that implanting produces. The Pope himself has issued a decree forbidding Catholics from being implanted. Evangelical Protestants are just as misled. They will forever be a thorn in the side of progress, condemning our people to a subservient life under the crushing heel of a false democracy and its perpetuators—all because of their pathetic religious beliefs.

"However, rest assured, their kind will not be with us long.

"But, on to better things.

"Our New Europe is being created in the likeness of the perfect society. Initially only those of leadership skills such as yourselves are being implanted with the most advanced models. In our experience, though, they are so effective and so respected that we have thousands flocking to us to receive the blessing of implantation. We want to do the same in North America. And we want to give you chosen people the chance to become our first echelon.

"Never before have the North American people had the opportunity to make such a giant leap for their nations. Never before have Mexicans had the opportunity to become equal brothers with their neighbors to the north. Never before have Canadians had the opportunity to take the lead.

"We have chosen Canada as the first North American country to become entirely implanted. Why Canada, you ask? Canada is well-known for its patience and extreme tolerance. While under the protective glove of the United States, it still has retained certain individuality. It is resource rich—diverse in European culture and accepting of a broad-based political foundation. It's also technologically advanced and politically stable. And best of all, its government is chronically slow-moving.

"By the time Canadian society is finished debating the rightfulness of implant technology, it will be in place. The technology will move far more rapidly than the legal system is capable of dealing with its implications. We will be funding both sides of the legal argument in order to ensure lengthy legal proceedings. Our lawyers will be implanted, and will of course win. No one will be able to fight the legal genius of the ages compiled into one human. "

The words flowed easily from his mind. Once in a while he would subconsciously reach to the back of his neck and absentmindedly stroke the small lump.

The speech went on for another half hour, but one observer left early and made his apologies at the door. His tape machine, hidden in the makings of his watch, would hold no more. The infiltrator made his way to drop off the recording at a predetermined drop zone. He pulled up to a convenience store and entered it. There he made his way into the men's washroom. Locking the door, he removed the chip from his watch and placed it under the sink where a small piece of gum held it.

The infiltrator then washed his hands and left the washroom. An elderly gentlemen immediately entered the washroom and reached under the sink, removed the chip, and left. He delivered it to CSIS headquarters in Burnaby.

A CSIS chief analyst listened to the recording. He sat in the privacy of an office that overlooked the ocean, far in the distance. Once finished, he scanned over the rafts of documents and emails laid out before him on a table. Many experts over the past several days had sifted through the information. Lawyers, doctors, and other advisors had rendered masses of reports and opinions. The results were troubling. He took the carafe of coffee he'd made earlier and poured another cup. As he stirred in the cream and sugar, he pondered over the implications of the occurrences of the last few months.

The legal opinions of how best to handle the marketing of illegally obtained human flesh in a foreign country were confusing at best. Apparently the implant-friendly Colombian government had taken the view that while the source of the brain tissue was an "unfortunate reality," the results of the experimentation were so positive that perhaps its origin might be overlooked. Other counties were asked, and it became clear that not all saw brain implantation as a threat. Mexico, the United States, and Canada, however, stood firm.

The analyst thought of the various alliances of countries that could take up sides. North America was a natural, given the relationship of the three closely knit countries. He wrote his report and submitted it to Joe Logan, his supervisor. He immediately sent copies to the Prime Minister's Office.

The PMO acted immediately and decisively. The advisors agreed that a political solution must be found, and all North America must be involved. The Prime Minister consulted his friends in Washington and Mexico City. Together they crafted together a simple plan. They would simply ask the people to vote, and the results would give the countries the right to declare war on COBRA or to concede defeat and allow all those who wanted to become implanted. The campaign began immediately.

The staff at the research laboratory in Bogotá had just finished installing the newest and most advanced model of implant into the upper cohort of COBRA leaders. Dr. Xavier Lyon, Henry Rexan, Lorne Browne each received this model, as did Werner Braun.

As the COBRA commander, Braun's implant was designed to command the other members under his leadership. He was their controller, the human mainframe. He, in turn, was to be controlled by the triad consisting of Rexan, Lyon, and Browne. Or at least, that was the way it was supposed to transpire.

The implantation procedure that had been perfected earlier was now relatively painless and was effective almost immediately. As Braun lay on the table, the surgical staff shaved a small square of hair off the back of his neck near the base of his skull. Braun felt the hair being scraped off and wondered what he would be like after the procedure. The surgeon opened the back of his neck and carefully excised the old implant. Braun's eyes rolled back in his head as the bloody wedge was pulled from his brain. Moments later, the new model cone-shaped implant was inserted.

He felt only pressure as the thin needle of the implant was inserted through his open wound. Self-anesthetizing, the implant wedge entered cleanly. The needle end found its home in the so-called reptilian brain located near the top of the spinal column and at the base of the brain. The rest of the implant was nestled just under the skin. The surgeon used a surgical staple gun to close the small wound.

After it was over, Braun sat up in the operating room, feeling no ill effects except perhaps the gentle easing of the sedative and the dull numbness in his neck. Braun's implant was the fastest and most highly evolved yet. Virtually a whole Internet's worth of information was instantaneously available to it. The stainless steel probe that was now inserted into his nervous system slowly began to "boot up." Braun found himself staring at the wall as Xavier Lyon entered the recovery room.

"How are you doing, Werner?"

"Fine, Doctor, I feel great...," replied Braun. Suddenly he felt slightly dizzy. Then a flood of thoughts entered his brain. "Why do I feel so strange?"

Lyon smiled at the puzzled look on Werner Braun's face. "Your new model implant is awakening already. At first it will be a little slow as it finds neural pathways that match your brain; soon, though, your implant will become an inseparable part of you, in a way that the old model could never be. But that is in the near future. For now you may already be able to access its power. You are making excellent progress, Werner. Just relax now and get used to your new abilities. But first, a few simple tests. What is the cube root of 729?"

"8.995882693," he replied instantly.

"What do you think of that?" Lyon said.

"Amazing. Yet, not unexpected," answered the new Braun.

"Perfect," was all she replied as she left the room.

Within a few days Werner Braun came to know himself in a new and different way. The new implant was far more creative and intuitive. He found he was able to understand, calculate, fix, remember, and communicate in the most fantastic of ways. An IQ test he wrote scored him off the chart. He tried the Law School Admissions exam and achieved an unheard-of perfect score. He then repeated the process with the Medical School Admissions Test with the same results. It seemed there was nothing he could not do. He read the *New York Times* virtually as quickly as he could turn the pages and felt like he could remember it all. He wrote poetry, and it was good.

As Werner Braun accessed the Internet, his understanding grew. He was virtually evolving into a new species—a hybrid—within weeks. Later on, he met the other implantees and soon realized that while they possessed many of his skills and abilities and were far more advanced than simple humans, they were nothing compared to him. He was soon introduced as their commander. The only people he felt vaguely inferior to seemed to be Xavier Lyon and Henry Rexan. Although these feelings seemed to defy logic, they were overpowering. He should never deny them; he knew that from the depths of his heart.

Werner Braun and the other New Europeans' recruits continued their training process under the watchful eyes of the leaders of COBRA. They would, in few days, be ready for their first task.

Jerry woke up to the sound of Leah speaking softly into his ear.

"Uncle Jerry, it's time to get up. Mommy says you have big meeting to go to."

Chen opened his eyes and smiled at the sweet little girl standing by his bed in a long flannelette nightie.

"Okay, Leah, tell your mommy I'm just going to take my meds and then I'll be right downstairs. Do you think she made blueberry pancakes?"

"How did you know? It was supposed to be a surprise!"

"Because I can smell them from here. I can hardly wait."

The little girl hopped happily out of room, glad to have Uncle Jerry and Auntie Rachel for a sleepover at her house.

Jerry went into the bathroom and saw his antidepressant and anti-psychotic drugs sitting there waiting for him. Despite knowing that they would slow his thinking, he took both, along with a long, cold drink of water. Then he went down to breakfast.

"Did you take your pills, Jerry?"

"I did, Jane. Besides, you know the stuff they gave me at the hospital will stay in my system for a while anyway."

"That's not the point," she said firmly. "You need to take your meds every day. Do you promise? Because if you stop, I'll be really mad at you."

"Okay, okay! I promise!"

"Good. Now eat up fast. Joe wants us down at the boat right away. Leah, can you go upstairs and tell Auntie Rachel her breakfast is ready?"

"Okay Mommy." Leah ran upstairs.

Within a hour or so, both the Calais and Chen family were ready to return to the boat, where they would spend the working portion of their day.

When they arrived, they were greeted by Logan and several CSIS agents, along with both CIA and Mexican security representatives. Once in the boat, Jerry and Jane pored over the latest technical and legal data. Edward and Rachel had some time to talk. They made some coffee and sat in the very galley where Jerry had come at Rachel with the knife.

"Rachel, we need to talk about Jerry."

She looked up. "Before you say anything, you need to know that I promised to love him in sickness and in health. Right then he was very sick. It wasn't him who attacked me, it was his disease. It's not his fault, you know."

"I know. And that's a good distinction to make. But you need to know we have information that a COBRA implant might just cure his bipolar disease permanently. "

"What? It might cure him? How?"

"The implants take over certain brain functions, and can be programmed to block the symptoms."

"How do you know this?"

"Henry Rexan called us personally, while you were in the hospital waiting for Jerry. Jane thinks the reason they want Jerry implanted is because they think they can control him with it."

"What does Jerry think?"

"He doesn't know yet. We wanted to tell you first."

"I want you to ask him, Edward. It will be too hard coming from me. Too confusing, since he almost hurt me."

"Okay, Rachel."

Downstairs in the makeshift work room, Joe Logan spoke to Jane and Jerry. "Okay folks. Let's take a few minutes' break."

Jerry went outside and saw Edward coming out of the galley. They stood together overlooking the ocean.

Edward looked at his friend. "I have to talk to you about something."

"I know what it is. I've seen the results of implantation on bipolar disorders. They call it a cure."

"What do you want to do?"

"Nothing."

"Why?"

"I'd rather die than lose my soul. And that is precisely the price of an implant. Edward, I know I will never miss taking my meds again. I know they slow me down a bit, but I'd rather be slow than not even me."

Edward nodded slowly. He was perhaps one of the few who truly understood the sacrifice Jerry Chen was making. "Tell me what you really believe."

"About what?"

"About why you think we are here on Earth."

"Are you talking about God?"

"Yeah, I guess so."

Jerry cocked his head. "Where did this come from?"

172

"I'm not sure. I guess it's just the way you run your life, and how you decide stuff. I don't really get it. Can you explain it to me?"

"I thought you'd never ask. I always thought you saw me as just weak and a little weird."

Edward exhaled. "Not weak, Jerry. I admire you. I just don't understand you...and yes, you are a little weird."

They both laughed.

"Okay Edward. Why don't you tell me what you really believe first?"

"I don't really know. I guess I believe in science, and I believe in evolution. I know you don't."

"What do you mean, you *believe* in evolution?"

"Well, I believe that what science says is right. We are the products of evolution. We didn't need a God to create us."

"Why do you believe the scientists?"

Edward lifted an eyebrow. "Well, for starters, they're smart, and most of them believe evolution created us, not God—and they have proof."

"So, in terms of eternal truths, if someone is smart, and has lots of people who believe in what he is saying, he's probably right and you'd have faith in him. Is that what you believe?"

"Well, no, I mean..."

"Lyon and Rexan are brilliant, and now they have lots of believers. Does that mean they're right?"

"No,"

"So tell me again why you believe what you do?"

"Point made, Chen. Okay, smart guy, what do you believe?"

"I believe we have two options. We either believe that we were made by God, or that we were made as a result of the actions of the universe, played out in what we call evolution. I believe that if we take option one, the God one, we have hope. If we take option two, it doesn't really matter what we do or believe."

"Of course it does."

"Not really. The no-God option means we're only recycled atoms. It means that the reason we want to survive is to protect our species, and that as individuals we are no more important than the animals, the plants, or for that matter, the rocks. When we die, we die, and at that point, it's all over."

"What's wrong with that?"

"I believe we are more than that: that we are all created with a plan for us, and that plan is perfect for us."

"How can I be sure?"

"I think most of us, deep inside, know there is a God who exists and cares for us. I think we know that our love for each other is more than just an inherited predisposition for survival of the species. Think of how much you love Leah."

"Okay, so what if you are right?"

"If you believe in God, there is good news, and bad news."

"Don't give me all that hell crap, Jerry."

"Okay, Edward, what are the options then? I figure there are two."

"You are so binary. Always two choices. Do you *really* believe we have a choice in what happens to us?"

"We always have the ability to choose."

"What are the options then?"

"Well, option one is that our choices matter for eternity, and option two is that they matter only for today, or for our lives on earth."

"Let's talk about option one."

"Option one is an exciting one." Jerry began to smile.

Just then Joe Logan reached the top of the stairs and called to the men, "We need you downstairs, guys."

"Can we finish this later?" Edward asked Jerry.

"Sure can." Jerry grinned. "Thanks for asking."

They both turned and descended the stairs, following after Joe Logan.

24

The assassin was ready, sitting near the end of the table, hand in his pocket, fingering the small plastic yet extremely lethal pistol that had been supplied to him by the CIA. He had the perfect view of his victim and only awaited the opportunity to take the shot. His neck had the telltale bump, but it was simply a silicon-filled fake inserted under the skin.

Henry Rexan sat in the meeting of his leaders and listened to the reports of those who where speaking today.

The Colonel in charge of communications was first. "I'd like to report that our website is receiving 100,000 hits an hour. Most are from people interested in becoming test subjects for the next round of implants. We have as many people as we can presently supply, knocking at our door and ready to go."

"Excellent work. Now, let's hear from marketing," said Rexan.

A young man in his late thirties rose. "Ladies and gentlemen, the news is good. So many major companies have requested access to the implant advertising component that the COBRA account managers could not keep up with the demand. In order to assure their place in terms of our ability to insert buying habits into the consciousness of consumers, they are prepaying accounts to the extent that we now have millions of dollars a day flowing into our funds. Of course, for the North American continent, the agreements are all subject to yes vote. For the rest of the world, we are a go as is."

"Again, excellent work," Rexan said, then added, "let us hear from public relations regarding the North America situation."

The vice president for public relations rose from her seat. "We are developing a multitargeted approach to winning the vote. Firstly, we plan to encourage the acceptance of free implants by allowing implantees to purchase goods and services directly through their thoughts. Nothing could be simpler. Also, we will be developing a number of products that will be able to be used only if one has an implant. The language translators are a good example.

"The advertising campaign will be a 'feel good' one initially. That is, we will show our audience how great the world will be for them and that they won't want to be left behind. The next phase will be highly emotionally based and negative. We will show our opponents as the evil ones, wanting to oppress people's freedom to chose.

"Finally we will host a campaign-like event, occurring simultaneously all over the continent and led by the best-looking, smoothest-talking, and most confident-appearing personality we can find. At the end of his speech we are hoping to convince the father of implants, Mr. Rexan, to make an appearance along with Xavier. After all, they are the ones who are making this whole thing possible." At that, she remained standing and began to clap. All of those seating around the table rose and joined her. Several had tears in their eyes.

Rexan rose and raised his arms, indicating for them to be seated. They did, hesitantly.

"You are truly a remarkable lot. I am very proud of you, all of you. And as a reward for your work, you will all be able to have first choice at the latest management-level downloads. What is better yet, they are ready today."

"Yes!" exclaimed several simultaneously. The rest simply smiled, cheered, or clapped.

Rexan subconsciously reached back and rubbed the small lump on the back of his neck. *It felt so good,* he thought. He scanned the room and looked at each of his people. All were handpicked, all successful, all part of the team that he would lead to Asia, his next choice of the part of the world to lead into the new beginning. He loved Asian women. Suddenly, a thought penetrated his skull. While looking away, a digital image seemed to play in his mind. It was an image of one of his VPs. A close-up and enhanced view immediately and spontaneously invaded Rexan's consciousness. It showed the VP's hand near his pocket. There was a bulge. That image too was immediately enhanced by the implant's image enhancer. It became clear he had a gun in his pocket. Suddenly Rexan knew he was the target of an assassination attempt.

Cautiously Rexan moved about the room, waiting for the assassin to make his move. The rest of the VPs began to slow in their applause. Rexan thought of several solutions to his dilemma, then selected one. He calmly went on speaking, once things had quieted down. He was careful to position himself with at least one of his people between him and the gun.

"Imagine the world we are about to create. Imagine a society so much more efficient than today's wasteful world. Imagine a world where there is no need for war, no starvation, and most, if not all, diseases are eliminated. The world's population will be managed through the use of thought and emotion insertions. Violence will be unnecessary and eliminated. Fear and greed will disappear. Scientific discoveries will occur exponentially. Not only will people feel happy, they will be intensely productive. It will be a perfect world. Only a few of us, like you for instance, will really need to have the freewill option offered by the latest round of managerial downloads. Freewill will have no need to exist in the general population."

The group once again began to applaud. The door to the room opened and Rexan's secretary came in and stood patiently near the midpoint of the conference table. Monika was a changed woman. In fact, she was a perfect example of what Rexan wanted implantation to produce.

Rexan raised his hands and the clapping stopped. "We do, however, have some foes who want to oppose the world we imagine. Once implanted, of course, those who are potential detractors would be of no concern. But what about those who wish to stand in our way by refusing implants? Most, we suspect, will be ill-educated fanatics, yet their presence would lower the development or evolution rate of the whole population. We must eliminate the Remnants. I've already ordered the process of cleansing to begin in Europe." He paused for effect. "Natural selection, for the good of our new world, might have to be accelerated."

As if those words were a queue, the assassin began his move. His hands reached for the pocket very slowly. Once the gun had cleared his pocket he stood and raised it.

A quiet pop shocked the air in the room. The people could not believe what was happening.

The assassin's eyes were beginning to roll to the back of his head as his knees crumpled. The bullet in his gun, which had never reached its objective, remained unfired in the gun, which fell from his hand.

Rexan's secretary and bodyguard kept her weapon trained on the brain of her enemy until his heart stopped beating.

Rexan spoke. "Ladies and gentlemen, it is clear that not all are ready to be trusted. There are those who will resist us, and will fail, just as this one did. Ultimately, it will call for some drastic action on our part. Are you with me? Are you willing to sacrifice to make the world a better place for you and your children?"

The applause began again, slowly in the beginning, then filled the room with the roar of victory against evil…at least in their minds.

Rexan dismissed his staff. The public relations expert remained and followed him into his private office. She entered his inner office after the meeting and beamed. "You were incredible in there. How did Monika know to come in?"

"One of the neat features of an implant is that you can communicate directly."

"Of course! That was awesome."

"Yes it was awesome, in every way possible," cooed Rexan. "Now come here."

She was indeed a perfect servant, he thought as she closed the door, locking it behind her.

Edward and Jerry took their seats around the massive granite-topped table in the makeshift meeting room of the yacht. Jane held the floor.

"Clearly we have enough evidence to bring charges in the United States, Canada, and Colombia against each of the principles of COBRA. The FBI is ready to move against COBRA in California; the CIA will be assisting the Colombian government in Bogotá. The RCMP and Interpol agencies are ready to move against them in Europe and Canada.

"One strategy the Columbian government is considering is to bring them up on charges of crimes against humanity in the world court or on abuses of human rights in the United Nations. Joe has played a huge role in orchestrating this. Have you read about what is happening in South American and Europe?"

Heads nodded.

"There are people from all over the world wanting to get implants. It's incredible. Like a panic-buying thing. Everyone is afraid that unless they get one too, they'll be left out." She continued passionately. "There are even rumors that the New European movement is getting huge shipments of implants, and that people living there won't be able to obtain Euro dollars without access via implants," added Edward.

"I'm not sure we can stop it," interjected Rachel.

"It would be like denying people telephones, computers, cars, or machinery. The stock market is going crazy on COBRA stocks. The implant system is hitting the roof. COBRA stocks are over 100 dollars and will rise tomorrow again bigtime, according to the news."

Joe Logan had listened to the discussions of the team all afternoon. He realized that they too represented society as a whole. Some wanted to ignore the past and move on to legitimizing the use of implants as a natural step in human development. Others wanted to attack COBRA legally, but also wanted to take the research findings in the hopes of finding a method of producing implant tissue sections without the use of human brains. And then there was Jerry.

At that moment Jerry spoke up thoughtfully. "Sometimes people are wrong, but their ideas can be worked with, consensus found, and a place found where all sides can comfortably exist. And sometimes people or ideas are just plain wrong. There is no room for compromise. This is the case here. There is no room for COBRA philosophy in a free and democratic society, at least one with moral standards that value human life as more important than progress. The COBRA system was born from greed, with no sense of limitations. The developers are psychopathic criminals whose only basis for decision-making is their greed or lust for power. By giving any edge to their product, we climb into the bed of amoral or, depending on your perspective, immoral servanthood. One can only serve one master. So one's conscience, or one's greed. Take your pick."

With that Jerry stepped away from the table they were gathered around and headed towards the bridge of the magnificent boat. Rachel soon followed, as did Edward and Jane. The four of them stood on the bridge, gazing through the tempered glass and over the darkening waters of the cove.

"You're right," said Edward, touching Jerry's shoulder. He went on to explain the call they had received from Rexan, offering the implant to Jerry.

Jerry looked shocked. "Rexan called you personally?"

"Yes. He left a message on our voicemail at home."

Jerry pursed his lips. "He's afraid of something then. His type would never make an offer like that."

"All right everyone, let's take a break and go out on the deck," suggested Edward. The four friends opened the exterior bridge door and worked their way to the bow of the yacht. They each took up a position leaning on the safety rail and breathed in the salty air, listening to the sounds of a peaceful ocean.

In the darkness, Werner Braun crouched on the shore, no more than 400 meters from Jerry's boat. A squad of other implantees, all under his direction, crouched low in the salal plants that hid them. Braun peered through the night-vision goggles at the yacht. It appeared as a greenish glow of heat through the lenses. His implant immediately transformed the vision digitally and enhanced its perspective. By estimating the angle and changing his view he was able to find the range of the boat to within one half a meter. It would take him and his team only few minutes to swim to the boat. They had observed the security groups surrounding the ship and had placed members of his team of New European soldiers in appropriate points. It would be a simultaneous hit. Highly planned and coordinated, each team knew their mission and their goal. Fear of losing their lives had been temporarily removed via the implant, although each had been given an overwhelming fear of failure. Each member felt invincible, confident, and motivated.

At the right moment, a signal was sent to all the members of the attacking force. On shore the muffled sound of rapid fire began. The Suburbans holding some of the CSIS agents were being pumped full of armor-piercing shells. Agents hiding in the surrounding forest hastily put on their night scopes and began to look for targets. Finding some, they fired. The body armor of the implantees, compounded with their amazing physical speed, agility, and ability to sense where and when fire would come from made them difficult targets. Several, however, fell in crumpled balls.

Jerry dove on top of Rachel, covering her with his body. Edward did the same with Jane. They lay, terrified, in the darkness.

The second wave of implantees attacked the two boats that were parked around and near the yacht they were protecting. Explosive charges blew holes in the boats' hulls just as their motors roared to life, plunging several of the occupants into the sea. Within minutes they had either been knifed underwater or burned alive on the boats.

Edward motioned to Jerry. Jerry nodded in agreement. They pushed their wives into the little room near the front of boat that held the crew's quarters. As Jane crawled into the room, Edward turned and looked into the water. Despite the darkness he was able to make out the image of a woman in a black wetsuit carrying a weapon and several pieces of other equipment as she climbed over the rail of the deck just below them. Once she landed, she crouched low and began a scan of the area using a night scope mounted on her automatic machine pistol. Jerry was awestruck and potentially in full view of the searching invisible beams. The woman turned just as Edward grabbed Jerry and threw him to the deck. Intermittent fire chattered from various locations on the boat as a pitched battle between the security forces and the attacking COBRA agents continued. Edward pushed Jerry into the room that held Jane and then forced himself into it as well. The door barely shut behind them.

The dozen CSIS agents onboard had jumped into action; many had appeared on the deck. As they did, two COBRA's on shore armed with high-powered rifles picked them off one shot at a time from a distance of 400 yards. They never missed. Within minutes the six agents whose job was to protect the perimeter of the boat lay dead.

Deep within the yacht, George and Tara listened to the attack. George's brain was screaming in pain as he gently pushed his beloved Tara towards the hall leading to the engine room of the yacht.

Joe Logan, holding his pistol in hand, covered George as they approached the steel-lined engine room. Bullets were bouncing and ricocheting everywhere. One of the agents, hit by a stray bullet, fell to the ground. George pushed him aside and led the way down the stairs to the door of the engine room. He opened the heavy fireproof door and ushered the others into it.

Joe Logan was last, his weapon at the ready. In the near darkness, all Logan saw was a brief flash. Suddenly he felt like he'd been kicked, and a huge weight was compressing his chest. In numbing pain he was forced to drop his gun. Radiating pain careened down his limbs, paralyzing them. He fell facefirst onto the deck. Without the use of his hands to break the fall, his nose first flattened and then broke. He collapsed with the full force of his weight and lost consciousness as he began to inhale his own blood.

As Werner Braun entered the main deck area, he recognized the man who had been implanted only recently. George was performing very well, he observed.

George saw his master carrying a small but powerful explosive device.

"Are they all in there?" he screamed at George over the rattle of the gunfire.

George stood frozen and did not answer.

A piercing pain sliced through George's brain as he processed what was happening. Tara was in the engine room. Jerry, Rachel, Edward, and Jane were probably hiding in another part of the boat.

A part of him wanted it all to stop. Yet an inner sense of urgency was compelling him to obey, and to answer the question. The natural part of his brain was waging war with the implant. At the speed of the fastest computer, the fight went on. He grasped the weapon in his hand and fingered the trigger.

Werner Braun observed with scientific zeal the battle that was occurring. George's implant was being ordered to download his deepest thoughts directly into Braun's brain. Braun was enjoying the moment.

As George felt himself losing his thoughts and soul to the watching Braun, he sensed he was about to disclose the whereabouts of the four survivors, his friends. He was about to have them murdered. This is what his betrayal had led to.

It was then that the Voice of Lisa spoke clearly to him and the world went silent. "Don't say a word, George. Just kill him," was all she said.

He raised his weapon towards the watching Braun. But Braun's hand was much faster. He turned his weapon and pulled the trigger, releasing a burst of bullets. The slugs stitched a line of horror across George's stomach, spilling its contents on to the deck.

Strange thing to think, thought Werner Braun as he watched George die, *before you are to kill someone, or to die yourself.*

The words downloaded from George's brain returned to Braun: *"I am come to send fire on the earth; and what will I, if it be already kindled?"*

Braun activated the explosive, opened the door to the engine room, and threw it in. He swung the heavy fireproof door shut and used a fire axe to jam the door handle, locking it from the outside.

He waited for the sound the explosion inside the room, then worked his way to the outside main deck, his work complete.

Braun summoned the remaining unhurt members of his team and instructed them to leave.

Stepping over a comrade writhing in pain, Braun and his group left the boat, satisfied they had accomplished their purpose.

Via a satellite feed, Henry Rexan had watched with relish the slow sinking of the yacht. He particularly enjoyed imagining Jerry Chen caught in the burning boat. Rexan loved a good roast.

The COBRA agents gathered on the beach and were picked up by several powerful motor launches that successfully ferried them to a number of small islands, where various helicopters and seaplanes awaited their arrival. Once it was known the number and identity of the wounded and detained implanted, Rexan ordered a signal sent to each implant that had been left behind. Within minutes, each of their hearts stopped.

25

Jerry, Rachel, Edward, and Jane crouched down in the dark, terrified, waiting for the shooting to stop. By the time it did, they could tell the boat was leaning and most probably sinking.

Edward whispered, "We have to leave, or we'll get caught in here and drown when the boat goes under."

"Agreed," said Chen.

"I'll go first and check it out."

"Fine by me," Chen answered.

Calais softly opened the door and peered out. He could see nothing other than the body of one of the intruders, still and lifeless. By then, the water was lapping at the upper deck where they were hiding. The boat was sinking fast. He beckoned with his hand and led the other three out of the room, over the rail, and into the cold iridescent water. They were immediately covered in oil from the blown-up engine room. Swimming through the debris created in the aftermath of the violent attack, they could see an approaching boat—its spotlight penetrating the black, searching for anyone left alive.

Calais and the others were in a state of cold shock as the Coast Guard vessels arrived and plucked them out of the water. Police, firefighters, and ambulance attendants swarmed them as the surviving members of the CSIS security force regrouped. The four were immediately rushed to Vancouver General Hospital, where they were treated for shock and hypothermia.

Jane cried out to the security detail to check on her daughter, as she feared COBRA agents might hurt her. A supplemental protection team was dispatched immediately to get Leah from safehouse she was in and assist in the reuniting of Leah with her parents.

After being checked out by emergency room doctors, Edward and

Jane sat waiting in the "bad news" room of the hospital. Finally their daughter arrived in the burly arms of an RCMP sergeant. The little girl reached out to her mother and Jane cried as she hugged her. Edward placed his arms around both of them and wept as well. They were safe, at least for the moment.

Joe Logan, with Jerry and Rachel supporting him, limped painfully towards Edward and Jane.

"George and Tara didn't make it. I'm so sorry."

Edward and Jane stood in shock.

"You should know," Joe said slowly, "that when they examined George...well, they found an implant."

Jane gasped. "Oh no."

Joe nodded. "He had an implant. He must have been part of the plot to attack the boat and get at you. You should know something, though. One of our men saw how he died. He seemed to be fighting the implant itself. He lost, though, in the end. And Tara died in the engine room, in the explosion."

They all stood together and cried at the loss of their two friends, then vowed to avenge their deaths.

Days later, Edward Calais sat reading the news from various places in the world. He reacted with revulsion at the forecasts that showed the spread of what was now becoming known as "the Implanted."

The European Economic Community was embracing Implant technology with utter abandon. Within a few weeks, two-thirds of the population was to be implanted or was on a waiting list for various models of humanware. For those people implanted, life was outwardly wonderful. Their needs and desires were not only being met, but indeed, were not even their own.

The economy was becoming controlled and entirely predictable. Supply and demand was beginning to be predicted and then matched. Workers could produce more at will; consumers would consume more, at will. The will in question, however, was the will of Rexan and Lyon and their advisors at COBRA.

The average person who was implanted was easily urged to consume and enjoy whatever commodity needed to be used at the time. Each person was entirely satisfied with whatever his or her lot in life was. Even to the death, their lives were not their own. Those Implants whose physical bodies were becoming expensive to maintain gladly removed themselves from society using corner store euthanasia materials. As individuals, their role was to accept and do, and they had given up their ability to question in return for chronic euphoria.

The European community was showing signs of being united for the first time in world history. Implanted politicians with an obvious common purpose and intent allowed for growth and a structure that was eminently efficient. From London to Moscow to Israel, one gigantic state was coalescing into a union that existed for the sole purpose of pleasing the European director, Henry Rexan.

Echelon data was revealing some relatively hidden facts about the reality of the new Europe and its defacto leader Henry Rexan. While it appeared the implantation program was becoming more successful than the wildest expectations, information was appearing that showed it was not enough for Rexan. Strangely enough, the man whose popularity was unparalleled seemed to lack a sense of completeness. There were still those who would not subject themselves to implantation. This sat on Henry Rexan like an annoying fly. He simply could not enjoy the day without planning how to eliminate some of the newest parasites of his continent.

Henry was making plans to accomplish this, using time-honored methods. Those not on the implant wait list would soon not be able to buy or sell goods. Medical care was to be denied. And soon there were no jobs for those who resisted the efficiency of implantation.

It was not enough. The Remnants, as he sometimes called them, were mainly religious fanatics. Apparently, they planned to live without the comforts of the new modern society. They wanted their own food and shared with each other what they had. They were moving to the countryside and out of the way of the Implants. Others were finding their way into the depths of the inner cities. It was particularly dangerous there because the uninformed were often "encouraged" to remove themselves from society during sweeps of the city by police forces.

In South America, the impact of implantation was quite different. Lyon's version of her perfect society was far more artistic and glamorous in nature. Her people spent less time working on economic prosperity and more time on expression. Lyon's influence on the governments of the day ensured that she controlled the cabinets of each of them. The model of implant she chose allowed most of the people to enjoy a relatively carefree existence. The controlled economy had brought the traditional inflation of South America to a steady and healthy 2 percent. This miracle was accomplished in weeks.

The arts flourished under her care. Great buildings were being built, gardens were planted, cities cared for. The poor were being given implants that allowed them to shun the drugs, alcohol, and glue sniffing that had softened their lives, at least in the short-term. Criminals were forcefully implanted and immediately freed. There was no evidence they would be a danger again. Many of them could be seen unconsciously cleaning up garbage as they walked the streets to work in the new factories. That notion was an added touch given by Xavier Lyon personally to the computer program that controlled the convict's implants.

The implant "encouragement" squads spent a large proportion of their time hunting down and "recycling" the brain tissue of those intellectuals who declined the implantation process. This was the source of the brain tissue necessary to implant the millions left who waited anxiously for their turn.

While the rest of the world waited uncomfortably for the new technology to have its impact on them, Edward, Jane, Rachel, and Jerry began again to work for CSIS and against an implanted society. Canada had made a political decision, along with the United States and Mexico, to stall the introduction of implants into North America. As a result, Henry Rexan had moved his operations into the Asian countries, and was relying heavily on the expertise and encouragement of the Chinese, who saw implantation as a way to bring China into the new age. Hong Kong provided the catalyst for Rexan's version of the implantation process. Hundreds of thousands of Chinese intellectuals had been implanted, and millions more were to come.

It was exhausting just reading about the impact that implantation was having on the world, so Edward grabbed some financial articles and headed to bed.

It was an early evening for Edward Calais. He settled into the giant bed alone. Jane was doing a little reading of her own in the living room. The business world had hugely changed since the outbreak of controlled economies in Europe and South America. North America stood on its own in many ways. "A bastion of freedom," some called it; others called it "an economic Titanic heading full-steam into the icebergs of an evolving world."

The articles spoke of money that had left for the new prosperity of Moscow, Lisbon, and Bogota. His office had received numerous calls from investors asking questions about the booming foreign markets and the seeming bust of New York and Toronto. The NASDAC had been especially pounded as it felt the overpowering competition from Implant technology on its local and highly technical companies. He leaned back into a huge down pillow, peering outside to enjoy a brief view of the city and the water. Then his attention was drawn to the television.

The announcer was steely eyed as he described a scene that had been recorded by a hidden camera.

"In Munich today a scene reminiscent of pre-war Germany was played out as our camera recorded an attack on a small church by pro-COBRA militia. The congregation of the Munich Baptist Church was holding a prayer vigil to pray for God's intervention. Their pastor had been very public in his opposition to implantation. This appeared to be a reprisal for his outspokenness."

As recorded by the camera, a gritty image showed the arrival of several vanloads of men wearing armbands of a cobra, coiled and ready to strike. The camera's microphone picked up the singing of hymns from inside the church as several COBRA agents threw gasoline bombs through the stained-glass windows. As the bombs exploded, the screams of the people inside could be heard. Two men spray-painted the letter *R*, for Remnant, on the beautiful oak doors. Soon smoke was pouring out of the broken windows. The front doors burst open and churchgoers fled the burning building. Edward watched in horror as COBRA agents beat them with bats and arrested them. When the story was over, he leaned back and thought about the unfolding world. He shifted in ged and gazed at the picture of his daughter and wife.

Soon Leah appeared at his side, and he quickly flipped the TV off.

"Mommy asked if you'd put me to bed, Daddy," Leah said.

He scooped Leah into his arms and carried her down to the bathroom. He watched as she brushed her teeth, and handed her a washcloth to clean her hands and face. Then he took her by the hand and led her into her bedroom. He smiled. It was a perfect room for Leah—picturesque...the walls bordered in delicate pink flowers and the ceiling was covered with clouds.

"Will you please tell me my favorite story Daddy?" Leah pleaded as she changed into her pajamas, then climbed into her warm, sweet-smelling sheets.

"Okay, little one, but this is a head-down story. Put your head down on the pillow and listen with your eyes closed."

Leah cuddled into her pillow and sucked her thumb, holding closely on to her "blankie," which was really just a small section of one of her mother's old flannelette nighties. She loved its smell when it was fresh from the laundry.

"Once upon a time," Edward began, "there was a little girl who was all cuddled into her bed for the night. She was sucking her thumb and resting, all warm and cozy, as her dad told her a night-time story. By the time he finished the story, she'd drifted off to sleep He kissed her on the cheek and softly tiptoed out of her room.

"The little girl was having a most wonderful dream when suddenly she awoke to a strange sound...the whinny of a horse, right outside her window! The little girl climbed out of her bed and carefully drew back the curtain. There, lit up by the light of a full moon, was the most beautiful and strangest-looking horse she had ever seen. It was a white, with a long mane and tail of silver. Along each of the horse's sides was a beautiful silver wing, covered in shimmering feathers. For some reason the little girl was not afraid as the horse bent its head low and seemed to beckon to her. She carefully climbed out through her window and pulled herself up and onto the horse's back. She wrapped her fingers around clumps on the horse's mane.

"The horse took two small steps, unfurled its wings, and leapt into the air. Its mighty wings made smooshing sounds as they pushed the horse higher and higher. The little girl looked down and saw her house get smaller and smaller as they climbed higher and higher. Soon the town they lived in looked like a blur of dots of lights. In another moment, it was gone.

"The horse continued flying. Soon they passed over a great ocean. The sun rose just as the horse and the little girl landed on a tiny little tropical island. The little girl climbed down from the horse and soon found herself running through the warm ocean, playing tag with her new winged horse friend. They played and played until the little girl got tired. It had been a wonderful day.

"Then, slowly the little girl climbed back onto the horse. He knew what she wanted. Immediately he leaped into the air once more and hurled up into the sky. She wrapped her fingers around her friend's mane and clung as tightly as she could. The sun set before their eyes. In a little while they landed in front of the house where their trip had begun, and the little girl, so very, very tired, somehow climbed up through the window and into her bed. She waved as the winged horse leaped into the air again, and then she fell fast asleep.

"When she awoke the next morning, she thought of the wonderful dream she must have had. Stretching out her arms, she looked down at her hands…and saw an *amazing* sight. Wrapped tightly around her finger was one long and beautiful strand of silver horse's hair. The little girl decided to use that hair as a necklace, and she attached a tiny little silver cross to it. She wore that necklace and cross always after that. And every time she touched it, she was reminded of how she felt when she was with her beautiful, winged friend. Safe and warm, always…"

Edward gently stroked his daughter's back as she fell to sleep. Then he tucked in the goose-down comforter that Jerry had given her. As he sat by her bed, watching her, his eyes moved to the window that looked into the darkness of the surrounding forest. Its pine smell pleasantly filled the room via a small opening in the windowpane. Edward leaned over for a good night kiss.

Returning to the living room, he sat beside his wife. The gas fireplace was turned up and the room lighting was turned down. The flames cast a flickering orange glow on Jane's lovely complexion.

"Jane, I need to talk to you."

She lifted an eyebrow. "What about? This sounds serious."

"I've been thinking a lot about what we need to do next."

"And what do you think?"

Edward went on to explain what was on his heart. The two of them spoke long into the night. It became clear they were both uneasy with the stalemate that had been reached with the implants. COBRA's marketing campaign was making further and further inroads into making implantation an acceptable alternative. Television, radio, and the Internet news services were filled with success stories of those who'd been implanted—and with the persecution of those who refused. More and more politicians were saying that unless Canada and the United States turned to implant technology, their countries would fall so far behind that eventually they would fail.

The latest American news described the open invitation being extended to the newest and most charismatic implanted personality, Lorne Browne. Browne was returning to Canada to speak at a convention of pro-implant forces. Edward and Jane were repulsed at the thought of seeing him again. Edward knew intuitively, though, that they must meet him and face his ideas.

Jane was not at all confident in Edward's ability to take Browne on, but chose to remain quiet at the moment. Instead, she merely joined him in listening to the news.

Outside of Leah's window, intruders finished gathering the information they needed, took a few more infrared pictures, and slithered into the black of the evening.

26

It was early morning when Lorne Browne's Lear jet entered Canadian airspace just off the coast of Alaska. He peered out through the window, reflecting on the difference between the Europe he had just left and the vastness of the land he entered. The huge forests, the fishing boats clustered near the outlet of a mighty river, and snow-dusted mountains that ran down to the sea reminded him of the opportunity that the resource-rich continent of North America presented. His implant began to gently instruct him on the most recent economic conditions of Canada. Similar to United States, her economy was suffering the effects of reduced trade with Europe and Asia. There, as opposed to North America, post-implant economics had produced a steady and controlled growth. There was no unemployment among the Implanted. The economics of supply and demand had been carefully matched. There was no waste.

Browne envisioned the future of his North America. With Lyon happily in charge of South America, and Henry Rexan enjoying his dominion over Europe and gradually exploiting Asia, North America stood ready for the taking. Browne ordered a light meal from the all-too eager-to-serve steward. As he munched on poached salmon and a bagel and drank a Colombian blend coffee, his implant filled his mind with the warmth and gentle, relaxed feelings of a Sunday morning. He soon nodded off. While he lay sleeping, his head propped up against the window of the plane, his implant continued its work.

Browne awoke refreshed and ready as the sounds of the plane landing intruded into his consciousness. He left the plane and cleared customs with ease. Gathering his luggage and descending the elevator, he saw the various locally hired security staff and vehicles that awaited him. He left via limo.

It was not a quiet ride. All along the route to downtown Vancouver from the airport, various protest groups had set up camp. Several anti-implant groups held signs and screamed slogans as he passed. Several threw plastic models of human brains at the motorcade. Eggs spattered on the windshields of the heavily armored limousine.

"If they only knew the world that awaits them," said Browne absently to the guard who sat beside him.

"A world where a computer controls your life?" replied the tall and muscular security man.

"No. It's a world where men like you can finally control your *own* future."

"Don't implants tell you what to do, and how to feel? I've been reading up a bit. It's been on all the news."

"Absolutely not. They are always under your control. Implants simply assist you. They are your slaves, not the other way around. If you want to feel better, and that will help you meet your goals, the implants can make some gentle adjustments to your emotional state. But you are always ultimately in control. You can turn them off completely if you wish, but trust me, you won't."

"How do they help you become smarter then?"

"First, they hold a massive database within themselves; second, they have access to download new information as it becomes available; and third, they fuse with your own brain tissue, allowing direct communication. No typing!"

The guard shifted uncomfortably, as if this polite, well-spoken, and caring person who seemed genuinely interested in explaining his point of view wasn't what he'd expected. "I heard you get brain tissue by murdering people."

"That, sir, is an absolute lie. All the experimentation and all current models obtained their tissue from organ donors and by cloning it. It is that simple. We aren't inhuman."

Browne looked deeply into the man eyes and knew he had won. It was child's play. One more vote in favor of implant technology moving into North America. He smiled and glanced out on the city he grew up in. It would be his soon. He closed his eyes and the music of Mozart softly entered his consciousness, granting him a few more moments of peace. His life was perfect.

The motorcade again ran into protestors as they approached the Waterfront Hotel, where Browne would be staying. This time, however, the crowd was a mixture of pro and anti-implant partisans. Lorne looked through the heavy tinted glass of the armor-plated vehicle and sized up the crowds.

"If this were Europe, I'd know what to do with these protestors. It's so much more complicated here," he said to no one in particular.

They were getting very worried. Jane explained to Joe Logan and the other Gang members her view of the latest data that Jerry's virus had collected. She spoke in hushed tones, almost a whisper.

"Below the leadership trio of Lyon, Rexan, and Browne, there exists a vast network of cell groups that have been gathered very quickly, mainly through Internet websites. Some of those involved are organized crime in the classic sense, but many are intellectuals such as researchers at universities, lawyers, etc. This group is more interested in the social improvement twist they are calling 'accelerated evolution.' They are the ones leading the spread of the implants."

"Why are they so persuasive?" asked the CIA representative.

"Faith," said Jerry, who had been quiet up until this moment.

"Faith! How so?" Logan said.

"They believe they are fundamentally right. They actually believe the world will be better off once everyone is implanted and under the control of COBRA. They have faith in what they are doing. They think it's the right thing to do. And what's more, the implant takes away their ability to think for themselves, so even if something within them knows it's wrong, the implant suppresses it."

"Scary," said the CIA guy.

"It says in the Bible Satan will be disguised as an Angel of Light, and that's just how people are responding to them. They see them as Saviors, but instead they steal their souls and turn them into machines."

"Indeed, but I don't think the Bible is going to help us now," said Logan thoughtfully, "Jerry, I think I know what we have to do. We have to get into their heads."

"What do you mean?" answered Jerry.

"We need to read their minds."

"How?" replied Jerry, keenly interested in a new spin on the puzzle game he loved so much.

"If we assume that the minds of the commanders of COBRA operate with no moral conscience, and that their implanted chips make decisions most favorable to them personally, their moves and strategies should be predictable, by a computer anyway."

"Of course," exclaimed Jerry. "I should be able to get Dinah to predict their next moves. The only thing is that it will only predict specific actions on a global basis, not an individual one."

"Why?" queried Logan.

"Because even within them there is the human connection, at a personal level; it is the creative part of the implant system. The implant suppresses thoughts that run contrary to its programming. However, emotions are not always entirely predictable, so one individual making one choice cannot be predicted as easily as the pattern of one thousand individuals making a choice."

"Are we lost then?"

"No, actually it is a positive!"

"Now I'm lost," replied Logan.

"Well, once we infect the Implanted, we can insert emotions that will create decisions that we can predict."

"We can control the Implanted?"

"I think we can, but the first thing I have to do is predict their next moves," said Jerry as he reached for the keys of his computer. He hesitated for a moment and bowed his head briefly. Upon opening his eyes, his fingers attacked the keyboard.

Several hours later, Jerry had fused loops from Leviticus and Echelon into a new program he called "Michael." After causing the computer to compile all the known data about the characteristics of COBRA and the current state of their affairs, he highlighted the "Predict" hot button and set the machine to work.

Moments later, a quack told Jerry its work was done. Jerry viewed the list of the five most likely initiatives that COBRA would take. His jaw dropped as he read the first one.

He screamed, "Edward! Jane! Joe! They are going to kidnap Leah!"

Only Logan came running.

"What? Who is?" said Logan.

"COBRA agents. I just ran the Michael program. It predicts that once they know we are on to them, they'll kidnap Leah. They'll hold her and threaten to kill her unless we stop!"

"Of course!" cried Logan. "That makes sense!"

He reached for his phone and dialed the Calais residence. The line was dead.

Just then a CSIS agent ran into the room. "We've lost all contact with the Calais residence, and our radios and cells are being jammed."

In the quiet of her home, Jane's pulse quickened as she studied the draft of the speech she was preparing for the Prime Minister of Canada's staff. It was to be given by the p.m. on the eve of the multinational referendum on Implant Technology.

It was difficult to imagine the words she had crafted being recorded in history. She thought of the great speeches she had heard in her time. Martin Luther King's "I have a dream"; J.F. Kennedy's "Ich bin ein Berliner"; and Winston Churchill's "We will fight on the beaches" speeches all came to mind.

These speeches, she reckoned, didn't appeal because of their logic, or reason; they appealed to the heart, to the soul. They spoke of great truths, of foundational values so profound as to be worth dying for. Sacrifice in the face of evil came to mind.

Outside the Calais home, the intruders, hidden by the night, moved into position. Through their night-vision optics, they could see Jane working.

Jane Calais knew as she made changes to her text that she could not do this alone. She was only human. It was too much responsibility. Yet the head of her government was going to deliver the final speech the people of North America would hear before they voted on whether to embrace implants or deny them.

"Mommy!" a voice from behind her called. "Mommy, I want you," it repeated.

Jane left her desk and went to Leah's room. She was sitting up in her bed, rubbing sleepy eyes. "I had a dream that you didn't need me anymore, Mommy," cooed Leah softly as her eyes shut once more. She cuddled into her mother. "I love you, Mommy. I love the way you smell."

"I love you too, honey," Jane said, a tear rolling down her cheek as she embraced her daughter.

Jane placed Leah back in her bed, tucked her in, and lay down by her side until Leah was fast asleep again. Then, kissing her softly on the cheek, Jane went over to the bedroom, checked the window and made sure it was locked, closed the door, and returned to her speech writing.

As the door to the bedroom closed, the three intruders all switched on their night-vision goggles. They peered into the girl's bedroom window from their hiding spots. At a signal given by their team leader, they began a carefully choreographed sequence. Two snipers raised their weapons and with five well-placed shots, eliminated the security detail posted around the Calais residence. A third member approached the window and electronically deactivated the alarm system. Using a simple glasscutter, he etched a fine line around the window, close to its frame.

198

Vacuum glass holders were then applied and used to remove the window.

One of the intruders climbed in the window and quietly stepped down to the floor.

Outside the house, the snipers took up new positions. They set their rifle sights on Edward and Jane, who had moved to the couch.

The intruder peeled off her goggles and her balaclava, and her golden hair fell to her shoulders. Dr. Xavier Lyon crept toward Leah's bed. In one swift motion she removed a chemically dampened cloth from a plastic bag and covered Leah's face with it.

Leah awoke to the feeling of someone covering her mouth with something. Her panicked gasp for air filled her lungs with chloroform, and she soon passed out from its effect.

The intruder left a note on Leah's pillow.

A no vote tomorrow means you will never see her again.
P.S. Her brain is perfect for us.

Lyon effortlessly lifted the limp body of Leah out of the bed and carried her, fireman style, to the window. She handed the girl over to a fellow COBRA agent and climbed out of the window and jumped to the cold damp grass of the manicured lawn. The agent carried Leah into the depths of the forest where, at a safe distance, a black van picked them up.

Once in the van they placed the unconscious little girl on a small bed. Dr. Xavier Lyon immediately applied a stethoscope to Leah's chest and listened carefully to her labored breathing. Lyon had never felt so alive. This was the ultimate intoxication. She smiled as she injected a mixture of drugs carefully concocted to maintain the child in a stable slumber.

As the van turned a corner, a portable implant machine fitted with a child's implant prototype slid out from under the child's cot and came to rest at her feet.

27

L orne Browne stood on the podium in the center of BC Place. The massive air-filled, marshmallow-shaped building was filled with supporters of COBRA.

"My goodness, is he ever good-looking," gasped a young fan as Browne's image appeared on the giant screen behind where he stood to speak.

It was a carefully orchestrated spectacle, and more entertainment than politics. Celebrities from Mexico, the United States, and Canada occupied seats on the massive stage. National anthems were sung, and an overly upbeat theme song played intermittently. The crowd was being primed.

Browne held up his arms and a hush descended over the stadium. "Thank you, Canada, for hosting us!"

The crowd cheered.

"My friends, whether you are in Mexico..."

An image of a huge crowd that filled a soccer stadium in Mexico City filled the giant screen; the people cheered as their country was mentioned.

"Or the United States..."

Los Angeles appeared next on the screen; they too were screaming.

"Or Toronto, or New York, or Tijuana..."

Multiple images flashed on the screen as these cities and their gatherings cheered.

"Welcome to freedom! We are here to announce freedom has arrived in North America!"

"Freedom!" echoed several hundred voices in the crowd.

"Freedom from pain..."

The crowd cheered.

"Freedom from worry..."

Louder cheering.

"Freedom from filth…"

Someone shouted, "Evolution now!"

"Freedom from discrimination…"

The crowd responded, "Ev…o…lution!"

"Freedom from disease…"

Cheers, chants, getting always louder.

"Freedom from suffering…Freedom from economic imbalance…Freedom from sacrifice…"

More cheers.

"Freedom for your children…Freedom for your country…Freedom for you!"

The crowd was in a state of frenzy.

"COBRA wants you to have freedom! COBRA means freedom!" Browne's words echoed through the building.

The people on the stage were on their feet and clapping.

Browne held his arms up high and paused. "But my friends," he said quietly, "there are those who want to deny your freedom."

"No, No, No," echoed voices from the crowd.

"They are lying."

"Liars!" screamed several.

"They claim that to evolve, and that to improve is wrong. They want to keep you from growing to your full potential as humans. They want to keep you slaves to oppression!"

"NO! NO! NO!" responded the masses.

"You must fight for your freedom! Sacrifice for the freedom of your children! You deserve freedom."

"Freedom!" echoed the crowd.

"You deserve choice."

"Choice!" echoed the crowd.

"You deserve peace."

"Peace!" echoed the crowd.

"You deserve freedom from worry, from anxiety."

"Freedom!" echoed the crowd.

"You deserve to be loved."

"Love!" echoed the crowd.

"You deserve to be free."

"Freedom."

"Fight for freedom!"

"Vote for freedom!"

"Ladies and gentlemen," Browne said solemnly, "we call you to a new generation of hope and of security, of peace and of love"—he waited for the crowd to quiet—"and all this comes from our life-giving COBRA technology. All this is within your grasp. Dare to dream the dream of evolution. Dare to share the dream of technology with those you love. Vote for Freedom. Vote for Implant Freedom. Vote yes!"

The crowd was clapping and swaying as the theme song was blasted from the speakers throughout the building and through all the stadiums in North America where all heard the same message.

Browne went on. "Ladies and Gentlemen, I present to you the founders of your freedom. The developers of COBRA—Henry Rexan and Xavier Lyon. They will set you free!"

The self-made super heroes exploded from the back of the stage, arms raised. The crowd applauded for what seemed like 10 minutes.

A young teacher in the crowd commented to his wife, "I can't believe anyone would vote no, especially after this!"

"I can," was her reply as she sensed the unseen darkness that filled the building.

Edward and Jane watched the proceedings in BC Place via live television.

"We have to stop them," said Edward.

"We will, Edward, we will. It's our day tomorrow. I have an amazing speech draft I sent off to the PM's office this afternoon." She smiled.

Edward turned to his wife. "If anyone can write a speech, it's you."

Jane elbowed his side. "I'm just going to check on Leah, then we should go to bed."

She walked down the hall toward Leah's room.

A second later, Edward heard her scream.

"Leah's gone! She's gone right out of her bed!"

Edward ran down the hallway and burst into their daughter's room. "She's what?"

"She's gone! I went back to tuck her in a little while ago because she had a bad dream. When I left, she was sound asleep."

"Look! There's a note!" said Edward.

"Read it," Jane began to tremble.

Edward worked his way through the short, vicious message.

"It's Rexan," she said. "I'm sure. Oh, Edward, I'm so scared!"

"I'll call for help!" Edward reached for the phone.

Jane collapsed, weeping, on Leah's bed. She touched the spot where, a short while earlier, her precious daughter's head lay.

Edward ended the call, then sat beside his wife, placing his arms around her. "Joe will get her back. I just know it. They are searching the woods now, and they've put roadblocks all around us. "

Jane looked out the severed bedroom window. The flashing red and blue lights of the police cars parked outside reflected in her eyes.

"She'll be so afraid," Jane moaned.

For the first time in his life, Edward Calais felt entirely helpless. He closed his eyes and mouthed the words, "God if you are real, show me now." He opened his eyes and looked up.

There stood Jerry and Rachel Chen, standing just a few steps down the hall, obviously praying. Both of them, heads bowed, mouthed an "Amen," then glanced up and saw Edward staring at them.

"Sorry, we were just..."

"I know, and thank you."

The room was full of the sounds of police, squawking radios, and faint siren and helicopter blades cutting through the air high above the home.

Jerry's tender voice began above the clamor. "I tried to call to tell you they might go after you guys. But I couldn't warn you in time. I was just a few minutes late. I'm so sorry."

"Why did you think they might go after her?" asked Jane.

"Michael, the program I wrote, predicted it."

"Just not in enough time," said Rachel softly.

"Thanks for trying, Jerry. Just get her back, okay? I have a new speech to write."

"You don't have to do this," said Rachel, stroking Jane's back gently.

"I have to now, more than ever," replied Jane.

Joe Logan pushed his way through the door and immediately took charge of the situation.

For reasons known only to their souls and its contents, Jane and Edward were at peace in as much as was possible. Jerry and Rachel remained with them as Joe Logan arranged for and then moved all four of them to the Waterfront Hotel, where they occupied an entire floor. Security was as tight and impenetrable as it was when presidents or royalty visited Vancouver and used the luxury hotel's facilities.

While being kept informed of the multinational search that was occurring for Leah, the four worked on the many tasks that not only had fallen their way, but also kept them occupied.

Jerry and Rachel spoke quietly in the room allotted to them.

"We have to do something more, Rachel."

"You're already working 18 hours a day on this. You need to rest. You'll get sick again," she worried.

His determination showed in his eyes. "It's not about us anymore. This is war."

"But how can we win—with what's happening in Europe?"

"I think we'll have to kill them."

"Kill them?"

"Kill them all."

"What are you talking about? Murder?"

"No, Rachel. I don't mean the people; I mean the implants."

"How can we kill the implants without killing the people?"

"Electromagnetic pulse. EMP."

"How?"

"The principle is to set off nuclear weapons that create

electromagnetic waves. They destroy computer chips by forcing energy through them and crashing the programming. We could have the bombs simultaneously launched into space and exploded there. No fallout on earth that way."

"Won't all the computer systems go down? We'll need our military more than ever. If it fails, we'll be at their mercy."

"Not if we modify the weapons slightly to produce a frequency that matches these chips individually."

She frowned. "Sounds too far-fetched."

He grinned. "Most of my ideas are, Rachel."

Jerry immediately sent an email off to his friends at the National Research Council. They could run the mathematical models necessary to confirm Jerry's idea.

The kidnapping of Leah had changed things. Late the next morning, Joe Logan cautiously approached the team of four as they broke from their work for lunch.

"The referendum team, and specifically the Presidents of Mexico and the United States and the Prime Minister, have asked me to ask you something," Logan said softly.

He shifted uncomfortably, first placing his weight on one foot and then on the other. He looked out the window and wondered where Leah was. His heart ached for her and her parents. He was amazed at the strength and determination he saw as he watched them work on the speech. Where was it coming from? He wondered?

"Go ahead, Joe. Is it bad news?" asked Edward.

"No, definitely not." Logan's voice quivered, and he stumbled. "They actually want you and Jane to deliver the speech."

"What? People don't know us from a hole in the ground," said Edward.

"The polls showed us at a dead heat," Logan explained. "However, Browne's speech last night was brilliant. We think it will sway the vote. As it stands right now, we think North Americans are ready to be implanted, or at least the majority is."

"How can one half of the continent be willing to let themselves have this happen to them?" wondered Edward out loud.

"Easy," answered Jerry. "No pain, no worries. That's very appealing."

"So is death, if you look at it that way," commented Logan. "Regardless, it is our side that speaks tonight. The Canadian government feels that if the world as a whole listens to you—the parents whose child was stolen to forward the cause of COBRA—they will see the wrong in it and the kind of people they are giving their bodies and minds over to, and people will vote no. It will be the ultimate character debate. We'll win."

"Nothing could be as powerful or as moving, if you can do it," added Rachel.

"It will make Leah's kidnapping make some sense, Jane," said Edward softly to his wife.

"They will kill her," she replied.

"I'll get her back," said Jerry, almost to himself.

28

BC Place indoor stadium was filled yet again. This time, however, the crowd was clearly anti-implant. Signs and placards denouncing COBRA were everywhere. Giant screens showed images of other major North American cities holding similar rallies.

Edward and Jane Calais readied themselves. They sat in the wings behind the stage and listened as the speaker began to introduce them. The audience was relatively quiet, although occasionally cheers erupted from them. Many of those in the crowd carried and waved protest signs.

"You'll be fine," said Joe Logan as Jane nervously paced the floor.

"I can't stop thinking of Leah," said Edward, who was sitting in the makeup artist's chair.

Logan answered the cell phone that gently vibrated in his breast pocket. A moment later he ended the call and told Edward and Leah, "I don't want to build your hopes up too much, but Jerry has a plan for Leah."

"Jerry?"

"Yes, he thinks he has found a way to hack into their system. The Implants are in constant communication with the mainframe or controlling system via satellite. They are networked together. Jerry thinks he can temporarily insert small program loops into the mainframe software. He should be able to insert commands into their brains that way. He is using Michael as a base."

"How will he get Leah back?"

"I'm not sure, but he seems confident enough, though."

Logan stopped to listen to the sound system. "Edward, it's time for your speech."

Officials hustled Edward Calais towards the glare of the camera lights. He saw out of the corner of his eye the images of the Prime

Minister of Canada and the Presidents of Mexico and the United States. Each said a few words by way of introduction. They spoke solemnly and calmly to their people.

The final words before Calais was to speak came from his Prime Minister. "And now my friends, some words from Mr. Edward Calais. He, perhaps more than anyone, has felt the weight and wrath of those who call upon us to yield our bodies and our minds to this new technology. Mr. Calais, we welcome you."

"Thank you, Mr. Prime Minister."

Calais paused to scan the crowd that filled the stadium, then looked directly into the camera and began to speak. "My friends in Mexico, and in the United States of America, and those here in Canada, today is a day of grave concern. It is a day that will be recorded in history. And you, my friends, are the ones who will write that history. It is to you that the question will be asked. It is to you that future generations will look to explain their lives.

"Why am I here today? I am not a politician, nor am I a medical expert. I am here today to expose a lie and to uncover the truth. We as a people, we as humanity, are being asked to grant permission to the proponents of COBRA to inject a device into our brains.

"This device contains living human brain tissue. A person who was once alive was captured, and while they still lived, and breathed, and felt pain, their brain was removed from their skull. The murderers who did this did not use any anesthetic, because it might have slowed down the manufacturing of implants. These slices, slices of human brain, were then installed in someone else's brain, just like a wheel of a car is installed in an automotive plant.

"You know this to be wrong. You can feel it in your hearts. No amount of benefit, no amount of efficiency, and no amount of progress can make this murdering scheme right.

"The device they have injected into many of our friends overseas and to the south of us has robbed them of their humanity as well. Like a deceiving serpent, it mesmerizes its prey, creating a sense of well-being while turning them into a machine—a machine that can be put to use at the controller's leisure.

"People of North America and the world, you and your children are more than machines; you are more than the product of evolution. Your past is not just the result of random acts of chemistry and of physics, and of time. You are more than atoms, of chemical reactions and nerve cells strung together. You have a soul, a spirit, a life that is yours and no one else's. You were created for a purpose. You are unique. You must not give that up.

"Over our history, men and women have sacrificed and died for the freedom to choose. Because of their sacrifice, you have that freedom. You must not give it away. The choice that you make tomorrow will be remembered forever. By voting yes you will have thrown your own soul to this band of snakes. Right now, ladies and gentlemen, eternity is staring you right in the face."

Calais stopped speaking. The crowd was quiet.

He began again, softly this time. "At this very moment, our little girl, our daughter, is in the hands of kidnappers. They have taken her and are threatening to kill her. She is two years old. Let me read the note they left on her bed:

A no vote tomorrow means you will never see her again.
P.S. Her brain is perfect for..."

After a few words, he stopped and tried to regain his ability to speak. He couldn't. He stood there, tears streaming down his cheeks.

A picture of Leah appeared on the giant screen behind him. She was picking flowers in a field.

On stage, Jane appeared at Edward's side, as did Joe Logan.

Jane moved to the podium and, while standing beside him, began to speak. "Henry Rexan, Lorne Browne, and Xavier Lyon have created a kind of evil that has never before existed. With it, they will control the world. They will do anything, tell any lie, hurt anyone, and even kidnap a two-year-old girl to accomplish their goals. We must resist them. Please, please vote no tomorrow. Thank you."

The crowd was silent. On the giant screen, the tape of Leah continued to play. As she walked through the park, she selected another flower for her bouquet. As she rose from picking the flower, she looked towards the camera.

"I love you, Mommy and Daddy," said Leah as she blew a kiss.

Slowly, people throughout the stadium rose in their seats, and began to clap. More and more joined them until finally all were standing. They weren't cheering, they were just clapping.

Edward, Jane, and Joe left the stage in each other's arms.

It was over.

In the Bogotá boardroom of COBRA, Dr. Xavier Lyon watched the performance of the anti-implant group. As the standing ovation began, she said to those of her staff who were watching with her, "They don't know what they are missing."

Her staff nodded in agreement, and as they did, the lumps at the back of their necks rose and fell.

A small child's voice called from the locked room next to the viewing room.

Lyon said, "Let's do her now. It'll be our first trial with this small of a brain. I'll get her."

Lyon left the staffers and entered the room that held Leah. The child sat quietly playing with some blocks.

"I have to go to bathwomb."

"Okay, I suppose. That way you won't pee yourself."

As Lyon reached down to pick Leah up, an inner Voice intruded into her consciousness. "Pick her up and take her to your car," said the voice in a strangely digital manner.

Lyon stopped and looked around to see who had spoken to her. She wondered what was happening. She picked Leah up and walked towards the implantation room door, forgetting about the bathroom.

The Voice returned, and it was even more compelling. "Take her to your car."

It was as if her father was giving her an order.

She stopped again, only this time, she turned slightly towards the other door in her office, the one that led to the outside. As she moved towards it, she stopped yet again, wondering what she was thinking of, heading in this direction.

But she couldn't stop herself. In a daze, she carried Leah past security and towards the door that led to the outside.

"Stop!" said one of the guards.

Lyon stopped and turned to face the guard. "You dare give me an order!"

"I have my own orders," said the guard, whose caution was immediately overruled by his implant.

Lyon focused her eyes on the guard and his badge number. All she had to do was think and it was done. The guard's implant responded to her unspoken demand and stopped the man's heart. He dropped to the ground, clutching his chest, gasping for air. Soon he was still.

Lyon, still carrying Leah, turned around again and stepped towards the closed doors.

The outside doors swung open automatically as she approached. They sensed and responded to the command issued from the chip resting just under the skin of Lyon's neck. Her Porsche sat waiting several hundred yards away, its top down. She carefully strode towards the car and, while cupping Leah in her left arm, reached for the passenger side door.

"Lyon! Stop!" echoed a distant scream from the direction of the building. Henry Rexan's voice was one she could recognize, even through the haze created by the inner Voice directing her actions.

"Get in the car and escape," ordered the Voice.

Lyon resisted. Her past fought its way from her subconscious and into her psyche. An image of her father appeared. He was pushing her away. She was only two years old. Lyon wanted to keep the child away from its parents, just as she had been pushed away from hers.

It was then that Lisa forced her way into Lyon's consciousness. "You will let her go, or I will kill us," Lisa said to Lyon.

In Vancouver, Jerry Chen's screen reported the hesitation that Lyon felt. He typed furiously, "Obey, Xavier! Get in the car and escape!"

As he hit Enter, the instructions were transmitted from his keyboard and instantly via modem to the microchip in her brain, through her COBRA interface, and into the base of Xavier Lyon's brain.

A searing pain shot through Xavier Lyon. She closed her eyes. All she could comprehend was the command. She felt as if her brain were melting.

"Get in and escape," ordered Lisa.

Lyon heard the footsteps of Henry Rexan getting louder.

"I will kill you both!" he shouted.

Lisa screamed into her mind, "Take the girl away!"

Lyon's hands carefully lay Leah down in the seat. She ran around the front of the car and leapt into the driver's side. She started the car.

29

Henry Rexan's will pushed his body beyond its physical capabilities. His implant forced the issue. Rexan's heart pounded, and as he ran, his already significantly high blood pressure rose even greater. The arteries in his heart stretched and swelled as blood rushed to meet the oxygen demands of his muscles. Years of accumulated plaque lining his arteries expanded and contracted with each heartbeat. A piece of plaque, tiny and soft, broke free and was immediately washed down the artery it originated from and towards the vessels supplying the heart muscle itself. As the plaque piece moved, clotting agents in Rexan's blood coated it with threads of protein. A clot formed and grew in his body.

As he approached the black Porsche where Xavier Lyon and Leah Calais were, Rexan pulled at the vintage Luger jammed in the belt of his slacks. Lyon responded to Rexan's presence by jamming the car in gear and releasing the clutch. The car leapt, then stalled as its engine lost a battle with the parking brake.

Rexan smiled as the weapon cleared his belly. He stopped running and placed both hands on his pistol, aiming it at Lyon's head. He was only a few feet away. He cocked the gun and released the safety.

Just then the soft, smooth clot, driven closer by each beat of his racing heart, entered Henry Rexan's coronary artery system. Another beat of his heart's muscle drove it ever more deeply into its own tissue. Slipping through the relatively open channels, the mucus-textured mass entered the narrowing passages of the heart muscle itself. Finally, it simply could not fit through any farther. It stuck, lodged in an artery, blocking the flow of blood into the straining heart muscle that lay beyond the fleshy dam.

His oxygen-starved heart muscle seized as the blood flowing to it stopped. The heart itself stopped momentarily, then began to quiver,

214

totally out of coordination. The pistol, however, was rock-steady and still aimed at Lyon's head.

Rexan stepped within a pace of Lyon. Leah was crying softly. As his finger began to squeeze the trigger, Rexan felt a tightening in his chest. His arm grew numb. His brain ordered his finger to tighten. It would not. He simply could not pull the trigger. It was as if a crushing weight had been placed on his chest. He was dizzy and felt strange all at the same time. He screamed in frustration. He wanted to kill, at least once more.

Lyon's eyes caught Rexan's momentarily. She leaped from the car and deftly kicked at the hand that held the gun. The blow knocked his wrist sideways. The gun fired, and the bullet carried harmlessly into the bush that surrounded the building.

Rexan dropped to his knees and collapsed to the ground, striking his head on the pavement. There he lay, grasping his chest and gasping, his eyes and mouth open.

Lyon, emotionless, looked down at her onetime business partner. Then she turned away and started her car.

Leah sat quietly beside her, in the passenger seat.

Rexan could no longer hear the sound of Dr. Xavier Lyon's Porsche as it carried her and Leah away from the compound and into the surrounding countryside. He was dead.

Jacko Rameze and another employee had followed Rexan out of the building and watched as two of his bosses fought. He strolled slowly up to the body of Henry Rexan, machete in hand. With one quick motion of the blade, he decapitated Rexan.

A laboratory assistant standing beside Jacko reached down and wrapped his fingers around Rexan's hair and lifted his head. "What should I do with this?"

"Freeze it. Dr. Lyon may want to have a look later."

The assistant casually walked away, bearing his horrific burden. A trail of scarlet droplets traced his path to the building. Once inside he placed Rexan's head in an ice bath, and following Jacko's instructions, put the head in the freezer.

Deep inside Rexan's brain, an implant gradually powered down and went automatically into sleep mode and rested.

As Jerry's computer screen relayed and interpreted the data Michael was sending it, he watched the rescue of Leah unfold. The Porsche carrying Lyon pulled over near an abandoned baseball diamond just as a sleek jet-black Blackhawk helicopter gently came to rest nearby.

The heavily armed specialists from the helicopter had immediately surrounded Lyon and the now sleeping Leah. They grabbed Lyon and handcuffed her. Leah was carefully whisked inside the chopper.

Medical staff immediately assessed the girl's condition. She awoke in the arms of a female U.S. marine sergeant who was stroking her hair and telling her not to be afraid.

"Where is my mommy?" she whispered sleepily.

"You'll see her in the time it takes to watch a baseball game," the marine sergeant said.

"I love baseball. Daddy says the Blue Jays are the best," she replied as she fell back to sleep.

"It's supposed to be an American game," murmured the marine as she stroked the little girl's head.

At the command center in Vancouver, Edward and Jane Calais cheered along with the others and wept tears of joy as the news of the rescue reached them.

Images of Leah's rescue were transmitted live to the giant screen in the stadiums all over North America. They also were being broadcast to every TV station tuned to the news.

Edward left his wife's arms and took several short steps towards Joe Logan, who was also teary-eyed. He reached up and threw his arms around the CSIS director.

"Thanks Joe," was all Calais could say.

Jane hugged Rachel and Jerry simultaneously. "Thanks so much, you guys. You saved her life."

"To let Edward begin that speech last night, knowing the risk, took amazing courage," whispered Jerry.

"I knew the angels were looking after her," Jane whispered back. "You helped with that too. Thanks for your prayers."

People all over North America stood in their living rooms, clapping, many in tears, as they watched the rescue of Leah.

30

The next day was referendum day. The team was assembled in the conference room, waiting for the last votes to be cast. At eight o'clock Pacific Standard time, the world would learn of its future.

As the clock on the wall struck eight, most TV monitors in the world watched the news. Military bases on both sides of the issue stood at high alert. Jet aircraft of all description left a multitude of bases and climbed to their assigned altitudes.

"This is indeed a momentous occasion," said the news anchor.

"It is indeed," replied the color commentator, "and here are some of the early results."

Joe Logan, Edward Calais, Jane Calais, Leah, Jerry, and Rachel Chen stood watching.

"Oh my goodness," said someone behind them. They all turned towards the big TV screen that was providing the results of the referendum as they were coming in.

"With 30 percent of the votes counted, as incredible as it seems, the vote is heavily on the no side!" exclaimed the silver-haired news anchor.

"Incredible, I've never seen such a swing. Just yesterday, it was too close to call, and yet today, North Americans have clearly responded to the impassioned plea from the Calais family last night and have made up their minds."

"It truly is remarkable. It's almost a miracle."

"Where does that put North America now?"

"I'm sure the heads of state are discussing their options as we speak...although I'm sure they wouldn't have predicted such a mandate."

In Washington D.C., the President of the United States of America spoke with his friends from Canada and from Mexico. They nodded in agreement. He was given a key and an open briefcase. Slowly he activated the contents of the briefcase and turned the key.

"The aircraft are ordered to launch the weapons."

The head of state and their staffs applauded.

Once given the go-ahead codes from the American president, the B52 bombers prepared the nuclear burdens that lay deep in their bomb bay holds. They carried a cargo of modified air-to-air missiles, each carrying an adapted nuclear-tipped warhead. The warhead had been set to explode at a specific altitude. The explosion would create and emit a powerful electromagnetic pulse that would destroy the computer chips that controlled the implantees. The missiles would be launched, then immediately rise to the level that would result in the greatest transmission of radiated energy. But it was all theory, of course.

Colonel Paul Allen, based in Colorado, was in charge of the operation, code-named *Mighty Thunder*. The Americans had provided the B52s and the Canadian Air Force provided air support. They were prepared for defensive attacks from implanted British and Russian pilots. The Canadians respected but did not fear their adversaries.

Col. Allen's staff had prepared the battle plan with utmost care. The computer systems that usually coordinated and transmitted the launch codes were not used in this case. Allen was concerned that the Implanted had access to them. He was correct. With little computer support, Allen used the methods from the precomputer days that his father knew. This meant regular radio transmissions were coded, single-use decoded books were developed and issued, and human couriers transported action and battle plans. In some ways, Allen enjoyed the extremely low-tech facets of this assignment. The planes were coordinated to take off in such a way as to cause as little suspicion as possible, so left their respective Air Force field intermittently. Many had to stay in the air for hours as a result. In the end, a network of planes effectively surrounded the earth.

At precisely 3 p.m. Greenwich Mean Time, the missiles were launched simultaneously. Each one fell from the bomb bay and for several seconds simply accelerated towards the surface of the earth powered by gravity alone. As soon as they were safely away from the aircraft, they ignited their solid propellant fuel engines and were propelled away from the huge aircraft that had carried them. Moments later they arced into the sky and headed towards the edge of the atmosphere. Tens of thousands of feet from the surface of earth they simultaneously exploded. Each one produced vast amounts of radiation at the specific frequency that matched the operating frequency used by the implanted chips found in many of the humans far below.

People all over the world looked up at the sky to see what appeared to be something similar to sheet lighting. For a brief moment, the entire earth was illuminated with a blindingly white light.

At the speed of light, the liberating rays headed towards the earth. Implanted people located all over the earth were immersed in a baptism of light. The waves passed easily into their skulls and those hitting the chip immediately were focused by and destroyed the delicate electrical passageways that had grown between the chips and their human hosts. The energy pulse overpowered the alignment of magnetic particles that composed the computer chips' memory and processing capability. The chips died immediately, unable to withstand the sudden pulses of energy that coursed through the millions of electronic digital passageways. Their synthetic memories were wiped clean.

The Implanted felt profoundly different because, for the first time since they had fallen prey to penetrating alien intrusion, they felt nothing at all. No more intrusive thoughts permeated their consciousness; no more answers to questions they never posed came to mind. Most had no idea what was going on and began to fear. That too was different, for true fear was something that had been filtered out of their minds. They were changed...at least most of them were.

Within minutes of the EMP pulse, waves of F-18 fighter-bombers targeted the factories that held the inventory of yet-to-be-implanted COBRA implants. One by one, each was destroyed. Theoretically, within 24 hours, the world was rid of the evil of implanted computer chips.

Werner Braun and the others had boarded the Chunnel train in England. They were placed in cars separated from the rest of the passengers. He and Georgio sat together as they always did since they had met, in the pre-implant days. As a sniper team they had trained and worked together. As the train entered the tunnel, the light of the British countryside subsided to the dull glow of the cabin lights reflecting on the walls of the tunnel. The train descended into the depths of the stone that distanced the train from the seas of the English Channel that lie above the Chunnel. By three o'clock, the train was separated from the outside world by the layers of chalk that the tunnel had followed. That, combined with the concrete casing and the hundreds of feet of water, produced an impenetrable barrier to the massive burst of energy that blanketed the rest of the earth.

Braun and the rest of the soldiers of the New Europe movement missed the change. Protected by circumstance, they exited the Chunnel in France with their chips' operating systems intact. Although they were not receiving updates over the Internet as they had usually, they still functioned as implanted soldiers should function.

Arriving in Paris hours later, they continued to follow the plans that had been programmed into their brains days earlier. At the nest of buildings that had been set up for them in the French countryside, they prepared for their mission. All the equipment they needed to do their duty was already there. The assassination teams gathered the materials necessary for their particular mission and left for the airports to the planes that awaited them.

Braun and his team arrived in Vancouver, Canada the next day.

As they drove the rental vehicles acquired at the airport, the team left the city of Vancouver and headed west, towards the camp that was prepared for them in the mountain wilderness. Upon their arrival, they set up the camp and began to prepare.

It was then that Werner Braun learned the truth. They were alone and disconnected. It was indeed a strange New World for them.

He and Georgio sat by themselves.

"Have you finished reading the papers?" Georgio asked.

"I have," replied Braun.

"So, what are we going to do?"

"We are going to find Henry."

"Didn't you read the paper? Henry is dead."

"Not the real Henry. He isn't dead, only frozen."

"I don't get it, Werner."

"While he was having his heart attack, his implant began to download the contents of his brain. His mind survived well after his body died."

"What do you mean he is frozen?"

"Jacko had his head frozen; that's what protected the implant during the change. There was no living brain to focus the EMP."

"How do you know this, Werner?"

"As his chip was downloading, it sent an email to me."

"We still have a chance then to accomplish our mission?"

"Absolutely, Georgio, absolutely."

Both men suddenly looked skyward.

The mountains that surrounded their camp echoed the characteristic sounds of military helicopters, and they were approaching at attack speed.

Epilogue

When the change happened, Edward, Jane, Jerry, and Rachel were watching the news. As reports came in from all over the world, they cheered as the remnants of COBRA in Europe, South America, and Asia were wiped from the face of the earth. Henry Rexan was dead; Xavier Lyon and Lorne Browne were in custody. Leah cheered too, although she didn't really know why.

They watched as the bombs hit the factories, and celebrated as teams of soldiers completed the job by destroying the remaining inventory of implants and brain samples. The samples were to be given a proper burial.

Edward was in the kitchen, putting together a celebration feast. The four adults and Leah gathered around the table. As Jerry gave thanks for the food, they held hands.

On the wall beside them was a picture of the Gang, at Hornby.

Jane shed a tear as she looked at the picture, focusing on George and Tara. "It's all so surreal. I can't believe they're gone."

"At least they died for a reason," said Rachel.

"And it's over now," added Edward.

Jerry Chen looked up from his meal and said only three words. "I hope so."

They ate and watched the news.

Jane patted Jerry on the hand. "You can relax. It's over."

"You're right, Jane," came the reply. "I'm sure you're right."

"Mommy's always right!" said Leah. "She told me so!"

The world rejoiced.

About the Author

RICHARD ALLEN WUNDERLICH's interest in technology stems in part from his many years of teaching and writing science and mathematics textbooks for the world's future scientists, engineers, and medical researchers.

"Being immersed in the minds of students who are much smarter than me," Wunderlich says, "often makes me wonder where the amazing technology they'll create will lead humankind." He also wonders, as many do, if technology is moving faster than our ability to decide if it's ultimately good.

Tomorrow's Paper, Wunderlich's first fictional work and the first of a trilogy, explores what will happen when a piece of technology is created that is so appealing, so enchanting, that its inherent evil is overlooked. Wunderlich, who lives and teaches in Southern British Columbia, loves to use storytelling to elicit interest and controversy in his classes. The intent of *Tomorrow's Paper* is to explore the conflict between what can be done and what should be done in an entirely plausible and terrifying venue. It will cause all who read it to reflect on their place in the universe, and to value and protect their innermost being, their soul.

Richard Wunderlich holds a bachelors degree in science education from the University of Victoria, B.C. He is a science and mathematics consultant and a program author for: *MathLinks 7-9* (McGraw Hill Ryerson), *Essentials of Mathematics 10-12* and *Experiential Science 10-12* (Pacific Educational Press), *Mathematics 10-12*, and *Applied Mathematics 10-12* (Addison Wesley).

For more information: **http://richardwunderlich.blogspot.com/ www.oaktara.com**

Printed in the United States
131859LV00003B/1/P